DEDICATION

This book is dedicated to the scores of boys and girls whose classrooms I have been walking into since 1997, who truly have inspired me to be the kind of teacher I have become.

THE LION OF HIND

POWER, PASSION, PATRIOTISM.
ONE MAN'S GUTS SENDS SHIVERS
DOWN THE MUGHAL SPINE !

VINZI ISAAC

Chennai • Bangalore

CLEVER FOX PUBLISHING
Chennai, India

Published by CLEVER FOX PUBLISHING 2024
Copyright © VINZI ISAAC 2024

All Rights Reserved.
ISBN: 978-93-56480-75-9

This book has been published with all reasonable efforts taken to make the material error-free after the consent of the author. No part of this book shall be used, reproduced in any manner whatsoever without written permission from the author, except in the case of brief quotations embodied in critical articles and reviews.

The Author of this book is solely responsible and liable for its content including but not limited to the views, representations, descriptions, statements, information, opinions and references ["Content"]. The Content of this book shall not constitute or be construed or deemed to reflect the opinion or expression of the Publisher or Editor. Neither the Publisher nor Editor endorse or approve the Content of this book or guarantee the reliability, accuracy or completeness of the Content published herein and do not make any representations or warranties of any kind, express or implied, including but not limited to the implied warranties of merchantability, fitness for a particular purpose. The Publisher and Editor shall not be liable whatsoever for any errors, omissions, whether such errors or omissions result from negligence, accident, or any other cause or claims for loss or damages of any kind, including without limitation, indirect or consequential loss or damage arising out of use, inability to use, or about the reliability, accuracy or sufficiency of the information contained in this book.

CONTENTS

Foreword .... *ix*

1. 1572-An Overturned Verdict 1
2. The Call Of Destiny 5
3. The Seeds Of War 9
4. The Bait 15
5. Perilous Statecraft 18
6. The Benefit Of Doubt 28
7. A Tantalizing Offer 32
8. A Final Throw Of Dice 39
9. Desperate Diplomacy 45
10. If Push Came To Shove 54
11. The Lull Before The Storm 60
12. The Final Stretch 65
13. Turmeric Valley – Shock And Awe! 81
14. The Soul Of The Sword 88
15. The Day Of The Jackal! 93
16. So Dauntless In War! 98

17. The Roar Of The Lion 120
18. Surprising Sparks! 130
19. Ripples On The Surface 137
20. No Time For Rest 146
21. Death By Dawn 151
22. The Sledgehammer To The Fore! 160
23. A Strategic Retreat 165
24. A Bolt From The Blue! 171
25. The Lull... 194
26. A Longer Lull? 202
27. A Refuge In The Storm 221
28. Obscured In Darkness 233
29. Desperate Times, Desperate Measures 245
30. Hiding In Plain Sight 259
31. A Daylight Dishonour! 270
32. Too Many Rods In The Fire 283
33. Into The Wild And Back 296
34. Peace, Total Peace? 319
35. Dawn In The Distance 324
36. To Every Man His Destiny 338

Bibliography & Social Media *352*

FOREWORD

This is a historical novel on the life and times of Maharana Prathap Singh of Mewar. Being a novel it conjures up what could have possibly happened in the life of the protagonist and his contemporaries. By and large this volume tries to stay within the parametres of historical facts. In Chapter 24 alone I have given myself a kind of poetical license to convince the readers to believe the events in the chapter based on circumstantial evidence.

This is my debut novel. I hope you will like it and that you will as myself come to appreciate and love the rich history, the culture, the diversity, the heros and the heroines who traversed through the length and breadth of this ancient land that is called India.

JAI HIND !

CHAPTER 1

1572-AN OVERTURNED VERDICT

A full moon rose over the Aravalli range that fateful night on February 28th, 1572. Down in the Gogunda fortress, flickering lamps threw giant shadows of the select nobles surrounding the deathbed of Maharana Udai Singh II. The dying king looked in askance at his favourite queen Dheerubai seated by his bed.

"Your son…" he said, inhaling heavily, "Jagmal will succeed me."

A faint smile mixed with grief crossed his consort's regal face.

"May he uphold the honour of Mewar," were the king's final words.

A moment later, one long release of Udai Singh's breath indicated his demise. Dheerubai let out a long wail.

Kishan Singh, one of the king's most trusted men, closed the royal eyelids. He left the king's closet to break the sad news to the waiting courtiers in the ante-chamber, "Maharana Udai Singh has joined his ancestors. May the king's memory be honoured!"

"Long live the king!" came the emotional refrain from the palace officials.

"Let the arrangements begin for the cremation" directed Kishan Singh.

The nobles hurried to the basement of the palace except for Rawal Singh, the apex general of the Mewari army.

Kishan Singh began musing in a soft voice, "Rawal, this coup shall defeat the manipulation of Dheerubai. The future of Mewar is at stake."

Rawal Singh's black pupils dilated with fervour, "You have my word," assured the overlord, his ribbon-style moustache rising in belligerence. He whistled and a large group of sleek-looking warriors came racing. "The commanders are all set."

The two nobles marched into the royal hall, followed by the posse. Blazing lamps on the walls of the empty hall illuminated a solemn-looking Jagmal Singh who had instantly seized power moments after his father's demise, seated on the throne of Mewar. Kishan Singh marched straight to the new king with Rawal and the army's topcats close on his heels.

"Prince Jagmal," said Kishan Singh as he placed both his hands on the regent's right arm, while a furious looking Rawal Singh already had his on Jagmal's left, "the throne is not yours!"

Jagmal Singh looked shocked, but not surprised. He always suspected that his rivalry with Prathap Singh would culminate in a cataclysmic clash in one way or the other. Was this the hour of fate? How annoying! How naïve on his part not to be prepared to counter his rival's confidantes!

They had perfectly been camouflaged like snakes in the green grass. Sweat began trickling down his handsome temples.

"My father chose me as king" he replied softly.

"Your brother Prathap Singh is the rightful king!" thundered Rawal Singh "If you don't vacate the throne… You shall face the consequences."

The successor calmly gazed at the armed entourage pulling the steel blades out of their sheaths. A few pointed lengthy steel-tipped spears straight at his face.

"Traitors! Backstabbers!" screamed Jagmal Singh standing up. They pulled him roughly. He was cast onto the red-grey ornate carpet. Kishan Singh brought his astute face close to Jagmal Singh who managed to prop up his person on his elbows. "Either bow to Prathap Singh or flee away! Forever!"

Jagmal Singh got up and stared into the eyes of the rebels as he surveyed them all.

"Flee?" he mocked Kishan Singh with a stare. "Alright, you robbers, just wait."

He hastened out of the hall in hotblooded fury. As he left, swarms of armed soldiers flashing sharp talwar swords surrounded the royal court, cordoning it off completely.

CHAPTER 2

THE CALL OF DESTINY

$\mathcal{P}$rathap Singh walked with Mewari pride on the cobbled stones of the Gogunda Fort driveway. He was almost a staggering seven feet, with amazing broad shoulders and a striking handlebar moustache to match. His royal gait matched with an excellent physique marked him out distinctly.

Now, he was about to leave the kingdom once and for all. His noble bluish-black steed, Chetak, stationed just outside the gates twitched his ears at the approach of his master's footsteps. Prathap Singh's wife Kanwar and their son Amar Singh were each already mounted on dark brown stallions flanked by his ever-loyal cavalry guards. The rest of his entourage and his other wives and their children were crowded in several horse carriages.

Would he ever return to these walls of Gogunda? What of Kumbalgarh and of mystic Chittor? He was about to mount Chetak when he heard a loud authoritarian, "Stop!"

It was Kishan Singh pacing very fast. He was being accompanied by Rawal Singh and the top generals.

"Your Highness, you cannot leave!" beseeched the trusted aide.

Prathap Singh made no answer.

"Kishan Singh, let me go into exile in peace" he said after a moment.

Kishan Singh looked at Kanwar and the young Amar Singh. "Sire, you are the next king!" he continued, fixing his attention back on Prathap Singh.

"That would be my brother Jagmal. He succeeds my father" advised Prathap Singh.

"Young Prince, Mewar has revolted…Prince Jagmal has abdicated the throne. His family has been awarded safe passage. They have fled" joined Rawal Singh, his eyes wide with excitement. "The people will have no one except you as their king. You are Mewar's choice. You have been their choice since your childhood. Do not disappoint them."

By this time, a massive crowd of soldiers and the public had surrounded Prathap Singh and his family. Hundreds more were rushing towards him.

Prathap Singh became concerned. Am I facing a slew of onrushing events? Things change in a matter of hours, don't they? He glanced at Kanwar. Her expressive eyes goaded him to believe.

The prince wished to ascertain nevertheless, "Kishan, Rawal, lead on."

He mounted Chetak and proceeded into Gogunda Fort rather than out of it, with reverberations of metallic horse hooves on the stone pavement.

Shouts of "Long live Maharana Prathap Singh!" filled the air.

Many lined up to throw rose petals on the approaching regent. Graceful Kanwar flashed a big smile. There were shouts of glee from Prathap Singh's children, the rest of his wives, his faithful bodyguards and the rest of the entourage. The die was cast. The throne of Mewar beckoned him. He had no choice but to say yes.

It was late afternoon when his tall figure walked into the royal hall with a measured tread along with Kishan Singh, Rawal Singh and the generals. He gazed at the vacant throne.

"Sire, we need to have the coronation before the sun sets. This has been our practice."

Feeling the weight of destiny on his shoulders, Prathap Singh said, "So be it."

"Summon the priests," commanded Rawal Singh to one of his generals who immediately hurried out of the hall.

With hardly half an hour left for sunset, Prathap Singh was duly crowned King of Mewar. Meanwhile, on the other outer reaches of the palace, the remains of Maharana Udai Singh II were consigned to leaping orange flames on a large pile of oak logs.

CHAPTER 3

THE SEEDS OF WAR

1573, Fatehpur Sikri

"Your Highness, Prince Jagmal of Mewar and his entourage," declared an imperial guard bowing before Emperor Akbar. The athletic monarch, a descendant of the Timur-Genghis Khan bloodline, was seated on an ornate throne about seven feet off the floor fixed upon a hexagonal metal base right at the centre of a wide wooden enclosure, designed with four eight-foot-high heavy, four-poster vertical beams upholding a rectangular canopy. To his right stood a large group of sharp-eyed veteran courtiers – Mughals and dashing rajputs sporting heavy moustaches. There were also a few commanders from the military dressed in ceremonial outfits sporting matching turbans. To his left stood a sizable number of young males from his extended royal family dressed in impeccable outfits apt for a royal court. One royal to his left held the emperor's sword sheathed in its scabbard, another bore his magnificent dagger which was sheathed in a sparkling green metal frame. Another Mughal behind him hugged his king's quiver to his chest while bearing the bow on his left shoulder. Two young Mughals standing way too close to the monarch were fanning him with exquisite strips of long, fine gossamer-like linen. Another young man wearing a beige outfit stood with a glove on his right that held a seated dove. A lone warrior remained upright with his shield and lengthy spear just off the throne. Immediately surrounding the throne were the members of his inner circle who were shining stars in their own right. On that lovely morning one of these men, Tansen, the poet-warrior, began reciting verses that he had penned in his king's honour. Akbar gestured at Tansen to pause his recitation at the announcement of the guard. The cabinet, the military command and the crowd of courtiers quietened their hustle and fixed their focus on the doorway to the Mughal court. There was a long moment of silence before Jagmal, Queen Dheerubai and their attendants humbly walked in to pay obeisance to the monarch.

"Long live the great emperor!" began Prathap Singh's younger sibling. "Your Highness, I, Prince Jagmal of Mewar and my company are here to pledge our allegiance to your rule over this vast land. May you reign from the Hindu Kush to the outer reaches of the Ganges and even to the eastern sea!"

Akbar was pleased with such a meek surrender. He grinned, raising his eyebrows.

"However, Your Majesty," added Jagmal in a sombre tone, "my brother Prathap Singh has conspired against this alliance and has taken the throne by force. We seek your protection."

The sovereign's eyebrows narrowed. So, Mewar has not changed its ways? He fixed his gaze at Jagmal Singh, "Son, you are welcome at my court. No one will dare touch you. Raja Birbal, my commander will advise you about your privileges and responsibilities on this deal. You shall leave for your quarters now."

Turning right he nodded at his standing courtiers who escorted the group out of the court.

The king looked at Abul Fazal, his grand vizier, "So close and yet so far," he said with a touch of regret.

The grey bearded vizier smiled, "Who knows, this Prathap Singh may walk into this court tomorrow and pledge allegiance despite him rejecting our proposals three times."

Akbar surveyed Man Singh, the rajput prince from the Amber region, his gem and military stalwart. He also happened to be the emperor's nephew. The rugged general, fixed his probing eyes on the throne, his massive horseshoe moustache perfectly adorned his winsome physique.

"Prathap Singh could rally our foes, especially the Afghan rebels" Man Singh began thoughtfully. "Mewar considers him hero. Ambition runs in his blood." He glanced at Birbal. There was a moment's silence again.

Then Birbal, the pale, wheatish-complexioned mastermind said, "Mewar is a divided house." The tough commander paused for a moment then raised his chin and ramrod straight nose at Akbar, "We have now gained a foothold on their kingdom. Prathap Singh's brothers Shakta, Sagar and now Jagmal are with us. His family's loyalty is wearing away. It won't be long."

Akbar took a deep breath. Was it time for his armies to unleash war on the rajputs of Mewar again? The last one which he led in person resulted in Chittor falling to the Mughals. The resulting carnage was horrific. About 30,000 Mewari troops who were the final line defending the fortress fell in the valiant endeavour to avoid the take-over. The defeat also witnessed Mewari women and children in the fort committing mass suicide. Maharana Udai Singh's garrison fought with zeal and valour. Nevertheless, they could not match the Mughal cannon fire. The emperor witnessed large sections of the fort go up in flames as the female inmates took their lives in a gruesome manner. Billowing black fumes and cries of anguish filled Chittor that February day in 1572. Maharana Udai Singh and his army chose a tactical retreat well in advance to avoid an all-out clash with the Mughal war machine, vainly hoping that Chittor would satiate the greed of the invaders.

Akbar posed a query to his cabinet, "Should I come down on Mewar?"

Todar Mal, always the one to wait for his turn quipped, "Send an emissary yet another time. We shall sense Prathap Singh's motives. If he does not comply, we shall wage war."

"My elephants and cavalry are raring to go," beamed Birbal.

"Should you not spread your canopy from the Hindu Kush to the Ganges as the prince observed?" joined in Faizi, the Yemenite, elder brother of Abul Fazl, donning a maroon turban and sporting a flowing red beard.

Akbar envisioned glory. If he could consolidate his grip on Malwa and Gujarat, Mewar would be encompassed. He could force them into submission. Then, he could venture deep into the Deccan…From the Hindu Kush to the Ganges and even to the eastern sea, certainly. The massacre at Chittor had tarnished his name per contra. It would not go unforgotten. Mewar would nurse the Chittor infamy for all time to come.

"Court dismissed," said the regent as he descended the steps. The aristocrats stood erect. As he walked past his courtiers, he raised his voice, "Man Singh, Birbal." He then snapped his fingers in the air, "You too, Todar Mal."

The three think-tanks hurried behind the regent as he made his way into the gardens.

CHAPTER 4

THE BAIT

1573 Fatehpur Sikri

The Moghul Czar walked in deep contemplation among the aisles of rose bushes surrounding the iconic Fatehpur Sikri Fort. He had his hands at the back, his fingers were interlocked. A cool breeze began to waft into the gardens that early afternoon. The three nobles followed in quiet silence. He swung around suddenly and addressed the prince of Amber.

"Man Singh" began Akbar.

"My Lord" replied the rajput war hero.

"You are related to the rulers of Mewar, aren't you?" continued the emperor.

"Yes, by marriage. One of the Amber royals married Maharana Udai Singh" came the calm reply.

"How much clout do you have over this Prathap Singh?" said Akbar as he stopped walking.

"That remains to be seen. The waters must be tested for their depth" proposed Man Singh.

Akbar paused for a moment. A nightingale started calling out its distinctive cries from the branches of a distant mango tree.

"I have been deeply perturbed by the massacre at Chittor. Not to mention the suicide of their womenfolk."

For a split second, rajput pride swelled in the bosom of Man Singh. He collected himself instantly.

"We shall tread softly, at least initially. Mewar must capitulate to Mughal rule. We will give them that chance to do it honourably. You shall meet Prathap Singh. Offer him our terms" counselled the crown.

"With pleasure," said Man Singh with a gleam in his eyes.

"But first you are to command the army to crush the rebellion once for all in Gujarat. On your way back, call on Mewar. If the waters are too deep, we shall drain them, Man Singh!" rumbled Akbar.

"At your service," bowed Man Singh who was born and raised in the Mughal court. His father Raja Bhagwan Das was Akbar's pointman over the Punjab province. Das also happened to be the emperor's brother-in-law.

"Birbal, what is your counsel?" questioned the throne.

"My King" said the crafty general as he ambled along his lord, "let us sharpen our swords for battle. Who knows how things will turn out?"

The magnate looked at Todar Mal to his left to elicit his opinion. The reserved administrator answered, "I feel we should give Mewar enough time. Repeated inculcation of goodwill could ultimately win them over. They are very suspicious after the Chittor episode."

The smell of roses hung heavily in the air. In the distance several dense rows of pink bougainvillea were stretching their strong thorny branches over angular wooden beams to spread themselves all over the periphery of the gardens.

Akbar fixed his gaze on a rose bud, "Man Singh, prepare to lead the army in five days. Proceed with the logistics" he said, turning to the general with a look of approval.

The muscular general immediately left, walking towards the far end of the fort.

Akbar bowed to smell the fragrance of the bud. He looked at Birbal, "Every rose has its thorns, has it not?"

Birbal smiled, "If the rose is to be desired sire, you have to deal with the thorns."

"My! Raja Birbal!" exclaimed Akbar as his eyes lit up with glee.

The three then strolled towards the dining hall of the fort.

CHAPTER 5

PERILOUS STATECRAFT

1573, Udaipur

The golden rays of the sun swept into every chamber of the Udaipur palace that summer morning as Maharana Prathap Singh read the scroll again in the audience hall. There was no expression on his face. He eased back on his comfortable armchair.

"You may wait" he said to the Mughal messenger standing ten feet away.

The man was whisked away at once to exit the royal hall.

"The Mughals have dispatched a message" said the king rising from his chair.

Prathap Singh thought for a while. Looking at Kishan Singh he opined, "Should we not honour rajput blood though such a man serves foreigners?"

"My Lord?" said his aide wishing to sense the dynamics of that morning.

Prathap Singh looked at Rawal Singh to his right and then again at Kishan Singh. "Man Singh Amber, Akbar's top commander is on his way here. The Mughals are up to something."

"Has not Akbar commended your brothers, Jagmal, Sagar and Shakta for betraying Mewar? Lands, titles, fiefdoms, what not?" chipped in Rawal Singh.

"Ignominy par excellence!" said a furious Kishan Singh. "Had Rana Sanga been alive, these traitors would have been quartered to pieces!"

"Cowards have no honour," said Prathap Singh as he gazed out of a window. He turned and looked at Rawal Singh intently, "We need to sense their intention for this visit."

"There is no smoke without fire," replied the top administrator philosophically, "Their hands are itching for war! They may demand a quid-pro-quo from you, My Lord."

"Can we forget the loss of Chittor?" anguished Kishan Singh, his eyes glaring, "These brutes slaughtered thousands of innocents. Not to forget our women and children."

Prathap Singh walked straight to a window and looked out at Lake Udai Sagar, "Mewar will not bow to the Mughals. We need to show our resolve. Let us however be courteous enough to honour Man Singh. I sense confrontation. Eventually these Mughals will show their true nature."

"My sword shall slay a thousand Moghuls!" thundered Kishan Singh as he partially pulled his razor-sharp talwar from its scabbard and sent the hilt slamming against the rim.

"My life for Mewar! Should I not spill the blood of these invaders to avenge Chittor?" exploded Rawal Singh.

The king turned to face his confidantes. His eyes were gleaming, his broad, black moustache like a sickle reaching to his sideburns began quivering with pride, "If these troublemakers attack again...We shall make them wallow in their own blood!"

Both top aides felt a deep sense of fulfilment when their king threatened to take on the Mughals. Their faces were filled with broad smiles.

"We shall meet Man Singh on the banks of Udai Sagar in the afternoon. Let not Man Singh set his eyes on this fort. We leave at once. Summon Amar Singh. Apprise the messenger."

In a short while, the gates of Udaipur palace flung open as Prathap Singh and his entourage galloped towards the rendezvous point.

On reaching the banks of Udai Sagar, tents were set and the cooking commenced as the sun broke through the clouds once again.

The sky was overcast with heavy black-grey clouds as thunder and lightning filled the atmosphere when the Mughal army – 30,000 strong – made its halt about 10 kilometres from Udaipur in the afternoon. At the head of this force was commander Man Singh perched on a small bamboo enclosure atop his special beast of war, an enormous Indian male war elephant that was almost thirteen-feet tall. It almost weighed about four tons! The army, neatly divided into legions was being led by able lieutenants. A few precisely-placed infantrymen carried lengthy green tapering flags. The Mughal battle standards were also carried by a few captains of the cavalry who followed the foot soldiers in battle formation. The general came down the heavily armoured gigantic beast on a rope ladder. He patted the pachyderm on its trunk. The huge animal made a long grunting sound of approval.

Man Singh summoned Asaf Khan, his deputy, "It won't be long. I shall be back in two hours. I don't expect a surprise attack from Gujarat. We have crushed them beyond hope. Nevertheless, dispatch lookouts in all directions."

The aide clenched his fist and placed it on his heart, "Your order shall be followed."

The gritty general mounted a dappled steed and took off towards Udai Sagar. He was accompanied by twenty cavalrymen carrying the Mughal standards.

Crown Prince Amar Singh could see the approaching horses from the lake. He was dressed in an impeccable outfit as he awaited the arrival of Man Singh. The horses pulled in. Man Singh looked at Amar Singh with a bit of curiosity. He then fixed his gaze at the eminent figure of Prathap Singh standing some distance away. He dismounted.

"Welcome to Mewar, General," greeted Amar Singh with a forced smile, "My father awaits you."

Prathap Singh now moved in briskly, "Greetings, Man Singh. May you feel at home among the rajputs."

"I am always at home in the land of Hindustan" said the General to Prathap Singh in a business-like tone as he greeted him. He then glanced at the arrangements in place.

After the customary washing of hands, the general was treated like a king to a vast array of delicious rajput cuisine. Hungry Man Singh and his escorts had their fill. Amar Singh, Rawal Singh and Kishan Singh stood a few feet away from the august personas.

Man Singh began sipping a glassful of sweet lassi. He looked at Prathap Singh.

"You are aware how closely we are related through marriage, Prathap Singh" commenced the general.

"I'm fully aware" replied the king of Mewar.

"We rajputs of Amber, made a decision to serve the Mughals. Not just Amber, but Marwar, Jaisalmer, Ajmer and the rest." He finished his dessert and wiped his mouth clean. "There is no power in Hindustan that can defeat the Mughal army." He paused for a moment.

"The Mughals have absolute sway from the Persian border, over all of the Afghan mountains, over the plains of the Indus and all the way to the outer reaches of the Ganges. Why, even to the eastern sea! We shall conquer the remainder of this land. We are venturing deep into the heartland too! They will genuflect before us as the grass bends to a rolling boulder."

"You mean… you expect no opposition?" quizzed Prathap Singh with a stern look.

"Opposition is futile, my son…Those who oppose must know they will not live to tell the tale! Why does Mewar have to resist us? Neither your father Udai Singh nor Rana Sanga, your forebear, realized this. What became of Mewar's resistance at Chittor? Your defiance will only result in despair, defeat and death! Why don't you accept hard reality? Just like the other rajput kingdoms who have—"

He was rudely interrupted.

"You expect me to follow suit? To follow the example of other rajputs into conceding my kingdom into Mughal hands? Should I morph into a mere subject of the 'Great Mughal'? Must I do his bidding as his servant and be ready at his beck and call?" countered Prathap Singh with a cold, composed face.

"We crushed your father's army at Chittor" warned Man Singh as he leaned forward, his eyes riveted on Prathap Singh, "Don't delay the inevitable. His majesty sent Jalal Khan Qurchi to meet you thrice. You rejected our offer on all three occasions."

"So?" replied Prathap Singh, his eyes narrowing in deep anger.

"The emperor wishes to give Mewar an honourable exit from repeating a confrontation. You surrender your sovereignty to the Mughal potentate and in return you will live your life at Akbar's court. Mewar shall become part of Mughal territory and your posterity shall continue to generations. What's more, you can even strike marriage alliances for your princesses with the Mughal household!"

Prathap Singh rose from his chair in fury. He fixed his wrathful stare at Man Singh.

"An honourable exit? Babur beheaded 500 rajputs at Khanwa and nailed their heads to wooden poles. Was that honourable? Your lord Akbar forced thousands of women and children to commit suicide by burning themselves when he ravaged Chittor with his artillery guns. You call that honour? You Mughals have no sense of honour!"

Anger and pride rose in his words. The tent was terse. A feeling of severe awkwardness began permeating the ambience.

Prathap Singh continued, "Rajput honour runs in my blood! We will never kiss the Mughal foot! And, should a ravishing beauty of Mewar produce children for a Mughal? Are we going to stoop so low?"

Man Singh's eyes widened in mild astonishment. He began glaring at his statuesque, well-built Mewari kinsman.

"We shall never concede. Either to you or to your fancy emperor! Mewar shall meet your so called 'inevitable' head on!" concluded Prathap Singh visibly enraged by now.

Man Singh now raised his handsome frame, "Choose your words carefully, Prince," he warned, his eyes frozen, his horseshoe moustache bristling with anger, "Your kingdom doesn't stand a chance."

"Chance?" roared the king like a lion. He advanced a step or two towards Man Singh, "These ragtag Mughals invade us from nowhere bearing strange designations like the Tajiks, Kazhaks and Uzbeks. Not to forget the notorious Turks, Mongols, Persians and Afghans—-and these are gauging my chances? I am sprung from the soil of The Hind! I am no foreigner! I am a direct progeny of King Porus! We defied the Greeks. We shall also defy the Mughals!"

Man Singh was fuming by now. His ingenious eyes were blazing with animosity, "You have your head in the clouds, son. You are haughty," he said as he spat on the ground, "Don't learn the hard way." His voice was slowly rising, "It will be too late. It will do well for you to learn respect for your masters!" He then walked away in a huff exercising extreme self-control in the face of such an outburst from Prathap Singh.

"There will be no submission!" thundered Prathap Singh. Man Singh's attendants instantly felt the reverberations of his voice.

As Akbar's stocky commander and his soldiers mounted their steeds, he aimed his vengeful eyes at Prathap Singh, "If I don't humble you, my name is not Man Singh!"

"I shall look forward to that day!" retorted Prathap Singh in a flash, "Don't forget to bring along your Uncle Akbar to witness the combat!"

The posse left the banks of Udai Sagar towards the Mughal camp, leaving behind a cloud of dust.

"I curse you, Man Singh!" muttered Prathap Singh in their wake, "You slave! You traitor!"

There was a pause for about a moment as Prathap Singh kept staring at the fading Mughal unit in the distance.

"This ground has been defiled by Man Singh and his entourage!" said Prathap Singh turning around, his eyes still glaring.

"Rawal! Kishan! Order this place to be cleansed with the water of the Ganges. Burn all things here. Get rid of every last whiff of Mughal odour from this place… We have slapped the Mughals. They will not take this lightly."

CHAPTER 6

THE BENEFIT OF DOUBT

Fatehpur Sikri, 1574

The audience hall of the Diwan-E-Khas was lit up by burning torches on the walls that early evening. Akbar's mind was deep at work. Birbal and Man Singh occupied settees to the right and Todar Mal and Abul Fazl to the left. Their eyes were fixed on their king. A few court officials stood to Akbar's right and left as usual but not that many as in the main hall of the court.

"So, the calf won't budge, will he?" said Akbar with a smile at Man Singh.

"His young blood is all excited, My Liege. Had he some taste of our might, he would have been forthcoming" replied a grim-faced Man Singh, his demeanour demanding war.

"There is no point in negotiating, My Lord. This is the fourth time Prathap Singh has rejected our overtures" quipped Birbal, "Why should we be mocked?" he said looking at Man Singh for attestation. The general gave him a matter-of-fact eyeballing nod.

"Raja Birbal," began Abul Fazl, "The Chittor deaths still disturb His Majesty. Those memories must first be put to rest before we launch a new campaign against Mewar."

The emperor rose and began pacing back and forth, "We have brought almost all rajput clans under our banner. They excel in every realm of the empire. Arts, culture, warfare and what not! We intermarry with them too. They are such noble subjects. Mewar alone has become a thorn in the flesh. Prathap Singh's brothers Shakti, Sagar and Jagmal are in our service. If we wage war against Mewar after what happened at Chittor, I feel it would shake the foundations of my relations with the rajput domains. Is not blood thicker than water?"

"If blood indeed is thicker than water, the rajputs would not be your able soldiers, subjects and counsellors. Should we not strike the iron when it is glowing red?" reasoned Birbal feeling certain that his king was in the wrong, "You now have the perfect ruse, My King!"

"Todar Mal?" said Akbar turning his head right, "What do you feel?"

The somewhat rotund gem nodded his head and said, "A worthy enemy will have the guts to challenge us. We could offer Prathap Singh yet another chance. Why don't we assign Raja Bhagwan Das to counsel Mewar?" Todar Mal looked at Man Singh to have his approval. "He has immense standing in the empire. He could sway Prathap Singh into submission."

Man Singh raised his arching eyebrows. His pride swelled at the mention of his father's name.

"Moreover, we are facing rebellion in the Hindu Kush, Bihar and Bengal. The Safavids of Persia are ever scheming to intrude into Hindustan via Kandahar. We need to firmly deal with these issues first and then turn our attention to Mewar." His husky voice reasoning with Birbal, Man Singh and the rest for acceptance.

"That seems right... Birbal, you shall carry tidings to Raja Bhagwan Das at Lahore. The issues raised by Todar Mal demand our immediate attention" observed an imposing Akbar presuming everyone at the council to fall in line. There was silence for a moment or so.

Akbar looked at Man Singh with pride, his thoughts now turned to dealing with issues concerning the military hierarchy, "I don't care what the army top brass believes. You are the one who will command my army, Man Singh!" he said raising his voice, "In a week's time you shall lead my troops into battle against those Afghan renegades in the Hindu Kush. Raja Birbal shall accompany you on this campaign."

A big grin broke on the face of Akbar's most trusted aide. Akbar took cognizance of Birbal's reaction and returned the smile in a reserved manner.

"Bihar and Bengal shall follow," he continued, "Then we shall fix our attention on Mewar and its king. My leniency has its limits. If Prathap Singh doesn't budge, he would meet the fate of Udai Singh's Jaimal at Chittor! Let us go."

The sovereign and his ministers got up and left the hall. They stepped into the cobbled courtyard of Fatehpur Sikri. The night was cool. A gentle breeze brushed their faces as the moon rose like a scimitar in the sky.

CHAPTER 7

A TANTALIZING OFFER

Mewar, 1574

The Kumbalgarh Fort rose like a city reaching for the sky that early morning as Raja Bhagwan Das stood with Prathap Singh on the battlements of the impressive citadel.

"I can understand your feelings, Prathap Singh" began Das as he took a few steps, "However, one has to balance one's decisions against the appeal of wisdom."

"And what would be that?" asked an impatient Prathap Singh as a huge band of clouds blocked out the sun.

Das stopped walking. He leaned on the parapet wall and looked straight into Prathap Singh's eyes.

A Tantalizing Offer

"If you decide to face down the Mughals... then, bloodshed, chaos, displacement, gory violence and in all likelihood your death on the battlefield would be the outcomes."

Prathap Singh shot back, "Would not such a death be the greatest feat for a rajput?"

"Your people will endure immense anguish and prolonged suffering at Mughal hands. Has not Mewar suffered enough?" continued Das, "Do you want to bring perpetual torment on your people? The weaponry and manpower of Akbar's army will annihilate you in all certainty. The people of Mewar will face the brunt of the oppression that will follow. Is it your wish to see that happen? Who knows if you would be alive to witness such pain? I'm trying to convince you that your war with the Mughals would be an exercise in futility! Bravado is one thing and facing the Mughal legions in military conflict is another thing altogether."

"You are suggesting that I prostrate at Akbar's feet? That I should think of comfort, leisure, pleasure and save myself from gruesome warfare with these Mughal nomads? Should I purpose to live till my hair is hoary with old age than to choose to have my dead body burn on the pyre? Should I watch the Mughal flag fly over my soil? Is that not humiliation by all means? A true rajput will never part with his honour! Let history say Prathap Singh chose warfare, battle and a valorous death rather than bow before the Mughals! As for my people, they are ready for any fate. We shall die together defending this land, this soil, rather than accept Mughal supremacy. Speaking of which, the Mughals don't belong here. They are invaders from the other side of the Oxus and the Jaxtares. Are they not an amalgamation of those so-called Turks, Persians, Tajiks, Uzbeks, Kazhaks and Afghans? Should I, a son of this land, acknowledge their military supremacy and bend my knee to this horde from the snow-capped Caucasian mountains? They intend to bring all of Hindustan under their dominion", Prathap Singh sounded intransigent.

Kanwar, his queen, watched the proceedings from a safe distance on the battlements clad in a shimmering turquoise saree, her face was half covered, exposing only of her elegant eyes. She watched with anxiety hoping that Mewar would somehow avoid war with the Mughals. She was not very sure if such a scenario could be averted.

Both men started walking on the ramparts. Das began gazing at the surrounding countryside and its idyllic features. The cloud-cover overhead moved away slowly allowing the blazing light of the sun to flood the massive fort.

"I have a proposition for you that could probably be acceptable to you and the empire" said Das after a pause in the conversation.

Prathap Singh locked his eyes with his interlocutor's. He raised his right eyebrow, "Go on."

"If you would depute your son Amar Singh to be in attendance at the Mughal court for a short period of time, it might soothe Akbar's anger against your perceived insolence. And I shall promise you that I would use my bearing to convince the emperor himself to return Chittor to Mewar's fold. It would be an exchange on both sides."

"He would return Chittor?" asked Prathap Singh with a bewildered face, "Would he?"

"I would reason with Akbar for the same. Though Mughal firepower is incredible on the battlefield, they are quite reasonable to strike a deal to avoid bringing such potency into play. This compromise looks like a win-win situation for both sides. You will certainly not lose face by any means!" assured the aging rajput governor, "Mewar's flag over Chittor and your crown prince in attendance at Fatehpur Sikri... Would you accept this arrangement? At least temporarily?"

Prathap Singh made no response. However, the very thought of redeeming Chittor raised his spirits. Chittor, the very nerve-centre, the very life of Mewar! He looked excited.

"If Chittor would be returned as an initial gesture and if the Mughals back off from the remaining Mewar domains, we could think over this to avoid conflict. My son Amar Singh would be deputed to attend the Mughal court. However, this gesture should not be looked upon as if I am succumbing to Mughal pressure. If things happen as you propose…" said Prathap Singh with a sombre face and not completing the sentence. He carried on, "Neither will I fight on behalf of the Mughals nor will Mewar's princesses be given in marriage to these foreigners. These clauses are definitely not part of this arrangement."

Das looked at Prathap Singh with Mughal gait. There are lines that I ought not to cross, he thought, "This is a good development. I can only hope that it leads to a truce between Mewar and the Mughals. I am imploring you to avoid the other scenario. It would certainly be not good for you nor for Mewar."

It had been becoming very overcast. Thick, grey clouds gradually blocked out the sun. Heavy drops of rain began slamming onto the battlements. The cool downpour turned into a deluge in an instant. Prathap Singh and his esteemed guest rushed into the chambers of the fortress.

After being seated, the Mughal emissary said, "Akbar feels bad about the course of the war on Chittor. He wants you to build a good relationship with him. As a mark of respect, he has sent this special shawl for you. You should wear this if you believe the emperor should be respected."

A Tantalizing Offer

He handed over a neatly folded shawl to Pratap Singh. The King of Mewar spread it out. It was greenish yellow in colour, about three foot long, interspersed with arabesque imagery.

"You expect me to wear this?" he asked Das.

"It's a choice you have to make. It will be taken as a mark of respect for the Mughals" replied the emissary.

"Thank you for the gift. It will be taken care of" said Mewar's champion without specifying what exactly he intended to do with it. He laid it on the armchair next to him.

The delegate began again, "I wish to make amends if Man Singh had hurt your feelings. We are rajputs at the end of the day, irrespective of whether we serve the Mughals or not."

After a moment's thought, Prathap Singh said, "If only the rajputs were united under one banner, instead of clamouring over clan loyalties, no adversary would have set his foot on our soil. The rajputs would never have sold their honour to aliens." Das locked eyes with Mewar's king for a moment.

"No offence meant, sire" added Prathap Singh correcting his censure.

"If the weather permits, I shall leave for Fatehpur Sikri tomorrow" observed Das.

"Amar Singh shall accompany you. The welfare of Mewar is my utmost concern. I hope that this 'arrangement', you put forth, works. Amar Singh's safety is your responsibility."

"Not a hair of head shall fall to the ground under Mughal protection!" assured Das.

CHAPTER 8

A FINAL THROW OF DICE

1574, Fatehpur Sikri

The Mughal sovereign kept gazing at the cool, rushing Jumna as he contemplated his next move. The wide banks of the river were overgrown with tall, green grass. He was lost in thought for a while. His throne attendees were standing at a short distance with utmost respect. A flock of cranes whooped in and swept pass the scion and his entourage as they camped on the banks of the watercourse.

"So, once again Mewar refuses" remarked Akbar addressing Bhagwan Das

"He has deputed his crown prince to attend the court, Your Highness" replied Das, "Amar Singh will be in attendance from tomorrow."

The monarch locked eyes with Das as the top official continued, "He is very firm on you returning Chittor to Mewar."

"Me, returning Chittor to Mewar? Is he insane?" retorted a wrathful Akbar, "Is he trying to rob me? Chittor is Mughal property. The fort is my jewel. He should forget it!"

Das glanced at Man Singh who raised his chin and pursed his lips in sheer irritation.

"My lord," started an angry Birbal, "this has gone way too far. He considers himself equal to you! Must we even trade territory? Is this a business deal?"

"I think we should consider his gesture in good faith" advised Todar Mal, "When his son returns to Mewar, he is certainly going to realize the goodness of the empire. The non-functionality of his impudence will surely dawn upon him. Chittor was won with Mughal blood. It shall never be returned."

At some distance, Tansen and Abdul Rahim Khan, son of Bairam Khan, Akbar's guardian during his cchildhood and adolescence, were tuning their instruments to a new song that Tansen had composed in honour of the emperor. The strains of the song seemed to soothe Akbar. Mewar and its revolting king appeared insignificant. Must he be infuriated at the prospect of a lone rajput king who was infatuated with himself? A rajput who thought it worthy to bargain with the mighty Mughals?

Albeit, he didn't want to be too merciful to him either. Court gossip was something he hated. Especially babble that projected him as indecisive.

"We shall not blow this issue out of proportion" observed Akbar, "Let his son be allotted lodging among the royals as a sign of courtesy. I shall however not grant him audience. I shall only meet Prathap Singh as a feudatory in my court. Mewar was expected to give up its self-rule. It is childish to think of striking a territorial deal."

Tansen and Abdul Rahim Khan kept straining their song relentlessly in the distance.

There was silence all around except for the sound of the song and the noise of the onrushing Jumna.

Akbar mused aloud, "He has obliged us in receiving my gift. Let's hope he gives up his frail expectations. Todar Mal, you shall accompany the young man back to Mewar after his service and serve notice in all seriousness. If Prathap Singh spurns me, my army shall slay him!"

"As you wish" said Todar Mal.

The king then looked at his nephew Man Singh and then at his favourite bureaucrat Birbal and said, "What of the Hindu Kush?"

"The pockets of resistance have been dealt with, My Liege" replied Man Singh, "Nevertheless, hundreds of these fighters have taken refuge in the mountains beyond Kabul. And your brother Mirza Mohammed Hakim still wields influence over these rebels. He is their inspiration. Hakim still dreams of the Mughal throne."

"He can keep dreaming for the rest of his life" chuckled Akbar, "What madness!"

Birbal grinned, "My lord, we need another campaign against these outlaws. Should not the Hindu Kush be free of these rebels? They must be pulled out by their roots."

Man Singh smiled with reserved seriousness. He could understand Birbal's eagerness for combat yet again. *The Afghan mountains are alluring Birbal,* he thought. *May be Kabul. Who knows?*

"A little yeast affects a jug of milk, My King" said Abul Fazl, "Don't overlook it."

A little yeast? Hakim as the yeast at the source of this insurgency? What does he amount to? Akbar reminisced his brother for a moment. *He is way too exclusive to be branded 'secular'. He is intolerant. The empire would implode to bits and pieces.*

"He must be shown his place. I know all too well that he keeps sending feelers to certain courtiers at Fatehpur Sikri to incite rebellion. We shall not fall for his cheap tricks" noted Akbar. He then came close to his vizier and fixed his eagle eyes on him, "My empire shall treat all faiths on equal footing. We receive all. We treat all with dignity. Hindus and Muslims alike. There shall be no discrimination. I shall deliver Hakim a stern warning. If he doesn't mend his ways, he will pay with his own life. I don't care him being my brother! I will burn Kabul to ashes notwithstanding my grandfather's grave!".

The decisiveness of the emperor towards his own brother's purported mutiny touched upon the members of his entourage, especially Birbal, in sharp contrast to his very flexible attitude towards Prathap Singh. Why this forbearance? Why show gentleness and sympathy towards Mewar contemplated Birbal. He turned to look at Man Singh to sense the depth of his thoughts. The general stared back at him completely baffled by Akbar's leniency. It was beyond him.

A huge swarm of low-flying storks caught everybody's attention that afternoon. Akbar looked up and gazed for a while. He mock-hunted the birds on the wing with a shot of his imaginary bow and arrow.

"Man Singh" said Akbar as he turned to him.

"My Lord" replied the highly favoured rajput soldier in the empire.

"We are deputing you to bring Bihar, Bengal and the Gangetic firmly under Mughal control. Raja Bhagwan Das here shall have a stranglehold on Punjab in your absence."

Both Man Singh and Das bowed their heads in humility.

"Once the dust settles down in these spheres, you shall ride to Mewar to conquer. We would have shown our kindness, if Pratap Singh does not mend his ways by then."

CHAPTER 9

DESPERATE DIPLOMACY

Autumn, 1574

Todar Mal took his time to take in the breath-taking view of the rich natural scenery surrounding the Gogunda Fort. He was stunned by the panoramic landscape that enclosed this Mewari high citadel built more than 1000 metres above sea level. He could see for miles around.

"This fort is incredible, Prathap Singh!" remarked Mal.

Mewar's king stood in silence. His lips stretched into a small grin.

"My kingdom needs peace, Your Excellency. We are a peace-loving people. We keep to our own affairs. Our swords stay in their sheaths unless it is really necessary to pull them out" Prathap Singh postulated.

Todar Mal fixed his eyes on Prathap Singh, "That is the very reason why I am here. We are offering you peace and prosperity. However, it comes with a price. The emperor wishes to welcome you into the Mughal fold."

Prathap Singh shook his head, "That is not going to happen. Mewar never wants to have peace and prosperity in the garb of glossy slavery."

"Must you not be reasonable, rajput? What do you gain for defiance?" reasoned Mal. "The Mughals are here to stay."

"We choose peace with honour. If we have to pay a heavy price for it, so be it" carried on the defiant king.

"I'm a man of war myself. I lead the Mughal army into battles. I fully size up my adversary before I fight him on the battlefield" observed Mal. "I hope that is how you proceed prior to confronting the Mughals, Prathap Singh. The odds don't favour you. It would be an overwhelming victory for us. We would be gloating over your defeat. Your insubordination would make some ribald songs then. Would it be a wise choice?"

Prathap Singh launched into a rhetoric, "A man must meet his fate in some fashion. If time and chance favour my enemy there is nothing I can do. I will however go down fighting. I face a horde that comes from far beyond the Hindu Kush. They have established themselves all too well in Hindustan. They seek a dynasty. They are already establishing their legacy. The rajputs have thrown themselves at their feet fearing annihilation. What wonder! Where is their dignity? Where is their pride? Why didn't they choose death by the sword? Were they too scared?"

Todar Mal continued his counsel, "You are too proud." He stretched his arms wide open and swung about 180 degrees. "With all due respect, we would take everything you own if we are to cross swords in the theatre of war."

He noticed a sleek-looking woman in royal attire walk towards them carrying a steel platter. He paused. Prathap Singh knew his wife Kanwar was approaching. Her heavy chiming anklets and her tinkling silver bangles announced her presence. Milk pudding and cold water accompanied her graceful presence. Kanwar bowed at Mal. The famed Mughal administrator was touched.

"Blessings," he said half looking at her, hesitating to make eye contact with the elegant queen as she raised herself. Kanwar smiled in a measured way and left the two men to continue with their deliberations. Kanwar's sweet sounding anklets and bangles began fading in the distance as she entered the royal chambers.

"You could lose it all, rajput!" bragged Mal as he began eating the pudding with a spoon. "Your wives, your children, your heritage...your lands and anything that makes Mewar what it is will be devoured." He quickly gobbled the dessert with great gusto.

Prathap Singh too finished his glassful of the sweet dish.

"At least for your family's sake you have to accept this compromise," reasoned Mal. "You must choose to do it from a position of honour. Not when you growl before Akbar in chains!"

"I have my manliness and my sword! Prathap Singh shall never growl before your Akbar!" exclaimed the King of Mewar. He controlled his anger at once and calmed himself.

Coming close to Mal he muttered, "I have offered truce if your king returns Chittor. In exchange, my son would be in attendance at Fatehpur Sikri. He has been at the court for some time, hasn't he? I have made my moves. Now, the Mughals must make theirs. We, however, shall continue to be a distinct kingdom of our own. We shall never become a vassal state of the Mughals."

"The emperor is not pleased with that offer, rajput" replied Mal in an equally low voice. "Chittor will never be returned. You need to attend the royal court, not your son. Your son is not the king at Mewar. You are."

Prathap Singh moved an arm's distance away. He sneered at Todar Mal, "This proud rajput shall not bow to the Mughals. I shall never attend your courts!"

He moved away to a distance and started gazing at the farmers and peasants on their way to work that morning on the slopes of the mountains.

Mal sipped his cold water. "I shall take leave, rajput. I am afraid we shall not meet again. I shall convey your stance to the emperor. The rest is up to fate."

Prathap Singh made no answer. He walked towards Mal. He stopped, nodded and smiled.

The Mughal envoy made for the fort exit. He was accompanied by Kishan Singh and Rawal Singh on the way out. From a window of the royal chambers, Kanwar peeped out with her half-veiled face. Amar Singh stood close at hand to have a glimpse of the proceedings. Mal's posse left in a huff just like Man Singh's except for the swearing by Mewar's King in their wake.

Nothing that he tried had placated the Mughals. Prathap Singh stood there, trying to figure how long the de facto rulers of the continent would take to launch an all-out war against him.

The familiar chimes of his queen's anklets and her clinking bangles approached his sensitive ears. She came and stood by him as he continued to stare at the mountains encompassing the fort. The perfume of her long flowing undulant hair filled his nostrils. She turned and looked at him with concern. He took cognizance of her gaze. His eyes kept wandering all over the scenic surroundings.

"They will come" said Kanwar softly. "I can sense it. They will be coming with all their might. May you prevail, My King!"

Prathap Singh turned. He scanned her liquid eyes.

"I shall be waiting for them." He pulled out his awesome, shinning talwar from its sheath and ran the fingers of his left hand across its length. "My sword shall drink Mughal blood!" he taunted. "I shall also slay those rajput traitors who have bowed before the throne at Fatehpur Sikri!"

He sent the sword slamming back into its position.

He peered into her eyes. "We are rajputs. We live for honour. We die for honour. My neck will never take on the yoke of these vicious foreigners."

He locked the fingers of his right hand with her left. He walked her to the royal chambers. The door was shut behind them by the guards.

They entered an ante-chamber with two antique-looking arm chairs. He had her sit on one and he sat on the other one, facing her.

"Kanwar, our lives are about to be turned upside down. The Mughal attack would commence anytime they wish. Ajmer is not far away. Their garrison there is teeming with troops. Albeit, I feel it would be sometime before they act. I do not know what hardship awaits us. I am concerned for you. I expect you to be brave. I want you to meet your fate boldly and live your life to the fullest. We are about to commence preparations for our defence. I am confident the Mughals won't get me. But then, in warfare, the sword kills the one and the other. Amar Singh shall succeed me."

He placed his hands on hers and gripped them firmly. She was smiling but two long streaks of tears rolled down from her exquisite eyes.

"You will live. You shall not die" she replied gently, her mellifluous voice struggling. "The lion shall not perish. Your foes shall fall before you. Your sword shall decapitate many heads, as you swore."

He gazed at her lovely visage. Her massive domed jumkis straddling her long wavy tresses made her look stunning. Would death separate him from this object of his affection, his passions and his pride?

He placed her hands on hers and gripped them hard. Her emotions were overwhelming her. She rose. So did he. He drew her close by her hips and kissed her forehead right where the partition of her hair glistening with a long streak of crimson vermilion met her royal façade. She raised her head and looked into his eyes, her bangle-bedecked arms instantly locking themselves across his neck in the blink of an eye. She lifted her person to meet his face, their noses touching, her breath deflecting off his visage, her body almost pressing against his, her perfume flooding his senses in onrushing waves. Her starry eyes kept holding him captive. She was about to thrust forward to hug him when he gently brought down her jewelled arms with their tinkling bangles. He turned and walked away closing the door softly.

She sat down on the chair and caught her breath, wondering what kind of events were to follow. Would it be like the massacre at Chittor, where her father-in-law's army lost to the Mughals disastrously? This time, her husband would lead Mewar into battle. What then? Should she and her household flee through the secret passageways? Was she thorough with their outlet locations and the procedures involved in such an exit?

Down in the hall she heard her husband's voice.

"Amar!" rose Prathap Singh's voice in a commanding manner

"Yes, Father?" replied the son.

"Summon Kishan and Rawal immediately. We are meeting for an important discussion. Proceed without delay!"

There was an urgency in his voice. The events which she thought would eventually happen were about to unfold one after the other.

I hope my death is swift if it comes to that, she thought. No Mughal shadow shall fall on my person!

She heard an amalgamation of voices and the sound of many footsteps. She arose and opened the door just a wee bit. She could see the army's top command hurrying down the corridor.

CHAPTER 10

IF PUSH CAME TO SHOVE

*T*hat night Kanwar felt the absence of her king on the royal bedstead. His strong arms were missing around her torso, his handsome muscular face absent against her massive earrings and cheeks, the nocturnal routine of him securing her body with his massive iconic bust, him toying with her lengthy, pointed fingernails on her stately fingers and the flaunting bangles on her striking brilliant-red henna-dyed hands, him interlocking her fingers with his, her bow-like eyelashes feeling his handles and et al. She tossed and turned, unable to sleep. She propped herself against her soft pillows which she laid vertically against the head of the bed. Her soul gradually transcended into a trance. A trance? Yes, she was carried away into a dreadful vision. Could she hear the beat of the distant drums in the stillness of the night? The blaring horns of the Mughals? The resounding rajput curved bugles? She could hear war cries and the trumpeting elephants. She could see prancing steeds, neighing stallions, the mad charge of the cavalry, smoke going off muskets, flashing swords, glittering spears, massive volleys of razor-sharp arrows, deafening cannon fire, men dismembering men on the gory battlefield, of blood-soaked earth, of lungs, hearts and livers thrust by spears, of gasping men drawing their last breath, of the victors and the vanquished...

She cleared her throat and made a hasty exit out of her disturbing hallucination. What were the odds of the Mughals ignoring the many chances they gave her husband? Mewar alone had defied the Mughal juggernaut. All the other rajput fiefdoms had toed Akbar's line one way or the other. Did her husband act without due consideration? The odds were overwhelmingly against Mewar. The kingdom could be wiped out. Who knows what carnage would follow at the hands of Akbar's military? Women and children could be easy targets. She shuddered to imagine.

Should it really come to that, I shall take my life. The flames shall have me, not these foreigners. Not just me but all the women and the children in Mewar shall do likewise. The consequences of punching the Mughals in the stomach will follow as dawn followed dusk with certainty. It shall be one incredible encounter! Mewar shall go down with its honour held high. No capitulation to these foreigners even under the threat of war.

This is my life trajectory, thought Kanwar. I was born for this and I shall face this with dignity and pride. Her painted eyelids rose high in shock. Prathap Singh, herself and all their subjects of Mewar were headed for a crescendo of cataclysmic proportions! Nothing was going to stop it.

She inhaled deeply and wilfully. Her soul-stirring eyes lit up, her erect nose gently tilted her head in pride...I am Kanwar! The blood of rajputs flows in my veins. I must be bold. I must be daring. I need a heart of stone. Am I not the queen? I will stare at death with gusto!

She got down from the bed and pulled the window screen. It was about half past two. There were men walking on the palace grounds. She could see what looked like bhil tribals from the mountains already arriving in the glow of the giant torchlights. Kishan, Rawal and the military command were receiving them. She could hear their muffled voices. So, things are falling into place, aren't they? Mewar did not boast of a big army. It needed reinforcements. That's why the bhil tribesmen, ever faithful to the Mewar ruling family, were being roped in. Who else? She often listened to her husband talk about some Afghan chieftains who were sworn opposed to the Mughals and in particular Akbar. Would they come too? Could Prathap Singh coax them into fighting the Mughal military machine? Who knows...

She walked across the massive ornate bedchamber, her heavy adorned anklets sending jingles of reverberation across the floor to the accompaniment of her tinkling gold bangles. Her round, diamond nose pin kept shimmering like a tiny beacon in the near darkness of the room. She drank a glass of water and then another. She laid down and closed her eyes, her heavy thoughts lulled her into sleep.

In a matter of two days, there were many bhil headmen arriving in a steady stream. Disgruntled rebels from Mughal-ruled neighbouring Marwar also landed at Kumbalgarh Fortress. A few nobles from Gwalior too joined these ranks. Leading them was a famed warrior from the royal family of the central region of the Hind called Ram Singh. All were lodged in the fortress awaiting the arrival of Hakim Khan Sur, the Afghan. And arrive he did with the company of two thousand swordsmen. How he managed to cross the Mughal-manned frontier with such a number of armed men was a mystery. The tall, heavy bearded Afghan was a direct descendent of Sher Shah Suri who had defeated Humayun and reigned from Delhi even though for a brief period. The crafty Mughals, however, toppled Suri and put an end to his rule. The Sur dynasty was not necessarily a friend of Mewar. They were hostile towards Prathap Singh's father, Udai Singh. Nevertheless, since the dynamics had changed on the geopolitical chessboard, Prathap Singh and Hakim Khan

Sur found themselves on the same page. Needless to say, Hakim Khan Sur saw eye to eye with Prathap Singh on the looming Mughal threat. He had a personal account to settle with the Mughals. Behind closed doors, huddled with the other invited allies, he made his views clear.

"They are out to destroy us all! They wish to grab the whole of Hindustan and the Afghan homeland. Their greed is endless. They wish to seize your silver and gold, your lands and forts. They want to force the people of this land into servitude."

"It's happening before my very eyes!" echoed Prathap Singh with utter seriousness.

"What a tragedy that all rajputs with only your exception have joined the service of the Mughal empire. Shocking!" noted the Afghan commander.

"Shocking indeed. Fate has chosen me to stand up to these invaders. I am strained for resources. I need more manpower. I need money. My subjects have been stretched to their limits. They have only their physical bodies to spare. We are left with what we have at our disposal" conceded Prathap Singh.

"I have a strong suggestion for you" continued the Afghan.

"What may that be?" posed the king of Mewar.

"No army marches on empty stomachs and thirsty throats. These Mughals would try to harvest your crops and drink your water" argued Sur.

"So?" demanded Prathap Singh with fresh curiosity.

"Get your people to immediately either harvest their crops or burn them down altogether. The same applies to water. All wells must be emptied or put out of use as early as possible. Unleash an emergency" continued an uncanny Sur.

"I understand" observed the king.

"Likewise, get your farmers to drain all irrigation tanks. Plug all sources of refill. If water sources cannot be drained, they must be poisoned." "Let's give these Mughals a taste of their own medicine, Prathap Singh!" exclaimed the Afghan with elation.

"Fantastic!" many in the session blurted out.

"The Mughals must suffer our vengeance," echoed a bhil headman. "What Hakim Khan says is absolutely correct. Starve them and may their thirst kill them all."

CHAPTER 11

THE LULL BEFORE THE STORM

Not a finger moved in the empire without the approval of the emperor. Akbar had total and complete control over the affairs of his ever-expanding enterprise. There were some, if not many, who wanted him to crush Mewar for good. The monarch had other concerns. The Hindu Kush affair somehow got his imagination into overdrive. He chose not to be concerned about possible Persian Safavid incursions through the Kandahar province in the Afghan highlands. Birbal and his subordinates were involved in hunting down the renegades on the Afghan heights with great abandon. The Hindu Kush campaign lasted two months. Birbal returned to receive his accolades and to sing his master's praises. The Gangetic, Bihar and Bengal consumed another five months under the supervision of Man Singh. He too came back with victory and was duly honoured. Punjab was firmly brought under control. Raja

Bhagwan Das saw to that. The dust settled down slowly but surely. Now, what of Mewar? Akbar was not propelled into action. The commanders thought the momentum needed to be carried on. He thought otherwise. Just another month or two perhaps and Mewar would surely come to its senses. Would not Prathap Singh hear about the campaigns? Would not fear force him into submission? There was to be no action on Mewar that year. Not yet.

February 1576:

Akbar thought he had given Mewar enough chances when there was simply no indication of Mewar's capitulation after him waiting for so long.

It was a particular Saturday, the Mughal chief chaired a meeting in the cool of the afternoon with his confidantes in the sprawling stone-paved courtyard of Fatehpur Sikri. His big guns and highly decorated military stars were seated in royal array and a host of courtiers were swarming behind the monarch in a hushed hustle. A notable presence in this array was the young prince Salim, who would be called by his future throne name Jehangir, seated on his father's lap.

Akbar addressed Man Singh, "This Prathap Singh has dishonoured me. He has challenged the empire. All our attempts at peace have been trampled under his feet. He must be eliminated. You are to commence our campaign against Mewar very shortly."

Man Singh looked intently at his king in his typical way. "Consider him dead, My Lord. He won't survive our onslaught."

"I am pleased that you are finally acting, My Liege!" said Birbal with smirking glee.

Akbar smiled at his favourite minister. His statesmen were in concurrence. It was time to act.

"A man is as good as his actions. Talk is cheap" said the monarch with a smile. "Raja Birbal, I shall need you here at Fatehpur Sikri, should you be required to return to the Hindu Kush once again."

"So be it, My Lord" replied the wily general who was way too ready to return to combat in the Khyber pass proximity.

The aroma of the lamb biryani from the not-so-distant kitchen began reaching their nostrils.

The royal lunch commenced. Everyone at the dining hall began taking mouthfuls of the hot aromatic long-grain yellow rice infused with lamb marinade and chunks of tender meat. Soon, many were helping themselves to a second portion. The emperor too had an extra portion to satisfy his appetite. Glasses of cold rose-milk sharbat followed as dessert. It was a feast fit for royalty.

Meal over, the cabinet ambled after Akbar on the cobbled stones.

"I wish you a swift victory" Akbar said looking at Man Singh. "May you bring honour to the Mughal realm."

The ecstatic general bowed his head, "May the name of Akbar resound through the ages!"

"So be it, Man Singh. My son Salim will be accompanying you on this campaign against Mewar" manoeuvred the emperor.

Man Singh raised his eyebrows. "Prince Salim?" he asked shifting his stare at the young lad standing by Akbar.

"We need to prune the branches as early as possible in his life, Man Singh. If the empire is to have strong despots, then we need men who are trained in the art of war right from their young age. He needs this military exposure quite early in his life. I don't want to spare him from this rigour. I need a worthy successor. Let him be present in the theatre of conflict. Make sure he is well shielded from the enemy's ammunition. Maybe you can place him in the rear with the reserves" deliberated Akbar.

"I understand, My Lord. He will be well cared for. You can rest assured on his account" replied Man Singh.

"I am also fielding Shakta Singh, the brother of Prathap Singh and Mohabet Khan, son of Sagar Singh, another brother of his, against Mewar. This act in itself would be enough to deflate his ego. We are turning brother against brother and rajput against rajput. Prathap Singh should lose a lot of confidence when he comes to know that his brothers and nephews are out to finish him on the battlefield" carried on the crown.

"Very well, My Lord" acknowledged the beaming commander.

As Man Singh was about to take his leave, his potentate came over, inclined into his left ear and whispered. "Remember the 10,000 gold coins. It might very well serve as the stimuli for some bold Mughal to account for Prathap Singh."

"I sure will, My Lord. I sure will" said Man Singh as he bowed in deep respect.

CHAPTER 12

THE FINAL STRETCH

Mid-Summer, 1576

Asaf Khan, deputy to Man Singh reached Ajmer in a week with a cavalry force of 30,000 made up of central Asian Mughul units composed mainly of Kazakh, Tajik and Uzbek tribesmen. Man Singh and Prince Salim followed suit about a month later leading another posse of 40,000 infantry, 5000 Uzbek, Tajik and Kazak archers, 5000 musketeers and 100 artillery guns and nearly 500 war-elephants. Preparations began in the garrison city in earnest for the forthcoming assault on Mewar. Briefings were held by Man Singh and Asaf Khan repeatedly to reinforce battle tactics. Obedience at any cost was emphasized, even at the loss of one's life. Swords, shields, spears, muskets, bows and arrows, and the cannons were all inspected for final quality clearance. The war elephants were given a medical check and dressed up for the grand spectacle. The cavalry's horses were put through trials for the final go ahead. The Mughal army stood in battle array with a strength of 80,000 men. Man Singh did a guard of inspection. The young lad Salim in full black military fatigues stood at his right.

"For Mughal glory!" yelled Man Singh facing them, raising his sword.

"For Mughal glory!" hailed the great host. The rajput commander felt thrilled. The mahout made the elephant kneel. Man Singh climbed into his small bamboo howdah with bubbling gung-ho. His sword was placed on his thighs and his bow and arrows slung over his right shoulder.

"Hey!" commanded the mahout and the great beast moved forward towards Mewar with determination. Salim, next-in-line, followed Man Singh on an almost equally massive war-elephant. The posse reached Mandalgarh more than a hundred kilometres south of Ajmer after a journey of about twenty-five days. It was a long halt as they had to wait for about sixty days for more reinforcements to arrive. Once the backings showed up, the battle plans were drawn up by the top command under the aegis of Man Singh. The young prince carefully observed the tactics spelled out by Man Singh, knowing that the day was not far off when he would either have to make such plans himself or would have to ensure that such schedules once made had to be carried out to perfection on the killing field under his watch. The battle array and formations were all set in mind. Mughal intelligence located Prathap Singh in Gogunda, his birthplace.

He thinks he can hide, doesn't he? Mused Man Singh as they reached the outskirts of Haldigatti about 35 kilometres south-west from Gogunda, by the banks of the Banas River. Man Singh had one long look at the rugged mountainous terrain all around that eventually meandered into the rough Haldigatti pass. Man Singh, Prince Salim and the top commanders immediately were off to have a look at the ravine out of a pressing curiosity. It was quite narrow. Prathap Singh would be committing suicide if he chose to fight here, thought Man Singh. It was spread out with large forest cover in several swathes of land and then into an open, spacious plain. He could also see valleys and clear running water in some places.

"The enemy is in Gogunda. He would advance from the west. There is no way he would come here to this valley" remarked Man Singh glancing at Asaf Khan.

Meanwhile villagers in the immediate vicinity of the Mughal forces sensed imminent hostilities on seeing such a formidable force and were seen leaving in large numbers. Akbar's men pitched their tents. Animals were tethered, equipment arranged in order and countless tents put in.

Man Singh summoned his commanders for a briefing in his tent, "Ahmed Khan, you will command the right wing with 20,000 troops, two divisions of 10,000 each." Ahmed Khan, the tall, lanky Mughal nodded.

"Ghazi Khan, you will be in charge of the left flank. I am entrusting you with this responsibility, given your long military service." The rotund Mughal maintained a poker face as Man Singh carried on, "You are commanding 30,000 troops, three divisions of 10,000 each, right?"

"As you wish, Commander" said Ghazi Khan finally managing a smile.

"Have you briefed your lieutenants, each?" Man Singh quizzed both Ahmed Khan and Ghazi Khan, both of whom replied in the affirmative.

"All set for battle. I simply can't wait" added Ahmed Khan.

"The 500 or so elephants are under your command, Madhav Singh" noted Man Singh as he trained his eyes on the handsome rajput to his extreme left.

"That's correct, sire" replied the addressee.

"You will have to scuttle back and forth on your horse leading the mahouts. I expect near-wholesome control of these beasts. If you deliver a good performance Madhav, the emperor will certainly honour you! He is particularly fond of elephants" goaded Man Singh.

"I shall, sire," replied Madhav Singh.

"Now, Mahtar Khan, you are in charge of the reserves. Not just the reserves, but Prince Salim too!" cautioned Man Singh. "We have assigned him an elephant among the reserves. This animal is also going to be shielded by four others forming a cordon. You better lay down your life if any harm were to threaten the prince."

"Over my dead body!" said the aging Mughal. "Nothing imperious would ever be allowed to approach the prince."

"All right, Asaf Khan will be positioned right in front of my central division. He will co-ordinate all divisions under my command. The 5000 musketeers, the 5000 archers and the field guns are within his reaching distance. The remaining 20,000 troops will make up the central unit under my command...I encourage you all to stay strong. The Mewaris won't withstand us. They will offer some initial resistance. But we will have the upper hand. We have superior numbers. We have the musketeers. They will be blown away like chaff. Now, the emperor personally offers 10,000 gold coins to the man who kills Prathap Singh! Would any man seated here be up to the task?"

The commanders glanced at each other.

"I have given my word to the emperor. Someone in our host has to do it. Prathap Singh is well trained in military warfare. He will certainly prove a tough warrior. He is my kin indeed. However, he has become my enemy. A foe who has dishonoured me. My priority is the empire and its welfare, not family ties. I expect one of you to personally finish him off. You can make an announcement about this offer to your troops during dinner tonight."

The prince of Amber got up from his seat, drank a glass of yellow orange pulp.

"Come along, Your Highness" he urged the young prince who had just finished consuming some black ripe jamun.

They left the tent. The top brass led by Asaf Khan waited for the prince to get on his horse. Man Singh led his staff all the way to the banks of the Banas river.

"We are quite sure Prathap Singh is in Gogunda" he began looking at the hills yonder and then at Asaf Khan. "We had better send the reconnaissance teams to scan the areas around us. We need to be prepared. We need to monitor his moves."

"He has sealed his fate in choosing confrontation. Can he prevail? Could he?" Asaf Khan roared in arrogant laughter as he arched his back.

"Sakta Singh!" ordered Asaf Khan.

Sakta Singh, one of the estranged brothers of Prathap Singh, immediately trotted forward, "At your service."

"You are very familiar with this terrain, aren't you?" demanded Asaf Khan.

"Very much" replied the smiling rajput.

"Dispatch teams for reconnaissance in the surrounding hills and valleys" said Asaf Khan as he leaned forward from his chestnut-coloured steed. He winked his left eye, "We are giving the final touches."

As Sakta Singh began leaving, the deputy whistled softly and sang sarcastically, "We are coming for you, Prathap Singh!" Pride simmered in his eyes.

As the intelligence teams in camouflage began dispersing into the surrounding terrain, high up in the hills, bhil tribesmen loyal to Mewar and her king, who had taken up positions well in advance as goat herdsmen and hilltop farmworkers, kept observing every moment and noise made by the huge force down below ever since their arrival. They were very adept at their own camouflage in serving Prathap Singh that even the best of the Mughal scouts could not make out that they were on Mewar's payroll.

Prathap Singh was at Kumbalgarh and not at Gogunda as presumed by Man Singh.

The Maharana had given final touches to his strategy and his tactics. His trusted aides, Hakim Khan Sur, Rawal Singh, Kishan Singh, Ram Singh and Bida Jhala were fully aware of their roles and positions. Fate, destiny and the stars were beckoning Prathap Singh to wage war. A war for honour, for dignity and for freedom. Prathap Singh could feel the intensity setting his blood on fire. Was it ardency or indignation? An incredible audacity filled his emotions. The Mughals must be given a decisive blow. They must feel the fiery wrath of this rajput. They must be forced to feel anguish and pain. Did they not underestimate his mettle?

He stood before the roughly 20,000 strong army on the afternoon of 20th June 1576. He felt humbled. Involuntary tears came down his valiant cheeks. After a long moment of silence he began, "You are men of honour. You have come forward willingly to put your life on the line. Many of you will return alive. Many of you will not. May your memory live forever! You do not owe your lives to me. I owe my life to you. May this land and its people remember your deed for all ages...The enemy we face is strong. His forces are massive. We are indeed outnumbered. However, the love we have for our lands and their customs is far stronger than his swords and spears! Our will can never be broken! The day will come when the Mughals and their army will disappear from this land. We shall always be free people! May we be blessed with victory! We shall engage them tomorrow."

At that very instant loud war cries erupted among the troops hailing Prathap Singh. Wave after wave of fervent passion filled the king.

He gestured at the soldiers. The Maharana had a word with his confidantes. They hurried to his study where battle array and positions were confirmed and clarified.

"As agreed, we need to prevent the enemy from gaining access to the Kumbalgarh mountains. We are all familiar with the Haldigatti expanse—its mountains, forests, valleys and streams by now. The narrow mountain pass at its entrance is way too narrow for the Mughals to move their army to reach Kumbalgarh. "The bhils and select warriors stationed on the high perpendicular cliffs should kill a lot of Mughals who succeed in getting into the passage to gain access to the Kumbalgarh valley. Their arrows and boulders should inflict as many fatalities as possible as the gully is almost two kilometres long. There would be a melee. On the other hand, we have surveyed the open terrain. There is no necessity for any surprises on the plain. Our numbers account for only 20,000 troops. "The Mughals have mustered about 80,000. My major concern, however, is the enemy's artillery numbering around a 100 cannons. An entire flank is also armed with muskets. The artillery is here for only one reason. To reduce Kumbalgarh and Gogunda to rubble! Akbar wants to raze both these fortresses to the ground! Since the artillery battery and the musketeers give the Mughals a clear tactical advantage, we need to cross the low-flowing waters of the Banas and engage the enemy at the crack of dawn. "My objective is to launch a devastating assault on their artillery and their musketeers to wrest the advantage. Everything hinges on this initial attack. This is fraught with absolute danger. We are going to lose a lot of men in this attack. However, it must be carried out. This would also produce a counter-offensive from the Mughals. They could probably launch wave after wave of retaliation. If no one volunteers, I shall lead the charge against the artillery battery and the musketeers myself."

Hakim Khan Sur who was listening with rapt attention, raised his hand, "Leave that task to me and my men."

Prathap Singh regarded him for a few seconds, shaking his head, immensely pleased with the audacity of the tall Afghan.

He then continued, "What if we are successful? Who is to know? They have a massive force. It is difficult to predict the trajectory of the battle."

He looked at all of them around the table. He could sense they wanted his decisions to be supreme. None at the table had the military cunning to outwit the Mughals one bit!

"The battle could swing in any way. We can only make plans. We can presume certain things. There is no certainty" went on Prathap Singh. "My main concern is Man Singh. If he decides to go all the way, it would be an all-out warfare. We need to be prepared for any eventuality... Now, it is my burning desire to exterminate Man Singh. Reports indicate the presence of a young Mughal Prince. We are not going to access him for any reason. In fact, he could actually be a distraction. Accounting for the Prince of Amber would be quite strenuous given the level of protection he would enjoy on the battlefield. However, I shall try to achieve my aim. Should not desires be satiated? It is dangerous not to. I need a substantial number of men to accompany me and to watch my back in this attempt."

Bida Jhala, his close aide and trusted commander raised his chin, "I would dare do that. I and my men shall be a wall of protection around you, come what may. You do everything in your power to neutralize that warmonger Man Singh. But why would they dispatch a young Mughal hatchling to the battlefield? Insanity, perhaps?"

Prathap Singh smiled, "Who could possibly know?" He took a deep breath and continued, "Hakim Khan Sur will lead the charge against the Mughal frontline with 6000 Afghans. Ram Singh is over the right flank with 3000 troops and you, Bida Jhala will be leading the left commanding 3000 troops too. I myself at the centre shall lead 5000 cavalry, 3000 infantry men and 150 elephants. The bhil archers will be just behind the right and left flanks. Should either I or you need help there should be clear communication. Keep your heads high. Act like men."

A light meal was consumed in near silence with commanders wondering if they were having food for the last time. Once done, Prathap Singh bid them rest and commanded them to be all ready by three in the morning.

Prathap Singh did not sleep that night. He stayed awake, cuddling Kanwar. She kept running her fingers through his hair as she gazed aimlessly at the walls. The yellow fire of the lamps gave the two star-crossed couple company. He kept playing with her silver bangles. He ran his index finger down the ridge of her stately nose. There was a long silence in that living room of the Kumbalgarh Fortress. Prathap Singh released himself from Kanwar's intoxicating embrace. He walked to an open window and gazed at the silence of the skies.

"Be careful when you charge at Man Singh. Beware! Do not harm the young Mughal prince in anyway. Command the soldiers not to!" Kanwar's concerned regal voice cautioned him as she rose from the couch. "The consequences of harming the prince are unthinkable. The Mughals would unleash inferno on Mewar if his life is compromised in one way or the other. I urge you to avoid running into the lad by all means." After a long pause she continued, "I can only hope every weapon aimed at you fails."

She buried her head in her hands, sobbing. Prathap Singh came over and raised her head.

"There is a price that we have to pay for our peace. We cannot avoid doing that. I tried in every possible way." He sat and enveloped her with his left arm. "May Heaven return me to you safe and sound. I am your love, your husband and your king. Nothing will ever change that. I will fight fate if it tries to separate us. As for this little boy, I will see to it that none of my forces ever go near him. Neither will I."

She got up, burst into tears and hugged him with all her might. He cradled her like a child for some time. He then released himself from her embrace. Then looking straight into her lucid eyes, he said, "I shall return. You can be sure." He kissed her forehead in his typical way.

She knew that her husband was a lion on the battlefield. His expertise in warfare was so immense that it would take a supernatural effort to kill him. His sword could behead five men in one go! Such was his physical prowess! His physique was simply awesome! His muscles were all steel. He was untouchable even by a group of 100 soldiers! Woe to them who raise their swords against him! These thoughts gave her hope. Hope is however still mere hope. Could someone attest for the certainty of hope?

Prathap Singh headed for the stables. His royal steed Chetak was all impatient to taste battle. At least that is what Prathap Singh sensed. The bluish, black horse neighed gently in the flickering lamps of the stables as it saw him approach.

He stroked its head. "My son, my love, you need to be at your best tomorrow. You will need to fly if need be, han?" said Pratap Singh chuckling. "Train your eyes and ears to make the right decisions. Your name will echo through the ages, my boy."

The horse grunted in approval. The animal was in the prime of his life. His strength and vigour were unmatched in all of Hindustan! The Mughals for all their assets could not boast of a horse like Chetak! Prathap Singh gave orders to have the horse all dressed up for battle to his attendants before three the next morning. He could see that the 150 or so war-elephants were all decked up for action. There was a sudden trumpeting from his favourite pachyderm, Ram Prasad. He went over and stroked its trunk. The animal put its long nose around the king.

"Yes, I know you too are ready." He looked into its eyes. There was love and affection like never before. He hugged his frontal left leg. He patted his sides. All elephants had their bamboo enclosures fitted large enough to house three soldiers. The warrior mahouts too were fired up for action.

The troops fell in line as per the battle array about three in the morning. Everyone was armed and ready in the darkness of the early aurora.

Kanwar brought out the platter for the fire waving ceremony. She stood surrounded by her female aides. The women folk sang a song of victory for their king. Prathap Singh's blood brothers stood armed and ready a short distance away. She circled the platter with the flaming camphor around the totally armed Prathap Singh right at the entrance to the royal palace. She applied the sacred vermilion exactly at the centre of his forehead.

"Victory to the rajputs!" shouted Prathap Singh.

"Victory to Mewar! Death to the enemy! Defeat to the enemy!" the top echelons of armed men in the room yelled.

The commanders stood assembled all set for action right in front of the fortress. As he mounted Chetak, he swiftly glanced at Kanwar before trotting off on his horse. The posse of 20,000 odd men - rajputs, Afghans and bhils - moved with Rawal Singh and Kishan Singh in the lead on their horses. About a 100 men playing the cylindrical wooden drums and flutes provided sombre music as the forces negotiated their way in the mountainous terrain to the Haldigatti pass. The music added the much-needed inspiration to the troops. The troops needed to traverse about 13 kilometres to reach the pass. The music was getting into the men and the horses. It sounded very ominous. As the elephants picked up pace in their own way, the ground began to resonate with the stomping of the massive beasts. The elephants were positioned right among the 8000 warriors at Prathap Singh's central command. The mood was gloomy as the army moved towards the flashpoint.

The seed had been sown by Prathap Singh long ago. A seed of defiance. A seed of pride. It was time for harvest or so the Mughals thought. And was he not ready, Prathap Singh? He was burning with hatred to unleash havoc on the Mughals and to blot out those rajputs who had changed their colours to save their lives! Wasn't he ready? He truly was ready!

CHAPTER 13

TURMERIC VALLEY – SHOCK AND AWE!

𝒫rathap Singh's army had to negotiate difficult mountainous terrain in the dark with flaring torches. While the walking was not so difficult for the troops, the elephants had to delicately balance themselves as they trod on the slopes of the Aravalli on their way to the rendezvous point. At certain places the rising grounds were sort of steep. The inevitability of their deed gave strength to the hearts of men and legs of the beasts to propel themselves forward. It was about quarter to six in the morning when Prathap Singh's company reached the entrance of the Haldigatti pass. The bhils and the rajput warriors entrusted with the defence of the canyon were already embedded atop the heights . The mountain pass meandered for almost two kilometres. Its walls were about 20 feet high in most locations on either flank. In certain places the rocky crags did reach about 40 or even 50 feet high making the place resemble bulwarks. The pass itself was so narrow that it was difficult for two men to walk together. At some points of the snaking pass, there were free spaces for troops or people in groups to traverse, but those were hard and rare. The pass almost shut down the valley and the plain that lay at the end of this lengthy, narrow ravine.

Mughal look-outs immediately sounded the alarm in their camp about quarter to dawn on picking up the sounds and sights of the approaching Mewari army. Commands were issued and orders were barked. The shrill calls of the clarion echoed in different places of the Mughal camp as they hastened to get their positions in order.

Asaf Khan galloped around shrieking injunctions, "Ahmed Khan to the right flank, Ghazi Khan to the left! Mahtar Khan, rally the reserves! Rally the reserves! The enemy approaches! Madhav Singh, double-check the elephant positions right away!"

The gunners ran to the artillery deployed on the banks of the Banas, the musketeers were ready in no time and the archers fell into battle lines with their bow and quivers. The rest of the huge army took that wee bit of time to get into alignment. The elephants clad in heavy armour stood in their war-like configuration as the mahouts climbed on their tusks to get onto to their necks. Elite sharpshooters armed with bows, arrows and quivers took their positions atop these pachyderms in the small bamboo enclosures made for them. These were firmly secured to the bellies of these animals. Man Singh had already put on his fatigues well in advance. He was atop his beast of war in the blink of an eye. His torso was covered with a heavy steel breastplate that was cleverly concealed under his normal garments. His limbs and head were quite exposed. He felt completely sure of not finding himself in harm's way up on the elephant of his. The rest of the Mughal commanding officers were all dressed up in their fatigues right from Fatehpur Sikri. The lad Salim, for his part, was covered in a full-mail gunmetal chain of armour that left only his tender fingers exposed. He donned a heavy, black, steel helmet with a dull pointed end projecting from the centre. He too got onto to the howdah of an ivory-tusker where he was enveloped by three heavily built Mughals who almost blocked his view of the action. His beast was encompassed by the reserves at the extreme end of the left flank.

While the Mughals were going about falling into battle formation at lightning speed, Prathap Singh and his army arrayed themselves into the pre-determined battle order with Mewar's 4-metre long, tapering crimson standards sporting a silver sun flying all over their assembly. Akbar's army was ready for warfare exactly at six in the morning.

As the golden rays of the sun began to light up the Aravalli hills that fateful morning of June 21, 1576, a falcon flying high in the azure skies could see the awesome firepower of 80,000 Mughal troops assembled bearing the 2-metre long rectangular black and green standards with the lion and sun insignia against a modest force of about 20,000 led by Prathap Singh. The Mughals deployed their massive horde of almost 500 elephants split into two divisions numbering 250. Each of these were positioned diagonally adjacent to Man Singh's central contingent. Akbar's troops numbering 30,000 were deployed on the left and 20,000 on the right of the main body of the army. Both composed of cavalry and infantry. The 1000 archers were right behind the 1000 musketeers who in turn had cannons interspersed among them right up front to inflict maximum number of fatalities on Prathap Singh's forces.

Mewar's 150-odd elephants were put into two divisions in similar fashion. Both elephant groups of 75 each followed Prathap Singh's central core of 5000 cavalry and the 3000 infantry at a 45-degree angle. Leading right from the front of this modest army however, were the 6000 Afghans. Both the right and left wings had 3000 infantry each followed by two groups of 300 bhil archers.

The booming call of the clarions on both sides were gradually rising to ear-splitting levels. The drummers on either side kept up the momentum with soul-stirring rhythms. The stallions in the cavalry divisions on either side began neighing and prancing in eager anticipation. The tusker-behemoths began trumpeting in an agitated manner. Mocking insults were hurled at each other's army. Jeering, howling, whistling and mad laughter followed to project power and strength.

Prathap Singh was dressed in a heavy metal-suit of armour and a shining steel headgear with a small spearhead at the centre. He bore two swords on his left thigh. Both were talwars. They were shinning, sharp, strong and vengeful to end the lives of all those who chose to come against him. Seated astride his Chetak his adrenaline began rising. As he began scanning the Banas' banks from behind the huge Afghan contingent, he had a clear view of the frontline Mughal positions made up of the cannons and the musketeers. He also had a glimpse of Man Singh's archers behind the musketeers. They were positioned a short distance from the banks of the Banas. Memories of Chittor falling to cannon-fire flashed in his mind. Akbar's musketeers had played a crucial role in the fall of Mewar's rajputs in that encounter. All of a sudden, out from nowhere, he could see a contingent of Mughal troops under the command of their don Bhalol Khan, numbering about a 1000, crossing the Banas in a hurry, heading straight for Mewar's army. He galloped towards Hakim Khan Sur and ordered him to engage the advancing Mughals.

As the Afghan contingent began moving to commence the attack, Man Singh cried, "Archers! Let loose!"

His archers fired their arrows on Prathap Singh's surging forces. The Mughal left flank unit immediately swung into action and headed straight for the river. Thousands of Mughal shafts failed to have a major effect as the Afghans took evasive action by grouping together under their shields. About a hundred paid with their lives for not being quick enough.

The Afghans swiftly slammed into Bhalol Khan's troops with gusto on an uneven stretch of land full of prickly shrubs just north of the entrance to the Haldigatti Pass. Swords flew, steely weapons clashed, spears lunged into hearts, lungs, livers and sides. Limbs were severed, bellies were disembowelled, fingers were chopped, ribcages got butchered, heads ended up cleaved in two and eyes were thrust through with spears and daggers. Decapitated heads and the grievously wounded began littering the ground as screams of anguish and hapless shrieking filling the air. It was Afghan versus Mughal in bloody combat. Blood drenched the outfit of many an Afghan and Moghul that glorious morning! Blood blending with the blood of fellow humans with no hatred, with no difference of opinion, with no cause for conflict! Quite a few Afghans fell to the earth like children falling in the rain, in the initial burst of cannon fire coupled with the musketeers' precision attacks and the deluge of Mughal arrows on Hakim Khan Sur's men. But once, the troops mingled into mindless hand to hand combat, the cannon fire, the arrows and the musketeers' shots ceased as it was impossible to open fire or shoot projectiles without killing both friend and foe.

The Afghans slaughtered the Mughals mercilessly. Bhalol Khan's contingent was surprised by the fierceness of the attack. An inspired Hakim Khan Sur and his forces were so superior that within half an hour of battle, about 700 Mughals fell to the vicious attack of the Afghans. Hakim Khan Sur's men lost about 200 men. The banks of the Banas were reddened with the blood of mankind, Afghan and Mughal alike. A badly shaken Bhalol Khan and his remaining men crossed the Banas and retreated behind the Mughal left flank.

This shocking reversal at the hands of Pratap Singh's Afghans shook the Mughals thoroughly. Their captains became apprehensive of what Mewar's forces were actually capable of. Though the Afghans prevailed, they failed to reach the Mughal musketeers.

Shouts of exultation rose from Prathap Singh's camp.

"Death to the Turks! Death to the Mughals! Death to the Persians!" and such cries exploded in the Mewar host in wave after wave of surging passion.

CHAPTER 14

THE SOUL OF THE SWORD

*M*eanwhile, as he began witnessing the deadly assault of Hakim Khan Sur's forces, Prathap Singh became a man possessed. A sense of euphoria flooded his mind.

He immediately yelled at the top of his voice, "Forward Mewar! Engage the Mughals!"

The entirety of his forces began approaching the river to head straight for the Mughals, by which time the Afghans had finished their grisly deeds. The forces of Hakim Khan Sur began reforming their battle lines to rejoin the rest of Prathap Singh's rajputs and bhils.

Mewar's king and his army rammed straight into the frontline Mughal units amidst a hail of cannon shells, musket fire, and sharp arrows. Many Afghans and scores of rajputs fell in the salvo of flying shells and whizzing bullets. The bhil archers on Mewar's side let loose a heavy deluge of their arrows successfully killing many Moghul sharp-shooters. Rawal Singh suffered a direct hit on his left shoulder from enemy cannon ammunition. His horse stumbled onto the ground, dead. The warrior was badly injured when he was run over by the train of horses advancing from behind. He did not survive. Not just Rawal, scores of onrushing Mewari steeds and their cavaliers perished in the outburst of Mughal cannon fire. The steed of Kishan Singh bled profusely on its right leg but kept speeding nevertheless. The rajputs of Mewar were however, in full swing.

The Mughal musketeers panicked and fled towards the left and right flanks of Man Singh's formation. Many fleeing musketeers were brutally butchered by the Mewari troops. Their field-guns were no match for the anger and the prowess of Prathap Singh's clans. The Mughal archers, being placed behind the gunmen, had enough time to scamper away and did not suffer from the brunt of Mewari forces' attacks.

Prathap Singh was itching for action. His talwar was raised in his right hand with Mewar's long crimson banners flying behind him in the scintillating light of that morning. His central unit of 5000 cavalrymen crashed right into the Mughal right flank led by Ahmed Khan. Prathap Singh's eyes widened with absolute ferocity.

"Attack!" he screamed. "Kill them all!"

His talwar sliced the hand of a Mughal off his shoulder in a microsecond. He decapitated another who charged at him. He swung his sword with awesome force at an Uzbek fracturing his head in two. His sword cut, slashed, sliced, beheaded, severed, butchered many a Tajik, Kazakh and Uzbek warrior. The shields carried by the Mughal cavalry were simply no match for the power of Prathap Singh's sword. Many of those shields were rent right down the middle in the full-blooded assaults unleashed by Mewar's lion. His sword became reddened with blood. He showed no respite. His hand was relentless in dealing death blows on numerous men and horses. Scores of Tajiks, Uzbeks, Kazakhs and Persians died at his hand! Blood began flowing down his right hand all the way to his elbow, dripping down to the ground. There was bloodletting on a cataclysmic scale that fair morning!

Prathap Singh sprang like a male lion on the Mughal cavalry. He became a blazing comet blazing over floating asteroids. Chetak moved with spectacular agility. Man Singh's cavalry of thousands fell back at the fury of this marauding rajput. What rage! What indignation! The rider on the bluish-black stallion was king and hero put together! The Mewari cavalry streaming like a river right behind Prathap Singh engaged the Mughal cavalry in pitched battle. It was some incredible bloodletting! It was also a long session marked by clashing swords, thrusting spears, piercing lances, charging horses, riders being thrown off their steeds and iron-hooves shattering the heads of fallen riders.

Ram Singh's right flank was engaged in intense battle with the Mughal left flank. There too scores of Mughals were decimated in the clash. Mewar suffered few fatalities. Concentrated hand-to-hand combat ensued in which the Mewari army gained the upper hand and pushed back Man Singh's left flank.

Ghazi Khan, in-charge of the left flank crossed swords with Ram Singh. As they were sparring, in the overcrowded left flank, Prathap Singh galloped across the battlefield brushing aside Mughal obstructions in his way and reached the right flank. He instantly identified Ghazi Khan as his target.

"You slave!" yelled Prathap Singh. Ram Singh instantly began engaging other members of Man Singh's cavalry at the sight of the approaching Prathap Singh.

On seeing Mewar's king, almost all of the Mughal cavalry pulled back granting him wide space.

"You die by my sword today, Mewari!" taunted Ghazi Khan as he went forward on his dapple-white horse to fight his adversary.

Mewar's star lunged forward. The Mughal put up a decent fight. Prathap Singh's strokes were swift and telling. The tired Mughal wanted to flee. Not a single

Mughal cavalryman stepped forward to challenge the King of Mewar. Such was his mastery! Prathap Singh's razor-sharp talwar finally managed to land on the head of the commander who desperately tried ducking his head to avoid decapitation. He suffered a long, lethal, deep fracture across his skull. His face was splintered diagonally across, axing his nose, cleaving his upper and lower jaws, chopping his large lips and inducing a grisly flow of blood all over his countenance. The critically injured commander fell backwards and was secured by Mughal cavalry reinforcements rushing in to bolster the left flank. The rest of the Mughal cavalry pulled back in retreat at this crushing assault.

CHAPTER 15

THE DAY OF THE JACKAL!

*A*ll this while, Man Singh and his clansmen were battling the rest of Prathap Singh's cavalry and infantry. There was tremendous loss of life on Mewar's side on this particular front as Man Singh's forces were made up of his own rajput clansmen who fought very fiercely. It was rajput against rajput on this part of the battlefield. It was horrific! In the chaos of that all-out war among the rajputs, friend killed friend and foe killed foe! Man Singh's forces gained the upper hand and pushed back Prathap Singh's central unit. This brought Mewar's momentum to a halt.

"Fall in line! Stay in your ranks!" Asaf Khan kept yelling as he darted around the theatre of war.

Pretty soon, the Mughals got their act together and assembled into neat battle array. The Mughals kept pushing their advantage and began slaughtering the Mewari central unit. Prathap Singh could see the tide turning in Man Singh's favour. He had to act. He needed to counter Man Singh's rajputs.

"Elephant charge!" decreed Prathap Singh.

At once, his elephant units following him charged with full force at Man Singh's rajputs crushing, killing, throwing, trampling, and bulldozing scores of Akbar's rajputs. Many died under the massive feet of Mewar's tuskers. This great assault was led by Ram Prasad, Pratap Singh's royal jumbo. It performed like the elephant version of Pratap Singh himself! The animal thrashed the Mughals right, left and centre, catapulting them straight into the air and crushing their ribcage under its feet. Man Singh's clansmen recognized the danger it posed. Asaf Khan coming around fired arrows killing its mahout. The mastodon also sustained wounds from arrows piercing its ears, legs and belly. A well-aimed spear from the Mughal champion got lodged in its right foreleg. The tusker lost control and ran amuck. It was eventually captured and led away by the Mughal mahouts in that chaos.

Prathap Singh felt heart-broken at the seizure of his royal tusker. The rest of his 150 elephants began ramming into Man Singh's forces one after another with incredible agility, wreaking destruction. His forces atop these animals were targeting both Mughals and their rajputs with arrows.

Man Singh pushed forward to wrest the momentum. "Madhav Singh! Engage the enemy!" he decreed.

His deputy Asaf Khan echoed the command very loud and clear to the elephant commander moving close behind Man Singh's troops. The Mughal trumpets blared out the signal for the elephant assault in tandem with the battle-standards being waved for the ramming-speed attack. Their mahouts immediately got their animals going.

What followed was carnage with Mughal elephants taking on Mewar's jumbos in mortal combat. Their shrill trumpeting pierced the air. Mewar's beasts issued their own loud aggressive calls. These behemoths slammed into each other with mahouts yelling on top of their voices. The concussion of these violent collisions threw many a howdah occupant into the air and to their death below. It was elephant versus elephant with many pachyderms entwining their trunks against their opponents in a show of strength. Some tried to pierce their foes with their long tusks. Many of these animals tumbled down in the impact of the head-smacking collisions. Many were speared after losing their balance. Many became easy targets for the archers from both camps in spite of their heavy armour. Many a rajput and Mughal was crushed to death by their stomping legs. Prathap Singh went around killing more Mughal-allied rajputs while encouraging his elephant division to fight till the end. Man Singh's beasts outnumbered Mewar's. They surrounded Mewar's beasts from all sides after a lengthy battle. The crafty general now ordered his remaining musketeers to rally around him.

"Move at will. Shoot their elephants!" commanded Akbar's general, which was echoed by Asaf Khan. This enraged Prathap Singh who wanted to kill Asaf Khan right away. The wily deputy kept clear of Mewar's king knowing fully well that if he were to cross swords with him, he would not live to tell the tale. He was scheming enough to play the cat and mouse game with the king of Mewar. It was a precarious gamble, but fate seemed to favour Man Singh's adjutant.

Mughal musketeers now scampered around and brought down Prathap Singh's elephants. They were trapped with no exit. The noisy rattle of the muskets could be heard across the battlefield as they killed Mewar's war-elephants. Like little hills upturned by their roots, the jumbos of Mewar crashed to the ground with their eyes staring aimlessly and their mouths open. Their crews were put to death by the Mughals and Man Singh's eager clansmen. All of Mewar's 150 jumbos were methodically annihilated by Man Singh's gunmen. It was slaughter on a mass scale.

The sight of his dead and dying elephants strewn across the battlefield deeply angered Prathap Singh. He could see Man Singh atop his elephant some distance away.

"Man Singh, you renegade!" he yelled at the top of his voice prancing on Chetak, raising his sword high in the air. The prince of Amber smiled when he heard Prathap Singh ranting.

CHAPTER 16

SO DAUNTLESS IN WAR!

*T*he Mughals sensed lip-smacking victory within touching distance. Their commander-in-chief decided to seize the advantage.

He yelled from atop his huge jumbo, "Asaf Khan! Forward with the reserves! Surround them!"

He leaned to his left and ordered Asaf Khan to convey his command while collecting a quiver of arrows from his confidante from a basket that was pulled up the side of his moving beast.

Asaf Khan along with Bhalol Khan galloped behind the central unit and commanded Mahtar Khan to envelope the principal units of Prathap Singh's cavalry and infantry caught in pitched battle against Man Singh's rajputs.

Trumpets blared directives to the reserves to encompass the rajputs of Prathap Singh. Battle standards waved urging the reserves to rush. They began moving in two units of 5000 each, made up mostly of the infantry with a few hundred cavalry.

The battle was turning in the Mughal's favour indeed. Their reserves began to close in on Mewar's dominant units. Those units - both cavalry and infantry - were feeling the heat of an overwhelming Mughal assault. The cacophony of swords clashing one with another was unbearable in the midst of it all. Mewar's rajputs began falling in scores. The only spot where this was not happening was where Prathap Singh was engaged in conflict. He continued to slaughter as many rajput clansmen of Man Singh as possible.

Sensing the need to do something drastic, Prathap Singh ordered the unit commanded by Hakim Khan Sur to move to the centre to counter Man Singh's rajputs. The Afghans had to put in some effort to shift themselves to the centre to counter the Mughals. They gradually began pushing them back with superior sword-wielding skills. Man Singh aimed a deft arrow at Hakim Khan Sur. It struck his armour, causing no harm to his person. Then he fired a spear at him, which he anticipated in advance and deflected with his metal shield. The tall Afghan neutralized many of his foes.

Man Singh commanded Asaf Khan to neutralize this clear and present danger, "Kill that huge Pashtun!"

The crafty veteran circumvented the battling hordes to come up behind Hakim Khan Sur. His massive blow beheaded Hakim Khan Sur in an instant. There was a roar of exultation from the Mughal forces, as the lifeless body dropped down from his horse. The Afghans and the rest of Mewar's forces felt their confidence had been dealt a severe blow at the loss of Hakim Khan Sur.

Prathap Singh made his way to his have a quick view of the mortal remains. He glared with deep wrath at the fleeing figure of Asaf Khan. He commanded his men to remove the body to a safe place and began trailing the perpetrator of the crime.

He breezed his way to catch up with the commander at full speed, unleashing a massacre of foe-rajputs and Mughals in his wake. Man Singh could see the peril his deputy found himself in.

"Target him! Kill him!" he commanded his elite archers.

A flurry of Mughal arrows whizzed their way towards their target. Most of them missed. Some hit their target but failed to have any effect. A few however happened to pierce him through the chinks of his chain-mail mantle. He gasped in deep pain as they punctured his person and made his blood ooze at three places-two on his back and from one on the left shoulder. The shafts remained lodged on his person.

Irate Mughals and foe-rajputs now began to target him with spears. His heavy iron-clad shield stood the test of time and defended his body from the searing spears and most of the arrows. Anyone in his way attempting to withstand him was slain in a fraction of a second. He finally caught up with Asaf Khan near the reserves and found he had to contend with Bhalol Khan from the Mughal left flank too.

Bhalol Khan for some reason left his estate and rallied to the defence of his compatriot with an upraised sword on his brown stallion. Prathap Singh lunged forward. Bhalol Khan froze. Mewar's King rose like a feather from Chetak and brought down his weapon vertically down on his enemy's right shoulder with crushing force from an ascent of about four feet. The strike was so deadly that it carved the enemy's body right into two. The spinal cord was severed down the middle like a ripe bamboo trunk being split on its axis. His vital fluid shot out in a crimson deluge all over the mangled body and over the horse's mane. It fell to the earth with a thud. The gory end of Bhalol Khan sent shock waves through the rival-rajputs and the Mughal ranks. The bloody, butchered body lay in a horrific mangle on the ground. The riderless horse ran disoriented.

Asaf Khan could not exit the heavy concentrated, confused mass of humanity surrounding him. He was the next to face Mewar's King. He had no other option but to fight. Armed with a spear he kept clear of Prathap Singh's swinging sword. His well-aimed lance, thrown very accurately, plunged into a quick-leaning Prathap Singh's muscles under the left shoulder blade with the chain-mail et al, causing a pronounced injury, but failed to lodge there.

Prathap Singh gained proximity towards Asaf Khan and screamed, "Death to the foreigner!"

Meanwhile, manoeuvring his elephant around, Man Singh could see that his second-in-command was facing the peril of losing his life. He cast a sharp spear at Prathap Singh from the howdah of his beast. The lance crashed into the heavy helmet of the king almost knocking him off-balance. Chetak, however, shifted his weight using its presence of mind and made sure its master did not land on the ground. The searing spear cut a long gash on his right cheek causing blood to gush right away. This attack intensified Prathap Singh's resolve to kill Asaf Khan for the loss of Hakim Khan Sur. He finally squared off with Asaf Khan. In the ensuing skirmish he hacked off the right hand of his adversary exactly at the elbow. Asaf Khan screamed out haplessly. His comatose right hand still holding its sword landed harmlessly on terra firma. He managed to flee the scene with a truncated right arm.

Prince Salim witnessing large-scale killing for the first time with a long spyglass was awed when he witnessed the deeply agonizing cry of Asaf Khan on losing his limb. His first reaction was fear. But it quickly turned to hatred for Prathap Singh.

"Why can't we get that man?" he asked his Mughal cohorts on his howdah in a contemplative manner.

"We will very soon, Your Highness," was the cautious reply.

"But when?" insisted the young lad as he stared at them.

"Pretty soon, sire" they responded.

Prathap Singh's anger became unbridled when he realized that it was Man Singh who had fired the second spear.

"Man Singh, you turncoat!" swore Prathap Singh turning around, as Chetak thundered towards the closely packed confines of Man Singh's ring of fire. His faithful entourage bearing the long tapering crimson flags with the silver sun, led by Bida Jhala, threw a wall of defence around him as he streaked across the battlelines.

His eyes were firmly set on the figure seated on top of the matt-black beast. He slammed his talwar back into its sheath. He now bore a long, gleaming spear that carried the onus of his vengeance.

He glanced at Jhala who had some resemblance to the king of Mewar, "Watch my back."

"We have your back, My King" replied Jhala in bated breath on his horse.

The elite cavalry unit composed of about fifty warriors now locked horns with the frontal troops encircling Man Singh's beast of war. These troops themselves maintained a healthy distance of about ten feet from the Mughal commander's massive black beast in armour as it kept swinging a five-foot long murderous sword to both its sides in an arching fashion to cut to pieces anyone daring to venture within the strike-zone. Its cunning eyes did not spare foe or friend. The commander and his attendants atop too kept killing their foes on the ground with precisely aimed arrows and the occasional spear for important foes.

A distance of 50 meters separated Man Singh's mammoth from Prathap Singh and his men. Man Singh knew that this was the day of reckoning. The hordes of the massing Mughal troops on both his left and right flanks along with the reserve contingents that had now come sweeping across the battlefield ended up obstructing the movement of his own central unit. The left and right wings were still battling the remnants of Mewar's army. The bhils were still shooting their shafts at the Mughals from quite a distance from both the right and left flanks of Mewar's debilitated central unit as they had some immunity from being set upon by the Mughals.

Prathap Singh and his fifty now unleashed a superhuman assault on the hundreds of Man Singh's clansmen on the forefront of his unit. The strike was astounding with heads, hands and limbs getting mangled in the brutal clash. Most of Mewar's fifty survived sans ten. Scores of rajputs on the Mughal side laid down their lives in defence of their commander. With only Sakta Singh to rally the troops, Man Singh's entourage ran haphazard at the devastating aggression of the Mewar unit. Man Singh could see the approaching threat and began directing his arrows at Prathap Singh and his small unit. A few daredevil Mewar rajputs made the ultimate sacrifice to shield their king in his hot pursuit of the Prince of Amber. After quite a slaughter of the hostile rajputs, Prathap Singh was within fifteen meters of his mortal enemy.

Both exchanged heated glances as the king of Mewar jostled around the Mughal war-beast for a perfect opportunity to accomplish his mission.

A clearly agitated Man Singh kept issuing commands to his men, "Nail him to the ground! Pin him down!" he thundered.

Heavy, savage javelins were thrown with pinpoint accuracy at Prathap Singh who deflected each of them with his heavy shield. Not even one of them broke through the defence of his bulky buckler. Chetak's sturdy, elephant-like face-covering too miraculously bore the deafening concussion of any spear landing on its head and then deflecting away. Prathap Singh closed the gap at about twelve feet on Chetak gaining ground from right in front of the beast as he zeroed in on the elephant at an acute angle. As the enormous animal swung its trunk to its left, Chetak leaped about ten feet with his king holding the upraised spear in absolute ferocity! As the bluish-black stallion rose high in the air, it landed its forelegs on the padded right foreleg of Man Singh's war-elephant. Prathap Singh flung the spear at Man Singh, who with his widened eyeballs tried to cower in the cramped howdah. His Mughal mahout, quicker than a lightning, launched himself between the tearing spear and its target and was impaled to death on the bamboo enclosure. The weapon managed to pierce all the way through the mahout's body and the howdah and stopped inches short of Man Singh's armour. As Prathap Singh landed like a feather cushioned by Chetak's powerful legs, Man Singh's tusker swung its sword to its right at that very instant. The sword's lethal swing caught Chetak exactly on the hind legs, severing his sinews and almost fracturing the legs. Chetak let out a cry of anguish.

Prathap Singh now swung his horse around realizing that it had been injured very badly.

Man Singh's elephant, traumatized from the encounter, veered uncontrollably. It turned left and ran wildly as it had a dead mahout transfixed to its howdah. The Mughals eventually found another and brought it under control. A shaken Man Singh still in his station decided to carry on commanding his troops.

The king manoeuvred his wounded horse away from the heat of the battlefield, away from the blade of Man Singh's beast.

"Leave for your life! Leave now!" cried out Jhala to his king who was himself bleeding from several places.

There was a steady stream of blood gushing from Chetak's battered hind legs. Out of nowhere, two serrated arrows flew in from the sky and pierced the stallion's right flank quite deep. The horse neighed and pranced with intense pain.

"Seek safety, My King. We need you!" Jhala raised his voice.

Prathap Singh trotted to another spot. They came to a halt at a spot dominated by his rajputs. Without any hesitation, Jhala removed the king's heavy helmet and placed his headgear on the king's head.

"Your Highness, leave now. You shall live to fight the Mughals another day. You can have your vengeance then. Would Mewar rejoice if you lay down your life today? Kishan shall accompany you" he urged.

Many voices around him echoed Jhala's counsel.

Ram Singh who had survived the Mughal onslaught thus far agreed fully, "We cannot afford to lose you, My King. Please leave right away!"

By this time, the entire Mughal army had completely encircled the central units of Mewar. Prathap Singh's right and left flanks were facing a monstrous threat as Mughal troops not only kept pouring around them but they had also shut out all possible exits for Mewar's remaining forces. The intense battle could only result in their death. The bhils were the only division on the right and left flanks who were free enough to fire their sharp weapons. But they were not enough to bring down the Mughal war machine.

Prathap Singh saw the inevitable before his eyes. He had to make a very difficult choice. He had to force himself to retreat whether he liked it or not.

"May heaven bid you success. Marshall the troops. Inspire them" he wished Jhala and Ram Singh.

The bhils, realizing that their king needed respite from the high-pitch hostilities, let loose a hail of arrows to keep the Mughals occupied from spotting the retreating Prathap Singh.

He cruised across on the seriously impaired Chetak, with Kishan Singh trailing behind him, leaving the battlefield sans his royal helmet, armour and the lengthy red tapering flags, a perfect camouflage that deluded the scan of almost all eyes of his enemy's troops. Well, except for two pairs of eyes in the Mughal camp!

He could not fool his brother Sakta Singh and Mohabet Khan, son of Sagar Singh, his erstwhile brother. Sakta Singh battled his way out and began pursuing the king and Kishan Singh, armed with a spear.

"Follow him!" ordered Mohabet Khan to a posse of three Kazakh horsemen when his uncle took off after the king, "Kill Prathap Singh! Off you go!"

They immediately began racing after the speeding king on their steeds. Mohabet Khan opened his mouth in glee at the prospect of seeing a dead Prathap Singh.

As he galloped after his brother, Sakta Singh's soul was instantly filled with nostalgia. His emotions were in total upheaval. Brotherly love started flooding his feelings. His conscience begged him not to harm his brother. The turmoil was unbearable.

Meanwhile, Jhala's ruse had worked perfectly. He fooled the Mughals into thinking he was Prathap Singh as he donned his king's helmet and his armour. His rajputs began speeding after his black horse just like they followed Prathap Singh with their long tapering crimson flags sporting the sun-shield. The Mughals thought the king had committed a tactical blunder. The lanky Ahmed

Khan from the right flank, took Jhala for Prathap Singh. He countered him and his soldiers with thousands of his own.

Jhala fought the battle of his life. Ahmed Khan's precise spear ploughed through the warrior-heart of Jhala. He fell to the ground with the weapon entrenched in his upper torso. His clansmen too were cut off with hundreds of them laying down their lives for Mewar and its king.

"Die, Prathap Singh!" barked the Mughal commander.

"We got him! We got him!" screamed the Mughals as scores crowded eagerly around the body of the braveheart to have a look. Ahmed Khan was found pinning the body down with his right foot on its head. Man Singh soon pulled up near the spot. One long look at the remains from his howdah told him that Prathap Singh had outfoxed him.

"This is not Prathap Singh!" he yelled. "This must be one of his commanders! He has fooled you all! Find him! Kill him!"

An earth-shaking roar let out by the Mughals and their rajputs filled the air as they raised their weapons in the air shouting, "Death to Prathap Singh!"

Concurrently, at a short distance from Haldigatti, Sakta Singh abruptly brought his horse to a halt after travelling almost one kilometre. He found that he was being followed!

"You may return to the command," he proposed to the Kazakh trio, turning around.

There was an awkward pause among the three pursuing Mughals. They understood his change of heart in no time.

"No rajput, we are here to kill the enemy" mocked one of the rugged warriors.

So, they had recognized him! Realizing the jeopardy his brother was facing, he retorted, "Either you return or I kill you!"

Consternation filled the mind of the tribesmen who now felt that Sakta Singh had betrayed Akbar's cause.

In the skirmish that followed, Sakta's spear accounted for all three escorts one after the other in spectacular fashion, just like his elder brother on the battlefield!

Breathing heavily, he continued the pursuit of his brother.

Prathap Singh did not realize that he was being followed but he nevertheless kept galloping on a critically wounded Chetak to reach safety. On hearing the sound of galloping hooves, he glanced back to see the charming rider on horseback in hot pursuit. A distance of about three hundred meters kept them apart. The king reached a wide fissure inundated by a flowing stream on a rocky hummock that that was about twelve feet wide.

"Let us leap over, Kishan" urged Prathap Singh as he backed up Chetak for the jump. He literally flew his badly limping Chetak across this fissure in one big leap and landed safely.

Kishan, coming to a halt at the edge, turned around and drew his sword out to fight the lone archenemy-rajput who was pursuing them.

Immediately after the incredible leap, Chetak collapsed on the ground in agony from the severed nerves. Prathap Singh pulled out the arrows lodged on his right flank. The horse was struggling to breathe from heavy loss of blood.

"Chetak, my boy!" cried the king as tears came down hot on his broad cheeks.

The horse gruntled as usual in love at the call of its name and blinked its eyelids.

Prathap Singh collapsed on his horse hugging its head and wailing loudly. He cried unashamedly as the last breath left the nostrils of his beloved horse. The king placed its head on his laps. He was absolutely inconsolable.

Albeit, taking cognizance of the pursuing danger, he gently laid the head of his dead horse on the ground, composed himself, pulled out his sword and was prepared to go all the way around the hummock to defend Kishan Singh when he heard a long-lost voice.

"Rider of the blue horse!" exclaimed Sakta Singh with excitement in his eyes as he dismounted his horse on the other side of the crevice.

Prathap Singh was taken aback when he saw his dashing, estranged brother standing on the other side of the chasm with a wide grin across his face.

"Sakta?" said the king in bewilderment.

There was a pause. He was torn at that moment between blood ties and love for Mewar.

After some hesitation he said, "Are you here to kill me brother, to appease a man from the Caucus mountains?"

Sakta Singh gestured at Kishan Singh to put his blade back into its sheath.

Looking across he said, "No, my brave brother. Does not my father's blood run in your veins?"

He paused for a moment, "Prathap Singh, you are a hero! Come down around the knoll. I wish to embrace you!"

The brothers came down from the little hill and embraced warmly, kissing each other.

Prathap Singh was moved to tears, at meeting his long-lost brother. "You belong in Mewar, Sakta, not at Fatehpur Sikri. Return home, brave son" said Prathap Singh holding Sakta's shoulders with both his blood-soaked red hands.

"I will, I will, brother. At the earliest opportunity I will return to Mewar, my home and to my ancestors. It has to be done safely. I have to be cautious about my wife and children. I do not want to place their lives in peril. I need to go back to the Mughals. I need to ensure that I am not a Mewar mole in the Mughal army. I shall return at the first safe opportunity. I shall come home, just as I went away from you." He jumped on his horse in a flash and was gone.

By the time Sakta Singh returned, the Mughals had almost clinically dealt with Mewar's army, killing scores of them at will. The weary, deflated Mewar troops were overwhelmed by superior Mughal numbers.

Ram Singh rallied the remaining troops and ordered them to retreat to the safety of the surrounding hills. Whatever cavalry remained galloped away into the green hills of the Aravalli. The remnants of the infantry and the bhil archers lost no time in hastening too.

However, there was no surrender of forces nor were any prisoners of war captured by the Mughals. The whole wide terrain was filled with thousands of the dead troops and huge lifeless beasts. Most of the dead were the rajputs of Mewar. About 12,000 brave sons of Mewar died on the battlefield to defend their honour that fateful day. The tally on the Mughal side was about 5,000 fatalities. Injured Mughals and their rajput clansmen lay scattered over a large expanse. Their moans and groans went unheeded. A little later, the Mughals put to death the critically injured Mewari rajputs on the field.

Man Singh had gotten off his elephant at the retreat of Ram Singh and his troops. He headed straight for the tent housing prince Salim. The topcats met in solemn silence.

"We lost Bhalol Khan and Ghazi Khan to Prathap Singh. Asaf Khan lost his right hand" observed Man Singh.

"So, is everything over yet?" inquired Salim in a mature manner.

"They will return tomorrow without fail" observed Ahmed Khan. "We should be on guard. Who knows? They might return tonight in the dead of the darkness."

"We haven't finished them yet with such huge numbers on our side?" asked young Salim rubbing his forehead with concern.

"The rajputs are gentle by nature but can be ferocious if aroused. Heroism runs in their nerves. It takes a lot to deal with them" replied Man Singh in a stoic manner. "I am told Sakta Singh is pursuing Prathap Singh. I expect good news. Mohabet Khan instantly dispatched cavalry to assist him at the very instant of this man fleeing the battlefield. Hopefully fate should smile on us."

"Mohabet Khan's eyes are as keen as an eagle's!" remarked Ahmed Khan as he drank a glass of water.

The heavy curtain of the tent was pushed open. Two Mughal soldiers entered with a vehement Mohabet Khan and his ever- smiling uncle Sakta Singh.

"He was expected to put an end to Prathap Singh!" screamed Mohabet Khan pointing his finger at the impressive rajput standing by him. "Instead here he is, cutting a very sorry figure!" he continued screaming.

Sakta Singh locked eyes with a stern Man Singh, "Mohabet Khan, leave!" ordered Man Singh as he switched to staring at Sakta Singh.

"So, is he dead? Your brother?" demanded Man Singh in his usual serious disposition after Mohabet Khan left the royal tent.

"I pursued him for about thousand metres. Three of our horsemen reached him before I could and drew swords. He killed the three and warned me not to pursue him."

"So, you just decided to return, Sakta?" probed an angry Man Singh still locking his eyes at the rajput with deep suspicion. "You could face death right here, right now, if you are found lying, son!" he declared. He rose from his chair, "Be a man, Sakta Singh. Should a prince find subterfuge in a clever lie? Are you not ashamed? Did you spare your brother?" He looked at his sword resting on the table and back again at Sakta Singh. "I don't spare traitors. You are lying, aren't you?" he glared.

Prince Salim intervened, "Commander, let me interrupt for a moment" he sounded too mature for a young lad.

Man Singh controlled himself and deferred for the sake of the prince.

"Sakta Singh," inquired the young Prince Salim, "I shall spare your life if, and only if, you choose to tell us the truth." He waved at Man Singh, "He shall not die. Not today."

"I..I chose not to kill my brother," faltered Sakta Singh softly addressing Salim. "He is my flesh and blood! You would have done the same if you were me. I cannot possibly kill my own sibling!"

Man Singh kept staring at the young prince. His agitated horseshoe-moustache was quivering for retribution.

"Should not Sakta Singh die for this?" ranted Ahmed Khan.

Prince Salim scowled at Ahmed Khan, "What did I just say?" The displeasure on the prince's face silenced Ahmed Khan instantly.

"You have betrayed the Mughal cause, Sakta Singh," said the young prince after a moment's silence, "I command you to leave the empire herewith. Go back to your brother if you love him. We don't need you. You shall die however, if we find you anywhere in the Mughal camp. Leave at once!"

Sakta Singh fixed his attention on the prince for a moment for an unuttered favour he was hesitant to petition.

"Yes?" inquired the young heir.

"Your Highness, my wife, and—"

"And your assets shall return to your homestead safe and sound," cut short the prince, turning away, not willing to make eye contact any further.

Sakta Singh bowed his head in deep reverence, "May your name resonate through the ages," he said.

He turned around, made his exit and jumped on his horse and darted towards Kumbalgarh on his chestnut-hued horse.

"Brothers, blood and bonds. Can we do anything about them? There is nothing on earth that will counter the love for one's bloodline! We should have known better" mused Mahter Khan.

A moment of silence followed as they tried to digest the events that would follow the outrageous bloodletting on the plain of Haldigatti.

"So, Prathap Singh has given us the slip! This is a blot against my name" observed a grave-looking Man Singh.

"We have to account for him at the earliest, now that he is weak, weary and wounded" chipped in Ahmed Khan.

"Why don't we pursue him tonight and be done with him? He must be either in Kumbalgarh or Gogunda," said Akbar's commander-in-chief as if he was conferred with sudden revelation. The prospect of killing Prathap Singh now looked very plausible.

"Yes, you are right, Commander!" concurred Ahmed Khan. "We should strike the iron while it is hot!"

"Shouldn't we?" asked Man Singh with alacrity.

"What matters is victory against the enemies of the empire. The earlier the better" admitted Salim. "You are the one to make all the decisions, General!"

"We shall strike tonight!" said Man Singh with cheerful eyes.

CHAPTER 17

THE ROAR OF THE LION

*P*rathap Singh reached Kumbalgarh Fortress early in the evening accompanied by Kishan Singh. He had used the horse lent by Sakta Singh. The citadel went wild with excitement at the arrival of the king. The iron hooves of a pair of galloping horses thundering in on the cobbled stones announced his presence. The courtiers gasped in disbelief to see him completely blood soaked without his armour or helmet and with arrows lodged on his back. Many rushed towards him to be of some aid. He raised his hand to signal that he was alive and conscious. Kishan Singh had to push back the palace attendees from coming too close. The noisy commotion in the falling darkness caught Kanwar's delicate ears on cue.

An attendant rushed into Kanwar's chambers, "My Queen, the king has returned!" she said out of breath.

Kanwar dashed like a hind deer towards the main hall of the fortress that led to the entrance. Her anklets chimed wildly to keep pace with her hasty steps down the flight of stairs. Her husband was seated all injured, wounded and pierced with arrows in the glow of bright yellow fire surrounded by the keepers of the fortress.

"The queen, the queen," said many as she approached slowly with large, astonished eyes at the bleeding figure of Prathap Singh. She prostrated at his feet, clutching them.

"You should all leave!" ordered Kishan Singh at the top of his voice. Everyone hastened out whispering loudly, hardly trying to control their happiness and rapture at the return of the king.

"I shall wait for your call, sire" he said, closing the massive doors behind him.

"Now I can die in peace" sobbed Kanwar as she rose and held his physiognomy examining the blood all over his face, her feminine, bangle-decked hands infusing an invisible elixir to heal him of the afflictions he had suffered on the battlefield.

She rushed to the door, opened them and summoned Kishan Singh.

"Call the physicians right away! Hurry!" she commanded. Then, she came behind him and gently felt the embedded arrows.

"Don't do that, Kanwar!" cautioned her king. She hurried and knelt before him.

"They will attend to me" he continued. "Now—"

"Is Chetak doing fine, My Lord?" she cut in amidst her tears.

Prathap Singh cried clenching his teeth. He then looked at his wife in remorse. She began sobbing again.

"Do not mourn for those whose time has come. I lost Chetak. Ram Prasad was captured!" he confessed, "Maybe, I shall possess them in another lifetime."

This news induced heaves and sobs from the queen.

The wounded king of Mewar went on, "Now listen, we are vacating Kumbalgarh and Gogunda tonight. Our forces have been famished. We lost more than 12,000 men today!"

Kanwar wailed hysterically. Her loud cries echoed through the massive fort.

Prathap Singh hugged her instantly and stroked her head. "Do not wail. Don't. Please don't. I live to deal with them another day. I will and I shall!"

The door flung open suddenly without prior intimation.

"Your brother Sakta Singh, My Lord!" announced Kishan Singh.

"Sakta? Here? Show him in at once" said Prathap Singh still cradling his queen, not letting her go.

A loud rumbling of hundreds of horse-hooves and neighing and jostling of horses next brought Prathap Singh's trusted lieutenant to the palace garrison.

"My Lord, Ram Singh has arrived with his men too!" added Kishan Singh.

"I shall confer with him in a while" the king confirmed.

"My dear Kanwar, Sakta Singh has defected!" he said joyously as he released her from his embrace.

"Sakta? What?" beamed a shocked Kanwar wiping her tears.

In walked the physicians. As they began working on the king, Sakta Singh ambled in with his typical boyish smile even at this crisis. On seeing his stately sister-in-law, he bowed to touch her feet. Kanwar's feelings once again overwhelmed her as her mind played flashbacks of the glorious days when she had been a young bride and Sakta Singh being infamous for his boyish mischief then.

"If I were a man, I would hug you, Sakta" she asserted with tears of joy.

Sakta Singh was moved. "I shall talk to you later" he smiled.

After a short period in which Prathap Singh's arrows and the gashes inflicted by the flying spears had been dealt with and bandaged, Sakta Singh and Ram Singh were in conference with the king.

"Sakta, you shall go with Kishan Singh to Gogunda immediately" began a wounded but very definitive Prathap Singh. "You shall be escorted by 3000 troops. Evacuate all including men, women and children as soon as possible. We will not allow the Mughals to satiate themselves by slaughtering us. They would definitely like to capture Gogunda and Kumbalgarh. We are going to abandon our forts for the present time. We shall leave a skeletal staff of around 50 men at both forts. If for some reason Man Singh decides to spare us, then we are lucky. However, the chances of that happening are remote. Ram Singh and I shall convey to you the rendezvous location. I wish I could go as far as the plains of the Indus and have the entire Thar between me and Akbar for quite some time. Let them gloat over us for now."

There was an intense hustle and bustle underway at Kumbalgarh after Kishan Singh and Sakta Singh left for Gogunda on horseback with about 3000 cavalry following them.

At Kumbalgarh, horse carriages and the stallions were made at the ready in a short time. In just about an hour, the king and Ram Singh led the entire company of the resident-clans of the king and the queen, the clergy, soldiers, courtiers, their womenfolk and their children, with 3000 horsemen in close convoy. They descended the Aravalli, trudging across hills and valleys in the darkness with only blazing torches for company.

As the caravan proceeded about 20 kilometres in the darkness, they could hear the gallop of horses gaining on them from behind. Swords and spears were at the ready. Prathap Singh felt more incensed at the prospect of being ambushed by the Mughals in the middle of nowhere in that dark night.

"At my word, men" he said drawing out his own sword that had slain numerous men a few hours ago. His horses came to a standstill.

A train of about 30 men carrying wildly blowing flames on heavy planks came to a halt alongside the entourage.

Bama Shah, the king's prime minister covered in tactical face headgears called out, "My King! It's your servant Bama Shah!"

"What brings you here, my man?" said Prathap Singh a bit relieved but intent on carrying on the journey.

"Where are you headed, My Lord?" the prime minister queried.

"As far as the banks of the sacred Indus, I hope" replied Prathap Singh heaving a heavy sigh.

"I know you feel like giving up. If you abandon us, who would fight for the rajputs in Mewar? Would not the Mughals swallow us up? Would they not force us into servitude and slavery?" questioned a concerned Shah.

"I would certainly fight these villains very soon" assured Prathap Singh.

"I have waylaid your entourage for that very purpose" the prime minister countered. "Here is 20,000 gold coins!"

Two horses bearing 10,000 gold coins in two heavy sacks on either flanks were slowly lead before the king. Prathap Singh was shaken. "I also wish to donate 25,000 rupaiya in money to aid you at this hour of crisis!" said Shah as a horse carriage carrying the amount creaked forward.

"I am amazed that you are doing this, Bama Shah" uttered Prathap Singh. "But, why now?"

"My Lord, eject the Mughals from our land!" he implored. "We have suffered enough! Must this agony continue endlessly? Use this capital to throw these invaders out for good. Let Akbar know there is a lion strutting in Mewar!"

He dismounted and bowed to his king, "I know a safe hideout about 12 kilometres from here among the craggy mountains. There is a network of tunnels and hideouts stashed away deep within those hills that no one knows except a few of my men. Your consorts and your chosen men can stay there with no chance of being detected! This place can house about 20 souls. Why do you risk going all the way to the Indus? You will be exposed on the banks of the blue waters. You could be betrayed. The Mughals won't spare you in the open. Do not fret about the rest of your palace inhabitants. I shall make sure that they mingle with the civilian community among the villages and towns of Mewar. I shall take care of that."

"Your proposition seems right" conceded the king.

"Father, uncle Sakta Singh and Kishan Singh are proceeding to the Indus from Gogunda!" exclaimed Amar Singh.

"Could you catch up with my brother and Kishan Singh and direct them to us?" enquired Prathap Singh.

"At once, My Lord. I shall dispatch my men right now to intercept your brother and Kishan Singh. The select few from their company shall join you. Rest assured. I have eyes and ears on the mountains that no one knows about. My men will certainly meet up with them before the sun comes up" confirmed Bhama Shah confidently.

There was a moment of total silence after which Prathap Singh began very slowly, "I am deeply humbled by your offering, Bama Shah. May your posterity walk in this land for many ages to come. I am exhausted from the battle and would need respite badly. I shall make a decision to move to the Indus after reaching the hideout you talk about. Lead us there immediately."

"Right away, sire" Shah replied.

The king instantly segregated his immediate circle of 20 and bade goodbye to the rest of the royal members from the Kumbalgarh Fortress, while a few courtiers from Bhama Shah's team galloped away to interpose with Sakta Singh and Kishan Singh and their cavalcade.

Bhama Shah and his troupe led the company gingerly over the slopes and valleys towards the safe place.

Shortly after one o' clock that dark night, two contingents of Mughal forces, each 10,000 strong, led by Ahmed Khan and Mahtar Khan headed straight for Kumbalgarh and Gogunda respectively on the orders of Man Singh Amber!

The Mughals came in with their cavalry armed to the teeth. The lanky Ahmed Khan led them from the front at Kumbalgarh.

"Has he abandoned the fort?" he asked his lieutenants as they began ascending the meandering pathway leading to the fort. The town surrounding the fort too had been emptied of its occupants.

"Or are we walking into a trap set by this fox?" he kept inquiring as they cautiously approached the main entrance.

A flurry of arrows was launched at them by the 30-odd die-hard rajputs left behind for the defence of the fort. The Mughals made sure their resistance did not last long. The same narrative unfolded in Gogunda, where another 50-odd rajputs lost their lives to Mahter Khan's troops. Man Singh's troops began inspecting the newly acquired forts for their lord Akbar. In the heat of excitement, Akbar's army hoisted the green Mughal flag with the prancing lion over both Mewar citadels in the dead of the night!

CHAPTER 18

SURPRISING SPARKS!

$\mathcal{B}$hama Shah led Prathap Singh and his band towards the shelter in the dead of the night. He conducted them through the chain of the green-brown Aravalli mountains. They finally reached a location between two quite lofty mounts, the second of which was blocked by the surging crags of the first.

"We need to climb the slope, Your Grace," he urged his king.

Prathap Singh and his cavalry followed in silence as they ascended the ramp in the light of the torches with some difficulty. The inclination led to the saddle of the height where everyone breathed a sigh of relief.

"It's just over there" he said pointing towards the shoulder of the mountain. "Everyone needs to dismount."

"Are we there yet?" questioned a concerned Kanwar feeling cold and exposed to the elements.

"I think we are almost there" replied the king.

The entourage finally climbed the shoulder of the mountain with some effort. The landing led to a very narrow, man-made pathway that ushered them to a huge iron door hidden in plain sight on the rocky face of the heights.

The camouflaged entrance, resembling the rugged surface was forced open by Bhama Shah's men.

"This way, My King" said a courtier as he walked in with his companions with the blazing torches.

Prathap Singh and his company entered a rocky hall with a high ceiling. At the extreme corner of this rock-cut enclosure the guide and his companions lifted a heavy, craggy rectangular-framed hatch which they had to drag with some difficulty. This entrance was wide open to allow a couple of people to descend down. A flight of twenty jagged steps led to massive parlours hewn into the rock one after the other, one leading into the other. There were five such lodgings. The prime minister led the king and his men down the flight of stairs. Prathap Singh could not believe what he was looking at.

"The last room has an exit out of the mountain on the other side. That too is completely obscured from prying eyes, My Lord. You should be safe here" observed Bhama Shah.

"Not only these halls, My King," he pulled a large ornate rug on the floor from under their feet and began rolling it, "Here you see" he pointed his left index finger to the floor where he and a couple of men lifted yet another large rocky stone that opened to a smooth lengthy slide reaching twenty feet down, almost invisible to the naked eye. This pebble smooth sliding surface led to a very narrow spherical tunnel. The tunnel was about one hundred metres long branching off left and right at its end, leading to their respective enclosures at the shoulder of the mountain.

"We shall provide you all with provisions you need without catching anyone's curiosity, My King. We shall never raise any suspicion. You need to be hidden here for the short term" said Bhama Shah.

The light of the torches threw elongated shadows all over the place.

"My Lord, the occupants of this subterranean refuge can leave for a breath of fresh air or to answer the call of nature without being detected. It is however better to be on guard and not be ambushed by the Mughals. Do not take things for granted. Exercise extreme caution every time anyone ventures out!" warned Bhama Shah's guide.

After spreading out the bedspreads and laying the pillows they had brought and stacking the gold and the coins at the corner of the third subsurface room, Bhama Shah and his men climbed the stairs again, secured the mountain door shut and left, leaving the king, his wife, children and his confidantes to themselves.

Prathap Singh sat down on the bedspreads on the rocky floor. A jewellery decked Kanwar who felt exhausted by the overwhelming emotions that were assailing her stood a little aside.

The king looked at everyone seated around him, "The diadem of sovereignty has been plucked from the brow of The Hind to adorn the crest of the Mughal!" he began, "Hindustan has ceased to have the paramount sway over her princes. A foreigner, an invader now wields the sceptre! We have become aliens in our own land! If only the rajputs had learned their lessons! Would they? They would not. Why would they? They have been this way ever since that Mahmood crossed the Indus to ravage us. Who could forget the brutality of Khilji and of Ghori? The rajputs can only think of arms, horses and hunting. We rajputs place priority on the constant bickering among our clans when there is no fire-breathing enemy to burn us all. An overbearing temperament, constant strife between rival factions and an irrational desire for vengeance against each other is what characterizes our realms.

"Alas, Hindustan! Alas, my mother! Is there no one to love you? Is there no one to cherish your lofty mountains, your sacred rivers, your striking tributaries, your breathtaking valleys, your ever-stretching plains, your sweet snow and your gentle clouds, the laughter of your girls, the humility of your men and the nobleness of your populace? Is there not one among your sons to defend your fame? Where is chivalry? Where is courage?"

Warm tears began pouring down his enraged face, "O Hind!" An impassioned king's voice rose, "You need a Vikramaditya, a Maurya, a Karna, a Duryodana, an Abimanyu or a Kanishka…Only such can lay to dust the pride of these invaders from the Caucuses! Only such can deal a death-blow to these trespassers! There was a time when we rajputs occupied the entire east bank of the Indus. We ruled all the way from Ujjain to the Oxus and the Jaxartes rivers! We have been pushed for decades on end by the Arab invaders and their proxies and now the Mughals have pushed us this far. What's more, the Amber, Marwar, Jodhpur, Jaisalmer and Ajmer clans have become sword-bearers for the Mughals! What an irony! Mewar alone chose not to compromise her honour and still survives the Mughal assaults."

He paused for a moment before continuing, "This son of Humayun wants me to become a spineless vassal! Wow! Should I not swing my sword against the face of this ruthless foe? There will be no peace until the Mughals sleep in their tombs and a son of the Hind ascends to power!"

"Father, don't lose hope. None among the Mughals can contest your raw prowess," encouraged his son Amar Singh. "Things are bound to change. We shall return to Gogunda and Kumbalgarh. Mewar's crimson and silver sun battle standard shall flaunt over our fortresses again!"

"Aye, it shall! What race would have maintained the semblance of its civilization, the customs of its forefathers in spite of repeated invasions by these hordes? The valour-brimming character of the rajput gave them hope to withstand the brutality of these invasions. So I will arm myself with the same rajput confidence and harrow the Mughals."

Kanwar came up behind him, stooped and placed her right hand over his left shoulder, "My Lord, you need to repose for some time. You are already drained by the battle. Why don't you sleep for a while and give your worries to the wind? We shall prevail ultimately."

Prathap Singh descended to one of the chambers below. It was lit with the glowing light of a lamp fixed on the wall. He lay down on something that resembled a rough mattress. Kanwar sat down by his knees fanning him with a thick dry palm leaf, her bangles pacing back and forth relentlessly in the action.

"Are you not going to sleep, dear?" he asked placing his left hand on her lap, his eyes still closed.

"I will, when you shall have slept" she replied in a cold manner, her thoughts engrossed elsewhere.

"It bothers me to subject the daughter of kings to this abject experience" he mumbled trying to sleep.

"It is my honour to serve My Lord in grandeur and in misery. I am sworn to that. I am bound to such an oath. This suffering matters not. You are my joy and my strength. I am more concerned about you than my discomfiture, My King," came the words of wisdom from the queen's red lips.

"You are my star. With you by my side, I shall live till I'm one hundred and twenty" he smiled with his eyes closed.

"May you sure do" she countered and laid herself across his slanting arms fanning herself and her king.

CHAPTER 19

RIPPLES ON THE SURFACE

𝒫rince Salim and a few trusted lieutenants, escorted by 10,000 thousand infantry, a 1000 cavalry and the remaining war-elephants reached Fatehpur Sikri on a sultry August afternoon.

Trumpets blared and courtiers lined-up to receive the returning prince and his entourage.

The czar was seated on his throne that was encompassed with bustling courtiers as usual in the royal hall when the prince walked in and paid obeisance.

"Proceed to your chambers. You must be exhausted by now" declared Akbar.

After his exit, the monarch addressed his court. "We have conquered Mewar. Gogunda and Kumbalgarh are under our aegis, yet Prathap Singh has given us the slip.

This man is far more elusive, now that he is aware of our hazards."

He paused for a moment, heaved a sigh and went on, "I provided Sakta Singh refuge. I fed him. I clothed him and cared for him. Yet, he turns against me and refuses to put an end to Prathap Singh. What a weakling! Would I not have accorded him a seat at my table along with my sons had he killed his brother? This betrayal hurts." He sounded very bitter.

Abul-Fazl, counselled the king, "Opportunity dares a man into doing things he would not do otherwise. Opportunity and raw courage are a dangerous combination, Your Highness."

"The empire would do well to test the trustworthiness of all refugees from princely states before admitting them into its care. Why should we fall on our own faces?" advised Mulla Do-Piyazo.

"We should probably demand they barter away their lives in the event of such betrayal well in advance of their admittance. What do you feel, My King?" said Birbal in a sarcastic manner. His displeasure was palpable to the dictator.

"I shall deal with this traitor Sakta Singh. He shall not get away with this. His family has already been expelled... Anyway, we are facing pockets of resistance from the rajput clans around the Mewar region. These are most likely inspired by Prathap Singh's actions. We also have a crisis in Gujarat with that hothead Mirza Mohammed Hussein[*] from the Mirza bloodline laying siege to Ahmedabad. I am deputing general Tarsum Khan to this troubled province…"

A sturdy-looking Moghul in black military fatigues and an ebony black, steel pointed helmet stepped forward and bowed lightly as his name was uttered.

"..to bludgeon these troublemakers around Mewar into obedience" said Akbar.

Tarsum Khan became the cynosure of attention in the crowded court as all the rajputs and the Mughals in the immediate proximity of the throne began staring at him intently.

Todar Mal, eager to express his views, joined the discussion, "My Liege, we have rebels rising up in extreme corners of the empire. Unless definitive and forceful action is undertaken, such forces will make a mockery of our commonwealth. I believe you should personally lead the army into Mewar and Ahmedabad and put an end to the antics of Prathap Singh and Mirza Mohammed Hussein. Then other mischief-mongers shall drop dead in fear when you project power."

[*] footnote: not to be confused with Mirza Mohammed Hakim, emperor Akbar's half brother

Tansen chipped in poetically, "Your sun shines in glory all over this land of Hind, must annoying honeybees block its splendour?"

"No buzzing honeybee will hover in my way," ascertained Akbar with a smile. "I shall personally take action. It's about time, isn't it?" He sounded determined.

"What is it you plan to do, My Liege?" demanded Birbal with his acqueline nose gently.

There was no response from Akbar who kept looking fondly at his favourite administrator.

"Take your time" continued Birbal, "But go with your feelings. Your instincts know better than any of us."

"Instincts?" questioned Akbar. "Instincts don't make sense right away. They are, however, proved right all the time. Should I not trust my hunch?"

Two weeks later, Man Singh, Asaf Khan and about 60,000 troops made landfall in Ajmer. The troops duly returned to their barracks. One week later still, Man Singh and Asaf Khan reached the courts of Akbar at Fatehpur Sikri.

October 1576.

It was a Friday afternoon. Akbar was seated on a magnificent armchair in the lavish corridors of the Fatehpur Sikri royal complex marked by its distinct wide

Persian arches. He was encircled by his confidantes. He looked across towards the rectangular pool in the centre of the voluminous courtyard. Its waters were gently moving in the swaying breeze.

"My silence has been taken for lack of interest. I shall lead the army myself to deal with Prathap Singh and Mirza Mohammed Hussein" observed the emperor.

"You shall strike fear in the hearts of your foes" remarked Birbal, adding swiftly, "I wish you would give me a chance to unsheathe my stinging sword."

The sovereign swung his head, "Raja Birbal, dearie, will not your blade taste blood? It sure will. Not in the mountains of the rajputs, but in the heights of the Hindu Kush. Fielding too many assets at the same location does not augur well, either for military or for the empire's wellbeing."

A robust-looking Man Singh was seated next to the right of the chieftain. His eyes fixed on his king with intense interest.

"Man Singh, I shall leave the planning and the tactics to you" said Akbar.

The mention of his domain forced a microscopic movement of Man Singh's lips in an undetectable smile.

"We must account for the heads of these two troublemakers who believe they are spearheading a revolution against the Mughals!" went on the monarch with wide-arching eyebrows.

"Revolution?" cut in Abdul Rahim Khan, the defence minister with a sarcastic chuckle, "Your Highness, what revolution can Prathap Singh unleash? Is he not whiling away his life in the name of revolution? He shall fall by your sword! We are leading an army of 70,000, backed by artillery guns, impressive cavalry, musketeers and innumerable host of elephants this time around! Does this rajput stand any chance? Whatever he had was ravished by Man Singh and our troops the last time we clashed."

A gust of wind blew through the wide arches, momentarily pausing the discussion.

"Prathap Singh remains a burning firebrand. That is something we cannot ignore. He is absolutely capable of igniting rebellion. He carries way too much charisma. A single ember of fire can set the dry chaff ablaze. We should never underestimate this enemy" confessed the king.

Abul Fazl the grand vizier chipped in, "Any failure on our part to eliminate the Prince of Mewar will be seen as a sign of our weakness. He must be accounted for among the dead."

Todar Mal glanced at Akbar and then addressed Man Singh, "This time you would nail him, Man Singh, wouldn't you?"

"The sun shall otherwise rise in the west" replied the Prince of Amber in a mocking manner.

"Raja Bhagwan Das is on board for this campaign to destroy the rebels of Mewar. The father-son duo should be a matchless gambit to put an end to Prathap Singh and then we shall strangle the throat of Mirza Mohammed Hussein" observed Akbar fixing his eyes on Todar Mal first and then at Birbal to imply that he still trusted his commander in spite of his many apprehensions that he had entertained after the first Mewar campaign.

Akbar rose and went down the staircase leading to the cobbled widespread courtyard, his hands locked behind him in typical fashion. His team followed suit.

"We shall reach Mewar in a week's time or so. We are leaving at the crack of dawn tomorrow."

"A quick victory awaits you, My Lord" said Mulla Do-Piyazo.

"As you say" smiled Akbar.

The long march to the Mewar region began with the first daylight. The vast army of men, weapons and animals shook the earth under its feet and reached its destination in just more than a week's time. The base was pitched about ten kilometres east of Gogunda.

Akbar's presence injected immense inspiration among all wings of the military. He spelt out the commands to his units, "Comb all the hills in the neighbourhood of Gogunda and Kumbalgarh. Probe every nook and corner of these mountains. He must be hiding here somewhere. I would love to capture him alive."

All roads leading to Gogunda and Kumbalgarh were blocked, barricades were set up in the streets and trenches dug up to trap Prathap Singh if he returned to storm the citadels. Tarsum Khan, having been deputed by Akbar for overseeing these cordons, went around almost daily to ensure the blockades were indeed airtight.

The emperor sat exuding confidence in his tent one late afternoon when a panting herald walked in. "My Lord, two units on patrol south of Gogunda have been ambushed! We have lost sixty men!"

Akbar turned to Man Singh on his right.

"I shall return with his head!" promised the impatient commander as he rose in anger from his seat.

"I have just lost sixty men. Should I lose my most decorated military soldier too?" answered an annoyed emperor.

Man Singh gave him the typical stare saying, "This crafty rajput is slithering back and forth like a noxious serpent across these mountains. Are we going to walk into his artifices?" he questioned quite upset.

Akbar replied, "You are wrong, Amber. Prathap Singh is no snake. He is one valiant lion who chose to confront us on this terrain. A lion who slaughtered scores of Mughals and rajputs… and if fate had not intervened, he would have killed the man I am speaking to right now. I dare say, in all of Hindustan there is no one as audacious as Prathap Singh! I acknowledge that. If only he had been enlightened enough to join my ranks. If only… I know this attack is his doing. No doubt."

Man Singh was taken aback by the praises his king heaped on his foe. He looked at his father doubtfully.

Bagwan Das now gave his view of things, "My Lord, the dragonfly will flit into the spider's gossamer one day or the other. If not today, tomorrow."

Akbar nodded in silence as he paced to and fro in the large tent with his hands at the back, lost in contemplation.

CHAPTER 20

NO TIME FOR REST

*I*t was a bright chilly December morning on the highlands of Mewar. Within the rocky confines of his hideout, Prathap Singh began chalking out plans to repossess his forts and to thumb his nose at the Mughals.

That morning, a private council gathered in the last chamber in the lower floor, located down the flight of twenty steps. Prathap Singh, Amar Singh, Sakta Singh, Kishan Singh and Ram Singh sat on the floor overlaid with a bedspread to cover the stony surface.

"It's welcome news, brother!" exclaimed Sakta Singh with a broad grin, "Akbar and Man Singh have left for Fatehpur Sikri! A massive entourage followed in their wake! This is a tremendous relief. This is proof enough that the mighty Mughal has bitten the dust against Prathap Singh, isn't it?"

"We are not going to relent" replied Prathap Singh in a nonchalant manner placing his right hand on his brother's arm. "We shall keep striking at the Mughal presence in our lands as we have been for the last five or six months. Gogunda and Kumbalgarh will have to return to our fold. The Mughals should be thrown out once and for all, even if it means throwing out their lifeless carcasses" spoke the king in great determination. "How many troops do we still possess?"

"We have about 6,000 troops. Of which a thousand are cavalrymen. If we choose to strike, it will come down to the Mughal numbers in and around the forts" replied Ram Singh.

"These men that we have should be worth the gamble. My information suggests that about 3000 infantry and 200 cavalry remain encamped in both Gogunda and Kumbalgarh" claimed the wide-eyed Kishan Singh. "The Mughals believe that the Mewari army has vanished into thin air! They are lulled into the comfort of complacency. We need to keep striking as you say."

Sakta Singh added, "Ahmed Khan is in charge of Kumbalgarh. His compatriot Mahter Khan has taken over Gogunda. The Mughals have left one Tarsum Khan in charge to coordinate their plans. He is one tough specimen."

"All three shall pay with their own lives for defiling rajput domains" said Prathap Singh as his eyelids widened fiercely. "They will not make it back alive to Akbar's court!"

"I presume you are planning a night-time strike on the forts?" asked Amar Singh.

Prathap Singh nodded. "In all likelihood, yes. We shall attack when they are least prepared for it. Not a single servant of Fatehpur Sikri should live!"

"How wonderful, Father!" exclaimed Amar Singh, "Back to the comfort of Kumbalgarh and Gogunda!"

"Don't be too hasty, son" cautioned the king as he waggled his right index finger, "We need to be ready to abandon these forts at a moment's time if need be. We are dealing with the Mughals. They will not take setbacks lying down. So, should they try to overwhelm us, we would and we should gladly abandon our citadels only to repossess them at a later time."

"So..." hesitated Kishan Singh.

"Once the dust settles down with Akbar and Man Singh's departure, we should be all set for the attack on the forts" proposed Prathap Singh. "Nevertheless, our preparation for the assault must not be detected under any circumstance by the Mughals. Keep the whole thing under wraps."

"Not a single mortal shall come to know of it, My Lord" assured Kishan Singh with all confidence.

"I need everyone here to maintain perfect camouflage when you blend with the populace in and around the cities of Mewar. None – friend or foe – should identify your persons. You shall die at Mughal hands if that were to happen" warned Prathap Singh. "And what of the horses and our troops?"

Ram Singh stepped in, "Our troops have been temporarily spread far and wide in all the towns and villages of Mewar with the only exception of the 600 that we use for the frequent raids on Mughal targets here. They have completely blended with the common folk disguised as farmers and labourers. No worries about that. We shall have them ready in a week's notice if we were to attack."

"The new moon comes up in seven days. It falls on a Sunday. It is perfect. Shall we?" questioned Prathap Singh with intense eagerness.

"Why not?" responded Sakta Singh, "The heads that are destined to fall on a Monday might as well fall on a Sunday!"

A wave of laughter echoed in the small parlour lit up by wooden lamps.

"Alright, Sakta. It is as you say" seconded the king. "We are set. We strike next Sunday an hour after midnight.

Our troops shall be spilt into two divisions of 3000 each inclusive of five 500 cavalry. Now, the 3000 heading for Gogunda will be under the command of Sakta Singh and Kishan Singh. Your troops will assemble in all readiness at Eklinji by twelve midnight. The other 3000 shall be under Amar Singh and my command. They shall assemble at Haldigatti so as not to raise suspicion. Let the forces remain split since the cavalry is also involved. I fear the Mughals might be tipped off into launching a pre-emptory strike on us due to the large presence of the armed forces."

"All clear" beamed Sakta Singh.

"Since you are very familiar with the layout of Gogunda you need to lead them into slaughtering the Mughals there, Sakta" reinforced Prathap Singh. "Ram Singh will secure solid intelligence on their movements at the fort in advance."

"Agreed, brother. You are the man I look up to" smiled Sakta Singh.

"We shall dispatch the rest of the Mughal force on our side at Kumbalgarh to their ancestors" mocked Prathap Singh.

CHAPTER 21

DEATH BY DAWN

*I*t was a moonless Sunday night. There was a thick cloud cover, though the bands of curling white clouds over the Aravalli range did not threaten to shower the terrain with rain. The common folk of Mewar had gone to bed early as usual about eight in the evening. Very soon the sounds of crickets, fireflies and nocturnal birds and other fauna began gently filling the air. Mewar's remaining armed forces now started gathering in the darkness of the night around eleven at both Eklinji and at Haldigatti. The cavalry had to walk their horses in an ambling manner so as not to generate the reverberations of advancing troops in any way. It was a risky proposition to assemble without being noticed but then there were not too many around to bother as to who would be preparing to assault the Mughal-controlled forts in the light of the far away stars. It was a bold gambit with absolutely no risk involved, at least at the assembling stage. The Eklinji contingent with Sakta Singh and the battle-hardened Ram Singh were moving ever so gently in the cool night towards Gogunda with the horses lagging behind deliberately to muffle their advance. Prathap Singh and Amar Singh led their unit from Haldigatti straight to the sighting proximity of the Kumbalgarh mountains.

At the vicinity of both the forts the elite units of about forty archers crept stealthily on the troops manning the barricades in the thick darkness and killed them with their daggers. There was simply no resistance from these Mughals who were either dozing or bored with the monotony of their assignment.

They were about 500 meters from the towering bastion at Kumbalgarh when Prathap Singh called out, "Halt!"

A moment of silence followed. He turned around in his black camouflage mantle, "Remember men, the cavalry under my command will only rush in after the sentries are dealt with. I shall wait for the blast of the conch shell. Now proceed."

Instantly the advance units completely covered in black coal dust headed straight for the high walls of Kumbalgarh. The night torches atop the battlements revealed the presence of the Mughal sentries positioned about a 100 metres apart. Some standing, some seated, some indulging in soft conversation and some gazing at the heavens above. In the flash of a moment, Prathap Singh's archers fired their arrows from a distance of about

50 metres and found their targets. The cry of Mughal soldiers on the walls of the fortress being struck by projectiles rudely shook the other units on duty below, numbering a few hundred. Not expecting an attack at that odd hour they hurried for their weapons. This short period of time saw Prathap Singh's archers climb the walls with ropes and anchors in the blink of an eye and unleash their swords against the remaining wall-mounted troops who were in total shock. These elite unit of archers ran down, slaughtered the oncoming Mughals, dodged spears and swords and succeeded in throwing open the fort's massive main doors. The conch sounded with a loud, dull reverberating sound in the stillness of that dark night. There was confusion in Kumbalgarh. Panic set in among the resident Mughals who were trying to catch some sleep far away from the comfort of Fatehpur Sikri.

Ahmed Khan, their commander was rudely shaken by all the commotion.

"We are being stormed!" shouted a captain as he put the armour on his commander's person.

Prathap Singh and his cavalry galloped, sprang over the trenches and swooped into the fort through the threshold like eagles landing on their preys. The loud clanging of the horse hooves on the cobbled stones produced a thunderous effect as his men crashed into the fort. The

Mughals, completely caught unaware by this surprise onslaught, were no match for Mewar's forces.

Tarsum Khan who for some reason kept awake that night rushed out of the rear exit from the main hall of the palace and found his way to the stables to get onto his warhorse. Mewar's infantry too by this time followed suit and were engaging the shell-shocked Mughals in bloody combat. Prathap Singh and his cavalry cut down any Mughal who dared to engage them that night. His razor-sharp talwar made short work of numerous onrushing Mughals. He loved slashing it down with lethal force to see their heads fall from their shoulders! Quite a few Mughal heads went flying in the air for a while before landing with a big thud. His new brilliant black horse moved like the breeze even knocking down many Mughals with its powerful hooves garnished with shiny metallic shoes.

By the hand of fate, Tarsum Khan wanting to make a name for himself identified Prathap Singh in the melee and headed straight to him on his horse in the courtyard after making short work of about twenty Mewari cavalrymen. Prathap Singh figuring the champion-like physique of the Mughal to be that of Akbar's man-in-charge galloped immediately to engage him in combat. It was a fierce duel between two evenly matched veterans, one rajput and the other a Mughal. As the swords clashed in mid-air, the king instantly understood that Tarsum Khan was a well-built warrior. Prathap Singh and his adversary did not take their eyes off each other as their stallions manoeuvred in circles to gain advantage. The Mughal charged at Prathap Singh who swung his blade right and left at his opponent's scimitar in devastating accuracy. Tarsum Khan could not believe the power in Prathap Singh's blows. His confidence began to shake as Mewar's champion zeroed in for the kill. In one long volley of clashing swords the Mughal champion's right knee felt the powerful impact of Pratap Singh's talwar. His right kneecap was shattered forcing him to lose his balance in an agonizing fall. He was surrounded instantly by Mewar's infantry who chopped him to pieces. One particularly enraged soldier, cut off Tarsum Khan's head, clasped it by the hair and raised it high in the air.

"Death to the invaders!" he shouted, which was followed by a noisy uproar with Prathap Singh brandishing his sword high.

It was a grizzly sight yet again with decapitated heads, lifeless limbs and dying Mughals, most of them Mughals, lying on the hard pathway of the towering fort. Cries of anguish and pain were heard everywhere in and around the fort. Mewar's troops swept in like a flood and fought in the halls, chambers and even in the bedchambers of the ancient citadel. The terrible onslaught resulted in the death of almost all the Mughals, except the lanky commander Ahmed Khan, who was captured and brought before Prathap Singh.

Ahmed Khan bleeding from many cuts on his person was forced to kneel before the champion of Mewar.

"The emperor shall come!" he declared in defiance. "My ruler Akbar shall come to tear you limb to limb, rajput! No one is going to save you!" He paused for a moment to catch his breath and then yelled, "Prathap Singh shall die before Akbar!"

There was silence for a long moment in that heavy night.

"I would love to die in battle against the Mughals. A valorous death is a great honour. Akbar, however, will never get me" came the calm reply from the king.

Prathap Singh raised his eyebrows. He looked at Amar Singh, "Your spear, son."

Amar Singh gave his king a long heavy spear with a shining spearhead. The king looked at the kneeling Ahmed Khan who realized what was coming.

The cringing commander began his rhetoric again in his final moments, "Death to Prathap Singh! You shall die, you—"

Pratap Singh plunged the spear straight through the heart of the genuflect Mughal, "You first, alien!" he yelled.

Ahmed Khan gasped for breath as blood gushed out of his breastplate generously. His lifeless body with the embedded spear leaned to the ground with his helmet still on his head, his inorganic hands hanging by his sides, his blood began spreading profusely over the floor, his eyes staring nowhere.

Prathap Singh pulled the spear out, placed his left leg on the head of the body and raised the weapon high in the air, "Rajputs! Kill every Mughal who dares to invade your soil. Would it not be an honour if you were to die doing so?"

Shouts of "Long live Maharana Prathap Singh!" filled the air.

"The Mughal alien will never own my land!" snarled Prathap Singh in response.

Mewar did lose some troops but not more than a 100. The Mughals lost their entire Kumbalgarh force.

"Amar!" called out Prathap Singh, "Round up all the horses in the stables. They would be invaluable in any future clash. Who is to know when that is?"

Amar Singh and his confidantes headed straight for the stables.

At Gogunda, it was a similar flow of events. Ram Singh and Sakta Singh followed Prathap Singh's plan to perfection. The fort fell with no major opposition. Mewar suffered only meagre losses.

A battle did follow, eventhough, the Mughals at Gogunda were totally caught off-guard just like the ones at Kumbalgarh and lost the initiative to the rajputs. Their response was meek and feeble. They fell before Sakta Singh and Ram Singh's men like a pack of cards. It was a gory slaughter at Gogunda in the halls, the pathways, in the royal kitchen, in the bedrooms and the living rooms. Heads, limbs and scores of dead bodies littered the royal fort that moonless night.

Mahter Khan lost his life in battling Mewar's forces and did not face the fate of his peer Ahmed Khan. Two hundred Mughals, too slow to get ready for the battle were captured alive and unarmed.

They were made to prostrate before Sakta Singh.

"My sense of justice does not permit me to kill an unarmed man, be it Mughal or rajput. It is against my core beliefs. Now get up, you scoundrels!" he yelled.

The captured Mughals stood dusting their clothes.

"Now I command you all to be off from our domain at once. Head back straight to your emperor. Tell him that rajputs reign in Mewar and not the Mughals!"

Shouts of exultation arose in the air from the Mewar forces.

"If we find you still in Gogunda by early morning you shall all die!" commanded Ram Singh, "Get going, you!"

The Mughals who were spared from the pain of death scampered out of the fort in the middle of the night, glad to get away by the skin of their teeth.

"Raise the battle standard by dawn, Sakta Singh," said Ram Singh with reserved happiness.

"I shall raise the crimson standard sporting the silver sun by the first light of the morning" came the reply from Mewar's royal son with a sweet beaming smile as usual.

CHAPTER 22

THE SLEDGEHAMMER TO THE FORE!

A war council sat at the meeting hall of the palace at Fatehpur Sikri. The air was tense and terse. The emperor kept staring at the empty space right in front of him for a while. His bureaucrats were seated right and left of the broad table. Akbar looked at Birbal and then turned to look at them all.

"This is failure. I would even call it a grand failure. He has kicked us in the face! Shame! Two full divisions of my force wiped out just like that in the middle of the night. How naïve have we been? He still maintains a miniscule army! Incredible!" complained the monarch.

No one spoke for about a moment.

Abdul Rahim Khan finally broke the silence, "He is crafty, My Lord. We give him that. He has to be crushed with overwhelming force."

Raja Man Singh did not speak nor make eye contact with his emperor. His mind was preoccupied with frustration in not being able to finish the Prathap Singh campaign. A stalemate that had put his position as commander of the Mughal army in the spotlight for all the wrong reasons.

"Who knows maybe he still has secret liaisons with those disgruntled Afghans in Kandahar? Who knows?" purported Faizi stroking his flowing red beard and sporting his typical maroon turban. "Otherwise, how do you explain his remarkable results?"

"The Afghans are not involved in Mewar, Faizi," came the brusque response from Abdul Rahim Khan feeling the heat as the defence in-charge. "The last of the Afghan involvement was with that Hakim Khan Sur who died in battle fighting us."

Birbal controlled his impulsive thought to request his emperor to dispatch him to Mewar to deal with Prathap Singh. An issue that was beginning to snowball at the moment.

Todar Mal too decided not to rub salt in the wound.

"Force is the only option we have. We have to resort to using disproportionate force. War and repeated wars is what will take the wind out of the sail. Is there any other option?" enquired Mulla Do-Piyazo.

Abul Fazl looked at the king with concern, "My Lord, we should not become a laughingstock in the eyes of the army. You must act even though we have failed. Even though we have suffered the loss of three of our trusted commanders and nearly 6000 of our troops, we must still choose to act. Certain trees suffer many blows from the axe before they fall."

Finally, Man Singh faced his master. His lord Akbar smiled at him kindly and said, "I fully believe in the wisdom and the understanding of my cabinet. Every one of you sitting here have my full confidence. That said, we need to come up with a clever solution to the Prathap Singh problem. He is becoming a major issue. We should not allow him to hog the limelight."

Abul Fazl spoke up, "If I understand the council correctly, I think the issue is our inability to locate his hideout in the mountains. If we could do that, Prathap Singh and his miniature government-in-hiding will be history."

"Would the fox hide forever in his borough?" posed Tansen with a mystic smile as he sat on his stately armchair. His rose-gold scabbard housing his dagger was tightly secured in his white gridle. His aquiline nose rose as his poetic muse got involved in the discussion.

"A lion in his den is what I would call him" came the rejoinder from the emperor. "It takes a lion to look the Mughals in the eye. That is what he has done, this Prathap Singh. He is daring. Way too daring."

"Do you have a solution, My Lord?" asked Birbal finally unable to control his desire.

Akbar nodded, "There is a solution for every problem, Raja Birbal. There is. If not, the Mughals would not have an empire against their name as of today. We do have to try certain things before we discover the right solution. That takes time."

"Success at short notice is sweeter, My Liege" winked Birbal.

"It sure is" admitted the emperor finally calming down a bit.

"Man Singh" said the emperor.

"My King" The rajput commander fixed his eyes resolutely as usual at his king.

"You shall lead the army this time too. You are still the man. Raja Bagwan Das and Abdul Rahim Khan shall accompany you. Shabaz Khan and Mughal Mir Bakshi are back from their campaign in Bihar and Bengal. Would you want them to assist you in Mewar? They could be like replacements for Tarsum Khan."

"Perfect, My Liege! I'm well acquainted with both. I am delighted to take them along" revealed Man Singh.

"These commanders may not join you immediately. You may proceed with your departure. They shall join the force in about two or three weeks" noted the emperor.

"At your convenience, My Lord" agreed Man Singh.

"Can you lay a trap for a lion, Man Singh?" asked the monarch in a mischievous tone. "A trap for a male lion in raging fury?" questioned Akbar.

"Lion-baiting is something I shall learn, My Lord" smiled the commander trying to restrain it instantly "I am still a skilled hunter of sorts."

"Scour every bit of the land. Turn the mountains upside down. You shall find this lion hiding somewhere. I am dispatching time-tested warriors to aid you. Trap Prathap Singh this time around. Even lions walk into traps. Good luck" wished the emperor.

Man Singh rose, bowing in deep humility he declared, "The Mughal lion shall prevail."

"They will pay for the 6,000 souls that perished in those forts. There shall be vengeance for my commanders. They could not have died in vain" declared Akbar.

The prince of Amber made an effort to smile realizing things were not as worse as he imagined them to be.

CHAPTER 23

A STRATEGIC RETREAT

Ram Singh, Sakta Singh and their cohorts galloped at top speed into Kumbalgarh Fort at sunrise. They he found the king standing on one of the mural towers unfurling the lengthy battle-standard of Mewar. Amar Singh stood by.

"Grand success, My Lord! You have secured a decisive victory! The Mughals were cast to the four winds!" declared the triumphant aide.

"All the more because of rajputs like you" said the king as he put his arm around him in affection.

The lengthy crimson standard began fluttering in the strong breeze, its tail-end moving like a fish back and forth.

They climbed down the steps into one of the chambers below, still smelling of the noise of the battle the previous night.

"The Mughals would be enraged by our operation" began the king. "We should expect retribution by all means. We cannot stay put in our forts to defend them. Neither should we haul the rightful inhabitants back in. It would be like handing Akbar the victory" confided Prathap Singh.

"So.." began Sakta Singh.

"We shall abandon Kumbalgarh and Gogunda in a day or two. It would take at least ten days for any Mughal force to make it here. They have a bastion in Ajmer but nothing happens without explicit orders from Sikri" said Prathap Singh as he crossed his legs seated on a couch. "We need to evacuate well in advance and make good our escape. Even our royal standards should be taken down. This time around not a soul in either of our citadels will sacrifice his life. I cannot afford to lose more men."

"How long are we to hide, Father?" posed Amar Singh.

"For the short term. We can abandon the hideout and return to these strong towers, if, and only if, the Mughals lose their interest in pursuing their goal of gobbling Mewar. They are absolutely determined not to do that in my opinion. At least not Akbar and his henchmen led by Man Singh Amber!" Prathap Singh's voice rose at the mention of the Amber Prince.

"A turncoat really. A man responsible for the death of thousands of rajputs. May their blood be upon his head!" observed Ram Singh.

"Would chance bring me face to face with this man to cross swords again, his head will not stand on his shoulders" mused Prathap Singh.

"Never bother, father. He would not descend from the howdah of his massive beast. He is dead scared of you I believe, isn't he?" declared the crown prince.

"He should be. After witnessing the carnage of his troops at the hands of Mewar's king, why would he not be scared?" argued Ram Singh.

"Ram Singh, we shall make our move tonight" spoke the king. "Sakta and yourself shall empty Gogunda well after midnight. Instruct the men to disburse perfectly among the common folk in our towns and villages. There should be no hint of any of them working for the Mewar forces. We shall likewise order our men here to do the same. The horses are to be well cared for. The stalwarts of Fatehpur Sikri may employ new tactics to capture or kill us. Obviously when one goes down the wrong track, one backs up and takes the other one, right?"

Both forts were devoid of their occupants by the middle of the night. The king, his aides, the infantry and the cavalry went into the night in the light of a nascent crescent moon. Prathap Singh and his trusted aides returned safely to their mountain hideout.

Two weeks later, a great Mughal force numbering 40,000 strong, led by Man Singh consisting of infantry, cavalry, artillery and about 50 elephants arrived at the outskirts of Kumbalgarh to wage war against the phantom Prathap Singh only to find the fort without a soul.

"The man has fled our advance, again" remarked Raja Bagwan Das.

"Something has to be done differently this time to catch this wily fox who thinks he is a lion. We shall teach him that lesson" boasted Man Singh.

A decision was taken not to occupy the fort in honour of the Mughals who had lost their lives battling Prathap Singh. In reality Abdul Rahim Khan was not in favour of being boxed in the fort in the event of another attack.

"We shall fight him in the open" he declared. "Let us weigh his guts against the Mughals out here and not inside a solid fortress."

The troops went about pitching their tents in close proximity of Kumbalgarh which now had the Mughal battle-standard flying high from its watchtower.

A scout party in disguise dispatched to spy on the Gogunda Fort returned to narrate a similar story two days later.

Man Singh, Abdul Karim Khan and Das sat in conference in their meeting tent.

"We need to show the emperor results" commenced Abdul Karim Khan, the defence in-charge of the empire. "All this show cannot be for nothing."

"We shall change tack this time" proposed Das. "Let us lull him into thinking we are planning something big. We shall not do anything too conspicuous in terms of scanning the terrain. Let us make this so called 'lion' come out in the open. He would inevitably come out. He cannot hide forever. What do you think?"

"I agree in principle" nodded Man Singh. "However, I think we should blend with the population in and around the forts to figure if Prathap Singh or his aides are living in plainclothes."

"Fantastic, General!" exulted Abdul Karim Khan. "No wonder you are the commander-in-chief! Not to sideline what Bagwan Das has suggested, we shall wait for about ten days. Maybe the 'lion' would choose to walk out without us looking for him. Who knows?"

The troops were wondering what had brought them to Mewar after having spent ten days without anything being done militarily.

A pose of 100 cavalry reached the Kumbalgarh force on the night of the tenth day. It was led by commanders

Shabaz Khan and Mughal Mir Bakshi. They handed a scroll to Man Singh.

"I am glad to have you here, commanders" confessed Man Singh, officially receiving the scroll.

It was from the emperor. It demanded that both Man Singh and Raja Bagwan Das return at once with the cavalry that brought the two commanders. No other details were provided.

A baffled Man Singh advised Das, "We leave with the posse of cavalry tomorrow morning."

Shabaz Khan and Bakshi now joined Abdul Karim Khan in their hunt for Prathap Singh.

"I recommend we go on a circuit in and around the two forts to familiarize ourselves with the conditions and the terrain" suggested Abdul Karim Khan.

"We will do that at the earliest, sire" replied Shabaz Khan.

A massive detachment of 1000 cavalry led by the three commanders began inspecting the forts and then proceeded to the surrounding terrain.

CHAPTER 24

A BOLT FROM THE BLUE!

June 1577

The Mughals began methodically combing through the population in the towns, villages and hamlets in and around Kumbalgarh.

"A reward of a 1000 rupaiya coins to the man who helps us capture Prathap Singh" declared Mughal Mir Bakshi from his horse to the crowd gathered at one particular town. "Dead or alive, you still get the thousand coins" he forced a smile.

The people listened intently. Many of them were Prathap Singh's men dressed perfectly to deceive the Mughal eye.

"We order you not to provide refuge for this man on the run. The emperor shall put you to death if you are found sheltering Prathap Singh or his men! Beware!" warned Shabaz Khan in a loud voice.

Both led the 1000-odd cavalry unit in circuit around the surrounding areas as planned. The same declaration and the warning were dished out in hamlet after hamlet, village after village and town after town.

Every patch of the mountainous terrain they trotted on was investigated for a possible hiding place and incidentally, including the one used by the king of Mewar. Its inaccessibility and the unbelievable camouflage of the hideout made it impossible for the Mughals to have had any interest in locating him there. It was an instance of 'so near, yet so far'.

After two long weeks of horsing around, the two commanders decided to halt the madness of it all.

"We might as well be looking for the proverbial needle in a haystack" remarked Bakshi trying to see the humorous side of it.

"If the emperor orders me to find such a needle, would I not do it?" shot back Shabaz Khan. "It just takes iron will to accomplish great things."

Back in his den, Prathap Singh knew he had defied death by a whisker.

"We were this close to disaster" he admitted to his family and top aides. "It's a wonder they did not find us here after repeatedly climbing up and down this mountain. Hundreds of them on horseback! Wow!"

"We should probably think of moving to a different location, My Lord. We have stayed here too long. We cannot afford to run this risk. The wolf is capable of locating the lambs even in thick darkness" counselled Kanwar as she sat fanning her king.

"Moving, My Queen? Not when the land is teeming with thousands of Mughals. They would eat you like cattle-fodder" cautioned Ram Singh. "We should lay low for the time being. Akbar's men are sniffing around with their noses to the ground."

Many months rolled by without any action from Prathap Singh. The Mughals were absolutely at their wits' end.

"What are we to do?" an impatient Bakshi queried Shabaz Khan one night in the glowing light of the yellow flames as they sat in the open for a breath of cool air. "Maybe the man has left the country never to return again. Has he exiled himself among the tribes of the Afghans, the Tajiks, the Uzbeks, the Kazakhs or perhaps the Persians? Persia is just across the border with Sind."

"It's very frustrating. I know. Unless Fatehpur Sikri makes a decision, we are grounded here" conceded the senior

Mughal with a light black beard. "We serve military orders. This order is from the emperor himself. We have no choice."

"Commander, all this eating, sleeping, military drills and scouting the hills for a non-existent enemy is so very monotonous. We are wasting our time!" implored Bakshi.

"You serve the empire. No questions are to be asked. You follow orders" came the terse reply from his senior.

March 1578:

Down in the lower deck of the hideout Prathap Singh convened his lieutenants for a discussion after more than half a year. "It's time for action. We should act again to propel the Mughals out of Mewar" argued Prathap Singh.

"And how is that going to be engineered, my brother?" demanded Sakta Singh, smiling as usual.

"I have a thought in my mind, an idea, that keeps coming back to me" mused the king.

"What is it, Father?" inquired Amar Singh.

"How many cannons are left on the walls of Kumbalgarh?" questioned Prathap Singh as he looked at his aides.

"There are twenty. About seven are located on the arsenal towers, facing south. The Mughals are pitched almost south-west. You mean…?" stretched Amar Singh.

"We must repay the Mughals in the same coin" smiled Prathap Singh.

"Could you elaborate?" asked Sakta Singh.

"It's in the rudimentary stage. Nevertheless, I shall give you the sketches" agreed the king.

"What is your plan, My Lord, with the cannons of Kumbalgarh?" quizzed Ram Singh.

"These Mughals are within the firing range of the cannons, aren't they?" began Prathap Singh with mischief in his eyes, "They are hardly five hundred metres away! I plan to open artillery-fire at these Mughals! A ferocious earth-shattering volley of cannon-fire targeting the Mughal masses housed in their tents close to the fort. An intense volley of fire that would completely take them by surprise," his eyes widened in expectation. "We need to unleash the artillery and then disappear in the chaos that follows. It would be risky. I want it to happen during daytime. The Mughals must realize that we can appear and disappear like ghosts! Enough to unnerve them for a while. We, however, must enter the fort from the other end during the dead of the night by scaling the high walls" he paused.

"Let's do it, brother!" chipped in Sakta Singh immediately rubbing the palms of his hands. "This sounds very exciting."

"The thing is, the base of the fortress walls is domed like onions. One cannot secure a firm grip to clamber up. Moreover, the walls are more than twenty foot high. We need to procure ladders to do the job. These props must be used in such manner that would still keep the Mughal army at ease while we climb and descend into the fort in the quietness of the night. Ladders could be abandoned if need be on the way out" reasoned the king.

"Ladders would be the best bet to get into the fort" advised a smiling Sakta Singh.

"This sounds spectacular, My Lord. Everything however must go with the plan" cautioned Ram Singh, "Do you intend to have all your forces again?"

"No, definitely not all of them. In fact, we shall be needing just about twenty elite troops or fewer and the four of us to launch this operation and get out as quickly as lightning before they can understand what had happened" said Prathap Singh, "I need a lean, mean team."

"Luck will certainly favour us, Father" cut in Amar Singh. "Kumbalgarh Fort is completely abandoned by the Mughals. Once in, we can easily access the cannon balls from the ammunition storage. The enemy is going to be blown to smithereens!"

"I love flying heads. I mean, flying Mughal heads. Not just their heads, but their limbs too" mocked Sakta Singh. "They are destined for such a death."

"This premise has to be worked upon. We need to plug all the loopholes. We have to minimize the risks. We need to thoroughly think this through" emphasized Prathap Singh. "I am going ahead with this only if I am perfectly sure it would work. There is no room for error. We would pay dearly, very dearly, if things go wrong. The Mughals are bound to tan our hides!"

"When are we likely to implement this plan?" Ram Singh raised his right eyebrow as he sat on the hard floor of the lower deck of the hideout.

"It's been more than six months since our last strike on the Mughals. You, Sakta and Amar Singh shall leave tonight to hand-pick the elite ones who shall secure the ammunition and fire the weapons" proposed Prathap Singh. "We would be needing just three ladders."

"We shall leave around two tonight. These Mughals would be having their blissful sleep at such a time. It would be easy to slink away" postulated Amar Singh.

"Fine. Stay put in your place wherever for a few days. The new moon rises in seven days. It would be perfect to vault into the fort in the darkness of that night and unleash fire. We would also need rope ladders that are about 15 foot long. One end of these should be tied to the bamboo ladders and the other end to the ornate merlons on the walls. This would help us both climb into the fort and then to descend down onto the bamboo ladders on our way out and make good our escape. I also fancy eight immensely strong, iron wall-anchors."

Once again, on a moonless night, 20 men slithered towards the rear sections of the Kumbalgarh Fort. The immense undergrowth made it easy for man and animal to stomp without making much of a noise or sound. The anchors bearing sharp edges muffled with tufts of green grass flew to their targets at quarter past one. They landed accurately and lodged themselves securely. The ropes at the other ends of these anchors were tied in taut manner to the bamboo ladders. The masked men comprising Prathap Singh, Amar Singh, Sakta Singh and Ram Singh climbed first on these scales and then climbed up the heavy rope ladders to reach the safety of the battlements. They were followed by the twenty-odd elites chosen for this assignment. Eighteen of whom went up like slinking cats. The other two remained at a safe distance with the tethered horses engulfed in darkness, well out of sight. Once in, the intruders gingerly went down to double check that the fort had indeed been abandoned by the Mughals before lighting the lamps in the chambers below. The ammunition storage was gently opened and the cannon balls were tenderly brought to the arsenal points on the walls, to the vicinity of the cannons.

As they were going about their clandestine work, they were completely caught off-guard by forward movement from the Mughal camp.

"Stay in line, men. Don't break your ranks!" yelled Bakshi on horseback in the faint light of the yellow flames in that dark night.

Seated on another next to him was his commander, Shabaz Khan.

"Alright, forward march!" ordered the apex commander.

The grim figure of Abdul Karim Khan in complete battle gear, was seated on his black stallion observing everything with a keen eye at that deviant shift of the night.

The armed band probably numbering a 1000 went marching away from the camp in the dead of the night. The other Mughals were all up and ready too, making quite a commotion. They, however, did not join this moving detachment. Neither did Abdul Karim Khan.

The rajputs on the walls immediately crouched at this development.

"Where are these heading at this time of the night?" whispered Sakta Singh loudly. "Looking for us?"

"I hope not" replied Prathap Singh as he squatted to hide his person from the view of anyone starring at the citadel. "Hopefully this is one of their military stunts to keep their army up and running for any eventuality."

"This is what I believe to be a 'search and destroy' operation by these Mughals to eradicate you, My King" counselled Ram Singh.

"They should be losing steam in one hour" joked Amar Singh as he peeped at them from behind the slits on the ornate structures. "Their weary eyes would drag them back to their tents in no time."

Prathap Singh looked at his son for a moment very sombrely in the dim night, "Never underestimate your enemy. There is always more to what meets the eye. Beware!"

Amar Singh's youthful face seemed to register his impulsiveness. He blinked his eyelids to admit that he had spoken without due consideration.

"Could they have located the hideout?" reasoned Sakta Singh anxiously, "The queen and her aides have to defend themselves!"

"Defend herself she will, My Queen" smiled Prathap Singh. "My gut feeling is that this is one of their routine drills to instil discipline among their ranks. The gait of these Mughals does not seem to indicate the identification of an enemy hideout. They are moving very normally. No hasty, jittery actions. We are safe. They have neither identified our presence nor are they heading for the hideout."

As the Mughals marched out and the remaining hordes went back to their beds, relative silence returned to Kumbalgarh and its vicinity. Prathap Singh and his men sat down behind the edge of the walls for quite some time till they were sure the Mughals were unaware of their presence.

The ammunition was ready for the firing at his command.

"My King, the ammunition is ready. Everything is set. Do we fire?" enquired Ram Singh.

"Why should we fire at the enemy who is blissfully sleeping? That would be cowardice, right? We need the enemy to be up and running about his daily chores. Then we can gloat over their failure. Not when sweet sleep has dulled their eyes" perceived Prathap Singh. "Let us be men while we fight."

Sakta Singh complained "Brother, we have three hours to go before dawn."

"I know. These three hours should fool them into thinking everything is just as usual" smiled Prathap Singh. "Such complacency adds to their fatality numbers."

"Come dawn, come death!" whispered Amar Singh to himself.

"This ambush serves them right, My King" spoke one of the elites from behind.

Prathap Singh nodded his ascent. The men reclined on the walls of the fort and whiled away their time discussing family, real estate and romance.

The cicadas, the crickets, the owls and other nocturnal creatures kept up their performance during the hours as dawn approached in the distance.

As the first light of the morning broke through, the hordes of Akbar's army, under the leadership of Abdul Karim Khan and his captains began stirring at the sound of a sharp bugle. They began moving about to gear up and face the day. In the commotion, no one paid attention to seven field guns atop the arsenal walls of Kumbalgarh oriented to face the masses of the Mughal army, none of the sharp-eyed Mughals cared enough to scan the walls. The fort was presumed abandoned and locked. So, it remained abandoned and locked in their minds and their imagination.

"On my word, men" said Prathap Singh as the cannon balls were loaded.

Just before the burning fuse came into contact with the gunpowder, the king could see the advancing Mughal force that had left hours ago in the night approaching from the distance. The contingent was approximately a kilometre away and was heading straight to the camp quite speedily.

Mewar's king was now in a dilemma. Should he target those top commanders and the detachment of troops they were leading or the huge mass of infantry and the cavalry left behind under Abdul Karim Kahn? As he spent a couple of a minutes pondering, the others were finding the discomfort of being detected unbearable.

"My Lord, we need to act now!" compelled Ram Singh with palpable tension in his breath.

Sakta Singh also felt the same. "Brother, the guns are facing the Mughals. This is too risky. We either fire or quit!" he urged, sparkling a bright smile as usual.

"Alright, we target the Mughals here" said Prathap Singh, reluctantly making up his mind.

A gun each was commanded by Ram Singh, Amar Singh, Sakta Singh with two elites manning them as crew. Each of the remaining four guns were manned by the other elite gunners.

As the advancing force under Bakshi and Shabaz Khan closed the distance to the camp at the outset of a yellow dawn, a blaring volley of cannon fire thundered from the walls of Kumbalgarh, raining fire on the Mughals camped below about half a kilometre away! The frontline Mughal masses took direct hits from the devastating fire directed at them. Heads, torsos, arms, legs, limbs and slaughtered human chunks went flying in bloody fashion all over the Mughal camp! Horror and shock took possession of Akbar's men who thought the end of the world was upon them! Body parts, intestines, and shattered bones and blood lay scattered all over their camp where a moment ago men were getting up to go about their morning chores. Screams of agony arose at once mingled with the brutal truth that they were under attack at that wee hour.

The advancing commanders were shaken from crown to toes when they saw smoking guns in the distance directing fire at the camp from the high walls of Kumbalgarh!

"What on earth is going on?" demanded Shabaz Khan as he kept staring at the fortress rising into the sky far ahead of him with a gaping mouth, his steed having come to a sudden halt.

"Someone is opening fire at our camp from the fort!" answered Bakshi as he too pulled up next to Shabaz Khan. "Could it be the rajputs? Is it Prathap Singh?"

Both commanders immediately deserted their detachment and galloped at top speed heading for the camp circumventing the eastern part of the massing troops so as not to become victims of the cannon fire themselves!

Meanwhile on the walls, the guns recoiled and moved back on their carriages. They were pushed back and loaded again with ammunition in a jiffy.

"Fire!" commanded the king with glaring eyes. The gunners rained annihilation on the forces a short distance away who were already running like mad march hares for their lives. The artillery unleashed accurate gory on the hapless Mughals. Masses of troops were blown to bits and pieces by the all-consuming firepower of the rajput cannons! Death came in an instant to many a man in the camp. There were stampedes in many locations in the camp as troops tumbled on top of each other fearing a massive rajput force had come upon them at that hour. Many were fleeing helter-skelter, half-naked in utter terror.

Abdul Karim Khan, rudely shaken by the tumult, was at a loss to deal with the rapidly unfolding anarchy.

He hoped on his horse in his night dress and called out to his captains, "Order the troops to fall back! On your horses, men!"

As the carriage decks were being moved forward for the third shot, Shabaz Khan and Bakshi who had by now reached the outskirts of the campsite, were torn between rallying their troops to safety and storming the fort. They chose the former as they figured that large-scale casualties could cause a delay in securing the citadel.

"Retreat! Retreat! Every one of you! Move back! Move! Move!" ordered Shabaz Khan at the top of his voice towards the central and the rear masses of his troops at the camp.

As the Mughals began to flee, the third round of ammunition were loaded into the guns and as the command went out of Prathap Singh's lips, the guns roared once again at the retreating Mughals. The third volley of fire caused little damage to Mughal lives except kill mortally wounded men who were too weak to leave.

However, there was an unexpected development on the high walls.

"My Lord, my gun would not fire!" exclaimed Ram Singh.

"What? Really? Back up, back up everyone!" yelled the king.

Amar Singh stood confused.

"Amar, I ordered you to move back!" yelled Prathap Singh.

As the gunners put enough space between themselves and their guns, Ram Singh's gun blew up, rising in the air with a vociferous, ear-splitting noise throwing those standing on the rampart to the battlements. The cannon ball in Ram Singh's gun had got stuck in the artillery barrel. As the weapons were being fired in great hurry, some debris got retained in his gun in the firing process. This resulted in the gun imploding due to the malfunction.

Prathap Singh and company were left aghast lying down. No one suffered any injury except for the trauma of the shocking explosion and some minor scrapes on the skin. The event left the rajputs disoriented for a moment with their ears ringing with repeated waves of shell-shocking noise. The cannon exploded into big chunks and crashed onto the ground below with a massive bang.

The disastrous explosion on top of the wall caught the attention of the Mughals as it sent ripples of shock into the surrounding areas.

Now, the Mughals were more or less in control of the situation on the ground. They managed to rally their massive army to safety.

Abdul Karim Khan raced towards his commanders on his black stallion, "Intruders! We have intruders on the fort! Kill them! Capture them alive! Execute them! Goons!"

"Let us storm the fort!" suggested Bakshi as his neighing steed screeched to a halt, joining Abdul Karim Khan and Shabaz Khan.

"What if the fortress is locked from the inside? Could our men climb?" posed Shabaz Khan. "There could be booby-traps."

Bakshi turned, and dashed forward shouting, "I need men to storm the fort! Can you men mount up these walls?"

Meanwhile, on the walls, Prathap Singh breathed out his command as he and his men gathered themselves again after the catastrophic explosion, "Off we go! We have made our point. Let us descend right away!"

The men promptly ran to the other end of the walls and began descending in a flash on the already fixed ladders. They landed in no time and began racing on the vegetation towards the waiting horses in the early morning glow and bounced onto their horses. They lunged at full throttle towards the mountain-hideout before their enemy could know where they were headed. All that they left behind were the bamboo and rope ladders along with their iron anchors still hanging from the fort walls.

The Mughals encircled the fort to secure it. They began ascending using the material left behind by the king of Mewar and his men.

"Prathap Singh! My sword shall behead you, you vagabond!" bellowed a blood-soaked Abdul Karim Khan in rage as he observed the climbing Mughals. "You just wait! You!"

The defence bureaucrat then galloped away to the other end of the fort.

"Prathap Singh remains a thorn in our flesh" observed Bakshi as he kept staring at the ramparts from his warhorse.

"You need a thorn to deal with a thorn. Don't you know that?" questioned Shabaz Khan, his horse giving its head a strong shaking.

"What a morning! Such disturbance! So many deaths! Chaos! Confusion! What are we to do?" implored Bakshi in desperation.

"You are a soldier, mind you" came the brusque reply from his senior.

Soon enough, the huge doors of the fort were thrown open and the commanders walked in slowly after verifying the non-existence of hidden dangers. The castle was now teeming with Mughals.

"These rajputs have come in so treacherously to wreck disaster on us! Snakes!" reviled Abdul Karim Khan still fuming with rage. He was accompanied inside by Bakshi and Shabaz Khan.

"I thought the emperor sent us on an errand to kill a lion, sir" rebuffed Shabaz Khan. "You can deal with a snake that startles you, but can you take on a lion that springs an ambush?"

"Oh, we shall very well deal with this so called 'lion'!" mocked Abdul Karim Khan as the three ascended the steps to the bulwarks. "Fate should destine him to die by my sword!"

"Fate brought him to you today. It did indeed. We were all taken by surprise. Had we been on our guard, we could have dealt with this 'lion'" carried on Shabaz Khan, daring to disagree with Akbar's top administrator.

They reached the arsenal tower, inspecting the cannons used for the attack still steaming hot from the use. Cannon balls lay strewn by the walls of the stronghold.

"With all due respect, sir, one fine day, I assure you, Prathap Singh and the Mughals will cross paths yet another time. It shall be a day of reckoning!" assured Shabaz Khan with gusto.

"I am sure it will be one such day! It sure will be, Shabaz. Will not your sword rise in triumph against this Prince of Mewar that day?" demanded Abdul Karim Khan surveying the vast expanse of the land from atop Kumbalgarh Fort.

"Pray that it would conquer" replied Shabaz Khan with restrain as he sent the Mughal green and yellow battle-standard with the embroidered lion fluttering over the bulwarks of Kumbalgarh.

That afternoon witnessed the sombre burial of about 300 Mughals who had lost their lives to the cannon-fire. They were mostly tribesmen from the central Asian highlands, the likes of the Tajiks, Uzbeks, Tatars, Turks and the Kazakhs. It also included a considerable number of the Persians and Indians alike. The camp was cleansed of the human remains. Shabaz Khan was lost in serious thought as the last of the bodies were lowered into their graves.

"You better hurry to Gogunda and secure the palace the first thing in the morning" suggested Abdul Rahim Khan as the commanders sat around that afternoon in his tent, "Shall I accompany you?"

"No! No.." came the reply from commander Shabaz Khan still deeply lost in contemplation about their next moves.

The burden of bolstering his reputation was weighing heavily down on him, "I shall go with Bakshi," he added in a serious tone. "Your presence is needed here. We don't need another attack by those ghostly rajputs. We shall become laughingstock in Fatehpur Sikri if that were to happen. I cannot hang my head in shame before my emperor. We are to give an account of today's events anyway. How can we avoid giving an account for 300 Mughal souls?"

Next morning, a heavy posse of 3500 cavalry carrying Mughal battle flags armed to the teeth left Kumbalgarh with the only intention of securing Gogunda Castle. Leading them from the front were Shabaz Khan and his second-in-command, Bakshi. Reaching the fort after a heady gallop in about an hour's span, the two commanders ambled into the palace and straightaway climbed the stairs to reach the top and had the Mughal battle-standard flying in no time. A sense of victory swept through the men as they sat at ease in the royal birthplace of rajput kings.

The entire palace was encompassed by the cavalry as a show of strength.

"We shall not take chances with this 'lion' Prathap Singh" began Shabaz Khan at his deputy Bakshi downing a glass of water. "I am leaving you in charge. Make sure you put up a fight if he were to storm the fort or commit an intrusion of some sort. I want sentries posted round-the-clock to ensure extreme vigil. Your 3000 men are more than a match for this spectre of a 'lion'. Your reply should be befitting if he shows up here in any avatar."

"Your command will be followed to the last letter" said Bakshi to his superior. "Our swords, spears and arrows are at the ready. Maybe I shall be the one to put an end to his life."

"Maybe…" nodded his commander with a bit of hesitation.

Shabaz Khan left Gogunda after midday escorted by 500 mounted troops.

CHAPTER 25

THE LULL…

August 1578

The cat-and-mouse game between the Mughals and Prathap Singh was beginning to fray Mughal nerves both in Mewar and in Fatehpur Sikri.

As he stood on the walls of his brick-red capital surveying the far-lying towns and hamlets on the plain of the Ganges that late afternoon, the scion sprung from the loins of Genghis Khan still wanted to project calm and equanimity to the members of the cabinet standing around.

"So, yet another brazen attack out of nowhere" noted Akbar.

Birbal held his peace behind him for a moment. His impulsive tongue however was goading him to go jingoistic, "Reputation once lost, is difficult to regain, My Lord…" he began very softly.

The Lull...

The Mughal chieftain stopped and turned with his hands still locked behind him.

His favourite minister smiled at him in a wily manner before continuing, "Esteem is easy to lose, but takes years to establish, My Liege."

The early evening breeze began to waft its way around the emperor and his aides.

"We must avenge the death of those 300 men who lost their lives" began Mulla Do-Piyazo stroking his greying beard as usual and carrying an intricate walking-stick, "Did he rain raw cannon-fire on our soldiers? This is barbarism!"

"Are we in confirmation that it was in fact the man himself?" inquired Abul-Fazl in a semi-official manner.

"Should there be any doubt about it, vizier?" posed Tansen, "Who else would have the nerve to climb those high walls and man the guns?"

"You need expertise in handling heavy artillery" observed Todar Mal. "Only Pratap Singh and his men could have unleashed the attack."

There was a pause in the discussion. A massive company of green parrots screeched incessantly high in the sky as they headed towards their nests in high trees in the woods in the approaching dusk.

"It is just an issue of luck favouring me" said the emperor as he swung his head around at everyone. "Just a matter of luck. The odds are very much in my favour."

A full, sluggish, golden, moon began mounting the sky in the east in the falling darkness.

The chief was still lost in thoughts. The evening air in the enveloping dimness was making the cabinet wonder at the reason for their monarch standing by the walls yet.

"We shall nail him eventually. Let's go down" directed Akbar.

The next morning saw the czar and the cabinet getting engaged in too many matters that demanded their attention. Prathap Singh and Mewar continued to bother many a minister though. In their imagination he remained a rajput prince who refused to admit defeat despite repeated Mughal attempts to crush him.

The emperor ordered the cabinet to attend an entertainment event that evening in the sprawling courtyard of Fatehpur Sikri lit up with blazing lights. It was marked by Turks performing swirling trances, Persian wrestlers wrestling to delight the audience, Egyptian Arabs performing numbers to the accompaniment of belly-dancers much to the amusement of one and all in the Mughal court and not to forget Tansen exalting the emperor as high as the sun in an eccentric recitation of his verse. This occasion was a welcome relief for the cabinet from the everyday affairs of the court. The only exception to this happened to be Man Singh who had been deputed by the emperor to crush upstarts indulging in rebellion on the borders of the Punjab on his return from Kumbalgarh.

The entertainment session was followed by a discussion on the nature of The Divine One. Jews, Hindus, Christians, Buddhists, Muslims and Parsees sat around to exchange views on their understanding of who God was and the means of attaining heaven. Later, the emperor went around with his guests showcasing the splendour of the fabled Buland Darwaza gate.

Special dinner followed. The emperor and the guests began to lay in.

Conversation flowed freely all around with the European missionaries evincing keen interest in the outfits worn by the dashing rajputs and the Mughals at Akbar's court. Women from the harem were present too, all decked up with jewellery and alluring mascara. The rare event brought all the emperor's wives and their ladies-in-waiting out into the gaze of the world in the glistening light of the torches.

Akbar's plan to get the elusive 'lion' out of his mind and to ease his thoughts worked well. Three days later, late in the afternoon, he summoned the cabinet for a briefing in the Diwan-E-Khas.

The great ruler began on a sombre note, "Let me put everyone here in remembrance. The tale of Mewar goes like this. Rana Sanga was defeated by Babur, Udai Singh capitulated to Akbar and Prathap Singh is on the run after losing his kingdom. The prince thinks he is a hero. Nevertheless, his fall is just round the corner. Mewar, has fallen and has become subjugated to Mughal rule. Why should I lose my peace because some warrior on the loose is playing hide-and-seek with my army?" He paused. "Will I not account for this wandering lion?" demanded the emperor as his cabinet sat around.

There was silence. No one wanted to voice out his views. Birbal could see the emperor and his cabinet coming around in endless circles.

"I realize that I am giving this man a more-than-a-life image" carried on Akbar. "Some kind of legendary importance, an iconic stature. Why should I blow things out of proportion?"

"We are going from strength to strength, My Lord" responded Abul-Fazl, "We definitely should not be distracted with sideshows like Prathap Singh. No power in the Hind has withstood the Mughals till date and Prathap Singh is not going to be an exception."

"You should capture him alive and throw him under the elephants, My King!" advised Raja Birbal angrily with arched eyebrows. "That would be an apt punishment for defying the empire!"

"Does he not deserve such a death, after unleashing such a bombardment on our troops during peacetime?" warned Faizi, mentor of the royal princes.

Todar Mal stepped in, "My King, let us continue with our presence in Kumbalgarh, Gogunda and the mountains of Mewar. It is the only thing that is drawing this lion out, even though that seems to be happening on rare occasions. One way or the other, we shall deliver the death blow! If we quit now, it would give Prathap Singh the time and the means to regroup."

"My Lord" began Tansen with hesitation, "the perpetual flow of water turns gravel into minute granules, doesn't it?"

"Aye, Tansen. We shall be consistent in our approach. Prathap Singh won't escape my net" assured Akbar.

Well after the cabinet had been dismissed, the emperor and his close confidante Raja Birbal mounted their horses that pleasant evening. Akbar sat on his dappled white stallion with a bow and quiver slung across his back and Birbal on his dark brown steed with blackish legs. They began to trot off in the company of the royal guard towards the open plains bereft of human presence.

They began galloping for some time and then slowed down to a steady pace.

"So, My King, are you seriously worried about this Prathap Singh menace?" enquired Birbal.

Akbar smiled. "Worried, Raja Birbal?" he laughed out loud for a few seconds, "We are the Mughals! We don't worry. Am I concerned? Yes, you could say that. Why would I worry about a man who is on the run fearing for his life?"

"Now, I know why you truly deserve to be called 'great'. A man of your calibre should not be worrying really," came the apt reply from Birbal.

They brought the horses to a halt. Akbar signalled to the guard to pause movement. He gestured at Birbal his willingness to gallop forward for some distance. They dashed forward in a short sprint and came to a halt.

"Man Singh Amber and Raja Bhagwan Das are in action in the Punjab, as you know. They shall settle things down and return. I expect some trouble in the mountains in and around Kabul again in the near future" spoke Akbar with great expectation.

"Your servant is always at your service, My Liege" replied a beaming Birbal.

"I shall give your stinging sword the action it longs for yet again!" confided the king. "Nevertheless, let's hope those mountain-dwelling Afghans call it off without us crossing swords with them."

He waved his right hand at the waiting guard who began to trot forward.

"Now dearie, let us race. Let us hunt" advised the king.

"So, we will!" chuckled Birbal. The two began rushing like warriors charging at the enemy, much to the confusion of the guards who also began zooming to catch up with them.

CHAPTER 26

A LONGER LULL?

November 1578

Kanwar could no longer bear the hardship of the molten-rock hideout after more than a year of hiding. Her king was very well able to see that.

"We should break cover and run the risk of staying elsewhere for a while" she proposed as she combed her long, black hair seated on the floor of the lower level. "I find this lodging too stuffy. The lack of ventilation is really telling."

"We hardly have options, my love" mused Pratap Singh propped up against the wall with his legs stretched, "I can only hope for Kumbalgarh and Gogunda in my dreams!" he laughed in a painful way.

The queen rose, made a huge bun of her hair and had it secured on her head with heavy hairpins. She dusted her saree with her hands, her chiming bangles giving her company.

She walked to her king, knelt down on her right leg, and propped up her person with her left. "You are so consumed with this effort in driving these aliens out of the kingdom that you pay little attention to your well-being" she whispered with concern placing her right palm on his left cheek. "My sovereign has lost his peace, his sleep, his land and his people. Why have things come to this?"

She looked deep into his black eyes. He took hold of her hand with his left arm and kissed her stately fingers. He examined her long, royal digits covered in brilliant red henna and then looked at her with devotion, "A storm is passing through Mewar, my dove. It brings lightning, thunder and extreme disturbance. The only way to endure is to go through it. I have determined to wait it out. I know the pain this has caused you. Why should my queen suffer the ignominy of living in a hideout? If fortune is kind enough to me, would I not house you in fair Indraprastha? This is all because of these Mughals from the Caucasian mountains who wants to own all of the Hind. Would their greed end with that? Are there any bounds to their avarice? Would I be able to stop them?" mourned Prathap Singh staring at her.

"Mongol or Mughal, who cares?" responded Kanwar. "We wish to see them out of our land, out of our realm. They have no business threatening us! We are the sons of the soil!"

"The Mughal would not accept your reasoning. For him all the kingdoms of the Hind are fair game. This marauding horde will stop at nothing until it brings the vast expanse of our homeland under its dominion" observed Prathap Singh. He pulled her close, made her sit on his rugged lap, and began fiddling with her heavy, ornate anklets to listen to their sweet tinkling chimes, "My forebear Rana Sanga fought Babur. My father Udai Singh battled Akbar and now history repeats itself. I am in conflict with this all-consuming multitude. Odds are, we are going to have a very difficult time ahead. Nothing is certain. Anything is possible. Death is just one hair's breadth away."

She tenderly placed her left hand on the flank of his right cheek, brought it close to her face and kissed his left cheek passionately for a while. Releasing him from her inebriating lips, she said, "Are you not the rajput who defied death, My Lord?"

Prathap Singh blushed, "Death, my love, shall come when it comes. Neither you nor I would be able to stop it. All we can hope for is a peaceful end."

She began stroking his thick black hair and examining his eyebrows with her fingers embellished with long pointed nails.

She brought her face close to the king's, whispering, "Why don't we depart to the Indus? We could cross the waters and live anonymously. These Mughals would never follow us there."

She put her arm around his shoulders and lay down her head on his chest, "What do you say? There would be no risk."

He raised her long wavy tresses which had become undone with his left hand despite the heavy clasps. He let them down and kissed her forehead, "Fate made you wife of Prathap Singh. Fate also binds you to his destiny."

She raised her head, turned and placed her right arm on his chest diagonally. "What do you mean, My King?" she said as she brought her face very close to his.

"Kanwar, it means that my destiny is to fight these invaders" he answered in a low voice. "I was born for this purpose. I shall do that whatever it takes."

His right arm took hold of her left hand and began smooching her palm very gently, "I can only hope your ancestors rest in peace knowing that their daughter in Mewar is in the safe arms of Prathap Singh the posterity of Rana Sanga. I deeply regret the discomfiture I am putting you through."

"Oh! My love is stronger than the hardships I endure for you, My King" she said triumphantly as she rose from his embrace. "Your dreams, your priorities and your desires are paramount, not mine."

The king heaved a big sigh, "Let me check if I can shift you and the children to some place close to the Indus while I have a free hand to deal with these aliens."

She smiled as she stood there gazing at him for quite some time. "Never put your life in harm's way for my sake." Her eyes began glistening with tears as she said that.

He rose, approached her and raised her face by the chin and looked deep into her divine eyes for a moment, "You are my life!" he uttered and climbed up the stairs to the top-level.

On the top-level, meanwhile, it was an unexpected visit from Bama Shah, the prime minister. "Your Highness, I hope things are going well…I hope you are secure in this place."

"I feel stashed away in this place. My only question is, should I shift elsewhere having been here for quite some time? The sense of being in one place for way too long is making me insecure. I think shifting to another more untraceable location is better than to leave everything to the odds" posed Prathap Singh.

"It's your call, My King" replied Bama Shah, "If you, for any reason, feel the Mughals would detect this location, it is better to leave. I will find a short-term hideout until the inmates here are safe to move permanently somewhere else."

Prathap Singh did not reply. He looked at the rugged floor for a long time.

"Would it be possible to have a hideout somewhere in the Sind, close to the Indus?" he probed.

"There are rajputs in the Sind region, My Lord" conceded Bama shah, "but not too many and with no proper antecedents. It is better to play it safe. Rumours have it that Akbar offered a ransom for your life at the Haldigatti battle. Money is a dangerous ploy."

"Money, han?" asked the king with a thoughtful smile, "The Mughals are faithfully following in the footsteps of Gazni, Ghori, Khilji and Lodhi who ravaged Hindustan's silver, gold and precious stones. The wealth of the Hind is something that could be bartered towards an end."

"They are teeming all over Mewar, My King. They are absolutely desperate to locate you. They are under the leadership of two commanders, one Shabaz Khan and the other is Mughal Mir Bakshi."

"I am aware. I have taken cognizance" replied the king. "So, these commanders wish to catch me like a kernel in a sieve, don't they?"

"What's more, now Kumbalgarh Fort has been thrown open and is being manned night and day since the day your opened artillery fire on these invaders. There is a big force on the lower level of the fort to make sure that not even a housefly makes it in. There are also inputs suggesting their defence chief Abdul Karim Khan has left for Sikri leaving the operations here at the command of these two high ranking figures" boasted Bama Shah.

Prathap Singh looked at Ram Singh seated to his left for a moment with sense of expectation.

"We are all too ready. It is for you to lay out the tactics and lead us into action" offered his confidante with sincerity.

The king turned to Sakta Singh to his right, "We need to scald these Mughals again. They should know they are not welcome here. Akbar must pay for his forays into my land. I will not leave this foreign race in peace!" thundered Prathap Singh as he spoke the last sentence "They are a scourge upon the whole expanse of the Hind!"

"We hardly have a thousand men, My Lord" cautioned Ram Singh. "The Mughals number about 50,000 men. What is your plan?"

"Would I ever take on a 50,000 horde with a 1000? Oh, never!" laughed the king in a conceding manner.

"The main body of the Mughal army is still half a kilometre away from Kumbalgarh, My King!" said Bama Shah adding fuel to the fire, "Our intelligence puts the Mughal numbers inside the fort around a 1000 troops."

"The new moon falls two weeks from now. If after repeated confirmation we establish the presence of the Mughals to be only about a thousand in Kumbalgarh, we need to neutralize the ones in the fort" suggested Prathap Singh. "What say you?"

"Akbar's army by now would be wary of new moons, brother. We have struck twice on these moonless-nights" cautioned Sakta Singh. "How about a day or two after the new moon? There would still be enough darkness before the budding crescent decides to shine her light."

"I know. We should not become too predictable. However, many new moons have passed without us doing anything. So, we shall strike and shed their blood" glared Prathap Singh.

"What of the modus operandi, father, if I may ask?" stepped in Amar Singh waiting for his turn to speak, "They would have certainly learnt from the blunders they had committed the last time we stormed the fort, wouldn't they?"

"We need to ascertain that only about a 1000 Mughals haunt Kumbalgarh" Prathap Singh said looking at Bama Shah again.

"My Lord, this information has been double checked" the minister assured his king.

"I would need about 300 cavalrymen, the best of the best. We shall ambush the fort like a desert storm and be out of it in the blink of an eye. It has to be that quick" proposed the lord of Mewar.

"My King, we need to take into account unexpected happenstance that might come our way" argued Ram Singh. "How are we to know we could leave in the blink of an eye? Are we that sure?"

"The only thing working in our favour is that the Mughals are still grounded 500 metres from the fort. With all the sentries and the early warning systems they might now have in place, the onus is all the more upon us to strike like lightning and leave like lightning" countered Prathap Singh.

"I just feel that the odds are stacked against us, brother" felt Sakta Singh. "Moreover, how are we to approach on horseback without being detected well in advance by those hawk-eyed servants of Akbar despite it being a night-time raid?"

"Father, there are too many loose ends here" cut in Amar Singh. "We need certainty that we would outsmart the Mughals."

"We should, my son. There is a little window of opportunity offered by fate which we should seize upon" said Prathap Singh. "I would rather brand it as a risky window of opportunity."

Everyone in the room arched their eyebrows in a sense of wonder.

"What may that be, brother?" asked Sakta Singh with a wide grin.

"The change of guard at the fort!" said Prathap Singh emphatically.

"The change of guard?" wondered Ram Singh. "What of that?"

"The change of guard happens every morning around 6 o'clock" informed Bama Shah. "The resident troops in the fort leave and are replaced with another batch of a 1000 soldiers. This is probably done to keep the Mughal army here on their toes."

"The fort is surrounded by thirteen elevated peaks on all sides" weighed in Prathap Singh. "If we manage to creep up to the blindside of the hills surrounding the fort without making much of a noise — I understand it is going to be difficult — if we can do that, then, we can charge at them about half an hour before dawn and take them by surprise."

"My Lord, the entrance to the fort is not a big one" admonished Ram Singh.

"We file in two in a row" said Prathap Singh as he arched his eyebrows. "The resident Mughals would be too busy with the preparation for leaving the fort at that wee hour. I guess that even the sentries on the walls would not be in their positions. We need to reach the surrounding hills by five in the morning."

"So, we shall" agreed Ram Singh. "300 of the elite, right?"

"Yes, 300 of the very best. Make sure they are armed to the teeth and that their charging horses are raring to go" goaded the king.

Two weeks later on the strike day Prathap Singh, his confidantes and their 300 left for Kumbalgarh Fort in battle gear about half past three in the morning on horseback. For strategic reasons, the group split into segments of fifty each and trotted as slowly as possible to mute their approach. As they began approaching the fort, the cavalry began to walk the charges in almost near silence to deaden the sound of the horse-hooves. It was in a sense maddening, moving like toddlers, but it was done with great efficacy. The cavalry spread themselves on the blindside of the mountains in perfect muteness. Although it was two days after the new moon, Venus was the only bright object in the sky that November morning, shining like a beacon in the near dark expanse of the heavens. The men reached the hills about five and could not locate neither cavalry patrols, sentries nor guards manning the watchtowers with their spyglasses. Had they overrated the much-touted patrols and sentries of the emperor? The Mughals tired of the proverbial wolf got fed up and abandoned their positions a full hour before dawn. The king found it difficult to keep the issue in suspended animation for too long. At a quarter past five, they slowly began to move in a long file of pairs of cavalrymen while the vast majority of about two hundred formed a large unit behind the long string of progressing troops. The slow trot led by Prathap Singh armed with his spear and his talwar in his scabbard began galloping on cue from the king. They negotiated the slopping hills, the gullies and the ruts with ease as they turned around the wide expanse of the surrounding hills making a beeline for the main entrance. And to top it all, the advancing party was bearing Mughal battle standards to bamboozle the enemy!

As the pink streaks of light began to spark in the east heralding the break of day, when darkness was beginning to make a reluctant retreat, Mewar's rajputs galloped around the fort, approached in racing speed and crashed into Kumbalgarh with absolute ardour! The few guards left to guard the entrance stood gaping at the onrushing cavalry mistaking them for Mughals. Only at the last moment did they realize that it was yet another brazen attack by the rajputs and by Prathap Singh himself! They froze in sheer terror!

Prathap Singh thrust his spearhead straight through the left eye of the Mughal who got up to flee, shearing his skull awkwardly and spilling its contents. Simultaneously, Ram Singh to his left sent his spear with great force into the Adam's apple of another Mughal guard. The other sentries who began fleeing were cut down mercilessly by the advancing rajputs. The rest of the Mughal army put up inside preparing to leave were aghast at being caught off guard yet again. Ashamed at being surprised they ran to alert others who were spread out all over the vast expanse of the fort going about their regime. Shouts, yells and screams filled the air as Prathap Singh and his troops began slaughtering the Mughals standing as a religious congregation who had left their swords in a safe place. Pandemonium prevailed for about two minutes with the Mughals trying desperately to come to grips with the overwhelming attack. Scores tumbled on one another in anxiety to get away from the storming rajputs.

Many Mughals decided to seek refuge in the palace complex instead of putting themselves in harm's way. Some climbed the trees in the complex to get away from it all. Others ran for their lives, many ran up the stairs of the palaces, while some others managed to reach the battlements and sound the alarm. In the space of about three minutes before the Mughal bugles sounded the alarm from the watchtowers of the fort, scores of Mughals lay dead, losing their lives to the spears and swords of Mewar's rajputs.

Prathap Singh and his troops went about clinically decapitating heads, cutting-off limbs, slashing deep wounds on faces, disembowelling, fracturing skulls and amputating fingers. The shrieks, cries and moans of the dying and the wounded shook the faith the Mughals had in themselves to the very core.

The moment they heard the bugles sounding the alarm, Prathap Singh ordered his troops into a retreat, "Rajputs, it's time to leave!"

The king of Mewar did not suffer the loss of a single soldier! His plan had worked to great perfection! The attack team was greeted at the entrance to the fort by the rear-guard who began hurrying their king.

"My Lord, the Mughals are advancing on horses! We have to hurry" said one of elites guarding the main gate holding a cylindrical spyglass in his hand.

"We leave at once!" agreed the king as his horse trotted and the entire group of 300 rajputs began racing towards the mountains surrounding the fortress at thundering speed. They well and truly vanished, dispersing into the safety of the summits, the valleys and the thick vegetation surrounding Kumbalgarh.

Meanwhile, a thoroughly shaken Shabaz Khan and his junior Bakshi pulled into the fort shortly after the attack. They were greeted by a very familiar scene of dead corpses, crimson blood splattered all over the cobbled stones, the critically injured in anguish, lifeless limbs scattered erratically and peevish looking Mughals cutting a sorry figure. The furious commander pulled up the man-in-charge and asked him, "How many did we lose?"

"I am yet to find out, sire" he answered.

"Well, do it at once, you blockhead!" yelled the commander who felt his blood rushing to his face.

How on earth was he going to explain yet another audacious attack by the rajputs to his emperor? And to Abdul Karim Khan too? Did not fate put Prathap Singh well into his path that morning and he had given the king of Mewar the opportunity to slip away? How ironic!

A while later, the captain who got the dressing down from Shabaz Khan showed up.

"Sire, we have lost 283!" hesitated the Mughal in-charge who had managed to save his life, "About a 100 are in critical condition."

Mughal paramedics came rushing in with necessary accessories to attend to the dying and the wounded.

Shabaz Khan spread his hands wide and looked up at the heavens. He then glared in anger at Bakshi who began feeling very uncomfortable at the heat in his commander's eyes.

"He is making fools of us all! We are all fools! Aren't we fools?" he began fuming. "Just think! 50,000 troops, two top commanders and 1000 inmate troops on guard at this fort cannot stop this.. this.." he began looking for the right word in his mind, "lion, yes, a lion! Shame on us all!"

He turned around and looked at the surviving soldiers in the fort, "Shame on you all lazybones! Can't 1000 well-armed Mughals stop this marauding band? Fools are you all!" he repeated.

"Commander, if he is attacking us this frequently, he must be hiding somewhere close by" counselled Bakshi gathering his courage. "Otherwise he would not be capable of this routine."

Shabaz Khan glared again at his deputy again, nodded very seriously, launched himself on his steed and admitted, "Yes, he is somewhere close by, no doubt, this lion will not get away all the time… and when I capture him alive..." he began grimacing and then yelled aloud, "Prathap Singh! You just wait!"

Within two hours of the pre-dawn strike, 5,000 heavily armed Mughals were pitched right outside the perimeters of the Kumbalgarh Fort to pre-empt any such future attacks.

Commander Shabaz Khan seated atop his horse began barking dictates as he went around the fort inspecting the ad-hoc arrangements.

"I just get the feeling we are beating a dead snake here" he sarcastically mocked as he stroked the mane of his stallion.

"Dead snakes are still known to have life in them, Commander" argued Bakshi. "We need to crush the head."

"This Prathap Singh saga seems unending. I am frustrated, I really am" said Shabaz Khan as he began breathing slowly.

As the dust settled down on the attack, both commanders returned to the comfort of the meeting tent to ponder their next move.

"We need to rattle every hill, every mountain, every valley and every gulley in the surrounding stretch and beyond the immediate vicinity" confided Shabaz Khan. "How come he eludes us all the time?"

"He is hidden under some kind of immaculate camouflage" confessed Bakshi grudgingly. "A snake in unsurpassed disguise. No wonder we are not able to locate him."

They began hearing the gallop of approaching troops in the distance. Not wanting to be clobbered yet another time, they instantly stormed out of the tent and swung upon their horses only to see the steady advance of a small body of Mughal cavalry in the short distance. The rest of the Mughals too by this time were up in arms falling into battle formation.

"Holt it! Hold it" yelled Shabaz Khan as he rallied around them with Bakshi. "It's the Mughals!" he cautioned them again.

The cavalry unit drew near and came to a halt near the two commanders.

"It's you Qutub-udin-Khan!" exclaimed Shabaz Khan. "What a surprise!" He heaved a big sigh of relief.

A well-built, middle-aged, athletic commander dressed in all-black grinned gently, "Peace to all," he began. "The ruler has dispatched me here with the sole intention of hunting down the elusive rajput Prathap Singh."

"You are in good company, Qutub-Udin" beamed Shabaz Khan. "We are indebted to the emperor."

The three alighted and headed straight for the tent where the new commander was briefed about Prathap Singh. He got up gung-ho, came out and surveyed the terrain with a spyglass.

"We shall be hunting rabbits in their burrows very soon" quipped Qutub-Udin-Khan as he pulled his sword out in pride.

Bakshi raised his left eyebrow high up in wonder. Here is a man with enthusiasm, he thought. How long will he be able to sustain that? A month? The mountains of Mewar would suck all his zeal into nothing, wouldn't they?

"I shall proceed to the fort to have a look around" wished Qutub-Udin Khan.

"Fine. Bakshi here will escort you" answered Shabaz Khan.

In a short while, both the commanders went galloping towards the fort accompanied by 400 mounted troops bearing Akbar's battle standards.

CHAPTER 27

A REFUGE IN THE STORM

*T*hree days after the assault on Kumbalgarh, a meeting was convened on a hot afternoon in the lower level of the hideout.

"There are two decisions that I have made that we need to act upon at once" said Prathap Singh at the attendees with a sense of foreboding. "The first is, Amar Singh is no longer going to be present with my family. This is for strategic reasons. If my family were to be captured or killed by the Mughals, my son will still theoretically perpetuate my line. Now, this is very important. In fact, this is supreme."

He looked at Amar Singh seated to his right who responded by closing his eyes for an elongated moment giving consent.

"Amar, you are to stay with Ram Singh in total disguise using a good alias for your safety" continued Prathap Singh. "The second decision I have made is that, we are abandoning this hideout that has wonderfully saved our skins for good. The Mughals will have by now postulated that my presence is located not very far from Kumbalgarh and would do anything in their power to restore Mughal writ and supremacy. If we are caught, there is no telling what would follow. The odds don't favour us. My wife and young children are also here. This is a gamble that I will not risk!"

The king paused and looked around, "Neither do I want the innocent people of Mewar to suffer in the Mughal quest to capture me. So, we leave with discretion, and once we have come to terms with our new hideout, we shall sort out the rest."

"For the sake of a hideout that cannot even be considered a hideout in its proper sense, the royal family would move to one of the empty mines in the old Zawar region" declared Bama Shah.

"Zawar mines?" debated Ram Singh alarmed as he winced his face. "My King, the mines are so dusty, dark and deep and who knows what resides there now? The dark dungeons there were abandoned long ago. Hiding there is not advisable!"

"If there is a choice between torture, death, dishonour on the one hand and being alive in an inhabitable mine on the other, I would gladly choose the latter" retorted Prathap Singh.

"Brother" began Sakta Singh trying to smile. "I have been to those mines once in my childhood. The place is quite cut off from civilization. It is surrounded by small forts from all directions. While these small forts themselves are now deserted and desolate, you probably would not be able to access food supplies like what you do here. How are you going to take care of sustenance? The mine would demand a constant use of oil lamps the whole day. There are other physical considerations too."

"My Lord! The vertical descent is at least a hundred feet deep, followed by an underground network of long, branching tunnels about ten feet high, leading nowhere" cut in a concerned Ram Singh again. "Some of them subsequently branching off to interlink with other tunnels. I have been there before. Once you reach the inner tunnels all you can expect is total darkness!"

"Would you reconsider your decision, brother?" asked a seriously concerned Sakta Singh with a mild grin.

"I know this is difficult for Kanwar, myself, the children and for the members of the cabinet present here, but I have no choice. I am definitive about this" Prathap Singh stood his ground. "I choose suffering to save myself from greater suffering… that's how I look at it."

There was a long pause. The place was quiet enough for people to hear their own heartbeats.

"The cavalry is safe and sound?" questioned the king, intending to shift the attention.

"Oh, every one of them is safe. Some dispersed as far as Sind, some into Gujarat and the rest into various locations on the banks of the Indus. We have left no trace for the Mughals" boasted Ram Singh. "They will not return unless you call for them."

"I might need them some time in the future" mused the king.

"Let me have advance intimation, My Lord, and we shall have them at your command" assured Ram Singh.

"You two take care of your other 'impressions'" cautioned the king glancing at Bama Shah and Ram Singh. "Akbar's military would stoop to any level to seize my patricians."

"We blend effortlessly with the local population, Your Highness" assured Ram Singh as he chuckled. "They would possibly find the proverbial needle in the haystack, but they are not going to catch us."

"What of you, Sakta?" enquired his elder brother.

"Oh, I would do penance masquerading as a Sadhu under a banyan tree well off the town limits at Chavand. I would be sporting a thick beard, a tapering hair-bun and long flowing matted locks too! You need have no fear. These Mughals would never take me for a royal Mewar rajput!" weighed in Sakta Singh. "If at all you need me, you will know where to look" he winked his left eye.

"My Lord, I shall leave late evening with the children, the queen shall be fetched two days later. Your Highness shall depart in the disguise of a clean-shaven brahmin priest to join the rest of your family a week later" advised Bama Shah.

The conversation came to an end abruptly as Sakta Singh raised his right hand in alarm gesturing at everyone to be silent. They could hear the distinct muffled sound of a Mughal patrol on the summit of the hill. It began drawing nearer and nearer.

Prathap Singh's signal sent everyone to the lower level in a jiffy. The king and Sakta Singh began waiting at the top four steps of the flight of stairs that led to the lower level with the heavy lid in a near -locking position with hardly a slit of space left to peer if the Mughals would break through the heavy iron-clad mountain door. Kanwar, her children numbering four, Bama Shah and Ram Singh were waiting by the other exit ready to flee if matters came to a head.

Outside the summit, a Mughal soldier pointed to the spot on the ground by the mountainside door, "She was standing at this very spot at three O'clock this morning," he asserted to Qutub-Udin Khan and Mughal Mir Bakshi. "I noticed her in the dim moonlight from that gulley below" he said, pointing to the narrow pathway that intersected the mountain-chain further down. "I am sure it was a woman. I also saw what looked like three children about eight to nine years old gesturing at each other. The dame dishevelled her hair and began combing it. After some time, she led the children to the other side and vanished into thin air!"

Soon, a patrol made up of twenty-five heavily armed Mughals on horses ascended the hilltop and dismounted.

"Are you sure it wasn't your eyes playing games?" demanded Bakshi.

"No, Commander. I even saw her feeling this mountainside with her right hand" replied the soldier.

Qutub-Udin Khan came close to the mountainside door, felt the surface overgrown with moss, weeds and tender grass. He then placed his left ear to the surface of the mountain door as if trying to listen to something audible. Moving back, he began pounding the door with his spear. He was joined by a few Mughals who also sent their medieval bayonets crashing into the door surface. Now, the mountain-hideout door was designed to withstand this kind of battering. The iron-door was heavily covered with natural elements to a depth of three feet. Hence it hardly suffered any damage except for a few rocky fragments falling off.

"They are hammering the door with weapons!" observed an increasingly anxious Sakta Singh.

Prathap Singh did not reply. His right eye kept peeping through the narrow slit. Should he flee or should he stand up to the intruding Mughals? There was no telling how many were waiting outside the heavy door.

The bulky Bakshi took a careful aim at an imaginary spot on what he thought was the hidden door and plunged his spear with mighty force. His spear failed to penetrate and deflected violently off the hard surface. The Mughals were left with a hard choice.

"Check the other side" ordered Qutub-Udin Khan at the soldiers.

The party went around and found they could not locate anything suspicious to investigate on the surface all the way around the broad facade surrounding the summit.

Qutub-Udin-Khan made up his mind, "We shall have this hill monitored for a few days. Should we notice anything abnormal, we would have to act. A woman with her kids in the middle of the night is something strange. Very strange if she really did make an appearance here."

After lingering there for five minutes, the patrol with the two commanders in lead left the place leaving a team of three soldiers to monitor the mount for any signs of human activity.

In the hideout, things were not returning to normalcy with the inmates still whispering to keep their voices low. They had no way of ascertaining if the Mughal patrol had given up or left to bring a greater army to force open the door.

Prathap Singh hurried to Kanwar and his children. He asked Bama Shah to leave for the first level.

"Kanwar," he said embracing her, "maybe our luck has runout. If it is the case, probably this is our last embrace and our last kiss." He repeatedly kissed his queen on her cheeks. "I believe Akbar has finally nailed us and will gloat over our dead bodies. I shall be your lord and husband in a thousand other lives! We die with honour. We shall die with dignity!"

Kanwar burst into tears. Prathap Singh picked up his kids and kissed them in turn.

"May the blood of my children be upon the head of these invaders!" he cursed.

He pulled out his sword, looked at Kanwar, "Farewell, my Kanwar. May your memory live forever!" he turned and walked in fury towards the flight of steps.

On the first level, he found Amar Singh, Sakta Singh, Ram Singh and Bama Shah waiting with bated breath and drawn swords.

The minutes became hours, the hours turned the day into night and the much-touted storming of the hideout simply happened to fizzle out.

Eventually, the inmates decided to sit down taking for granted that the Mughals had in fact left. Or were they silently crouching just behind the door to pounce on the inmates leaving the hideout? There was no sound of human or animal movement outside. They could not be sure. What were they to do?

After a tiring wait, the king sent his sword back into its sheath, went downstairs, hugged Kanwar again and wiped her tears and cried as he kissed his sons and daughters.

No words were exchanged. He simply nodded and went upstairs, gestured at everyone to tiptoe downstairs which they did at once.

In the safety of one of the lower-level chambers, he had his men sit down, "The evacuation is put on hold for about three or four days. We need to be sure of the happenings in the immediate environment."

"Agreed, Your Highness. There is no way we are going to run that risk. We shall stay put" conceded Bama Shah.

"Your valiant ventures towards the Rana Sanga lineage are deeply appreciated" said Pratap Singh with utmost humility. "We are indebted to you and Ram Singh."

"We are at your service, My Liege" declared Ram Singh. "The Mughals can only touch you over our dead bodies!"

Prathap Singh stared at Ram Singh for a few seconds, his eyes conveying his gratitude in all their fullness.

Three days later, Shabaz Khan, Mugal Mir Bakshi and Qutub-Udin Khan raced to the observation position in the gulley below the mountain hideout accompanied by 50 cavalrymen.

"Anything to report, men?" demanded Bakshi at the ten soldiers stationed in the improvised hut put up for them.

"Nothing, Commander. Nothing at all! No human activity on this mountain" answered a captain, "All we could see was field labourers going about their work in the distance in the morning. No sign of man, woman or child anywhere on these heights. Neither in the night nor in the day. I assure you of that."

Shabaz Khan produced his typical annoying look at Bakshi gruntling, "I feel our troops are beginning to hallucinate during the night patrols, aren't they? Reduce the number of night convoys in these areas. They don't do any good."

He gazed at the hilltop for some time. "Wait here," he commanded and began ascending the mountain on his horse. Reaching the top with some difficulty and locating the purported spot of woman being seen standing with her children, he loitered for a while and then descended carefully. Reaching the gulley below, he ordered the Mughals in the observation hut, "Men, you are to pull down this hut, pack everything up and return to the camp."

He looked at Qutub-Udin-Khan and remarked, "The court should not be split to their ends at hearing we are chasing ghostly apparitions on the mountains of Mewar instead of snaring flesh and blood rajputs."

A good five days later, the hideout door opened at three o' clock in the morning. Prathap Singh, Sakta Singh, Amar Singh, Ram Singh and Bama Shah stepped out with caution surveying north, south, east and west with great discretion.

After a few minutes, Bama Shah and Sakta Singh, leading two children each descended the mount eagerly. The children waved looking behind at their father and mother standing in the doorway. Once in the gulley, the men hoisted the children one each on their shoulders and began walking cautiously towards the safety of their compatriots in the nearest hamlets for the safekeeping of the royals.

Two days later, Ram Singh in the camouflage of a shepherd escorted Kanwar dressed as a shepherdess devoid of all her jewellery in the dead of the night to the children.

Within five days, Prathap Singh masquerading as a brahmin priest and Amar Singh equally posing as his apprentice, made good their getaway in the middle of the night.

The hideout was locked from outside by the loyal Bama Shah with nothing on the inside betraying any human presence except for the smell of cooked food hanging heavily in the air.

CHAPTER 28

OBSCURED IN DARKNESS

*T*wo weeks had passed since the day Mewar's royal family and the king's aides fled the hideout in the mountains. Mughal patrols in regular frequency kept combing the open terrain, farmlands, towns and villages for any possible sign of Prathap Singh and his confidantes. The make-believe appearances of Mewar's stellar personalities had worked so well that Akbar's men could not see through them for their true selves.

A full month later, Prathap Singh decided to move to Zawar mines deciding that oblivion would afford a better protection against Akbar's servants. He preferred such a choice so as not to be on tenterhooks about their cover being blown anytime.

"We shall leave inconspicuously, drawing no attention, making it look like the movement of men, women and children who go about carrying out their normal daily lives" insisted Prathap Singh, still sporting his shining bald head with a little tuft of black hair entwined in itself right on the dome of his skull. "If we are stopped or questioned anywhere enroute we shall give the perfect excuse and remain calm and composed in the face of those arrogant servants of Fatehpur Sikri."

Sakta Singh, already sporting a growing beard and thick, spiral locks dangling all the way to his waist, replied, "I don't expect to be stopped by these creatures who think they bear the world on their heads" his lips smiling in a mocking manner.

"Ram Singh, you shall accompany the queen to the mines" instructed the king. "And for all practical purpose she is your wife, so to speak" laughed Prathap Singh.

"She will be brought safely to you, My Lord" said Ram Singh with a reserved smile, not being the one to smile at such meetings.

"Sakta, stay safe at Chavand. Do hurry when I send word" beseeched the king.

Sakta Singh nodded with his perpetual boyish smile.

The first to leave were Ram Singh and the queen ambling across the fields and the hills as a husband-wife duo on their way to visit relatives in the south all the way to Dungarpur, with two of Prathap Singh's children. As they walked gently towards the nearest hamlet for refuge before nightfall, they came across a Mughal foot-patrol in the afternoon whose soldiers evinced a passing interest in the pair.

The next day, the pair left early in the morning with the two children towards the next hamlet walking as usual, with Ram Singh and Kanwar carrying a child each on their arms.

About midday they ran into Shabaz Khan and Mughal Mir Bakshi leading a posse of about 200 cavalrymen. The contingent pulled up right in front of them.

"Where to, brother? The sun is not very kind today, is it?" enquired Bakshi of Ram Singh.

"Greetings, My Lord. I am headed for Dungarpur" came the meek reply.

Shabaz Khan cast a cunning eye at both enquiring, "Ever came across the fugitive Prathap Singh?"

"Our king?" questioned Kanwar, covering half her face with her plain-looking saree and refusing to make eye contact, "Oh, he is on the run, sire. Some say he has disappeared." She lowered her head in respect.

"A great reward awaits people like you if there is any lead that can help the empire apprehend him dead or alive. You get money to last you for a hundred generations!" suggested Bakshi.

"What business beckons you in Dungarpur?" probed Shabaz Khan of Ram Singh and glancing at the children who by now were clinging to their purported parents.

"My father-in-law is ailing, sire" said Ram Singh pointing to the queen.

Shabaz Khan was impressed by the striking features of the woman. She didn't appear to be common folk. Should he investigate them further? Maybe this is an anomaly and this man got very lucky to have such an elegant wife. He decided to give them the benefit of the doubt.

"You may proceed" he said and spurred his horse. The whole contingent began trotting forward.

The husband and wife did not exchange words nor did they express any signs of relief even well after the disappearance of the cavalry patrol.

Late in the afternoon, they reached the next hamlet, which afforded them safety. They did not come across either Mughal cavalry or footmen on patrol after the encounter with Akbar's military top brass.

"That was close, My Queen!" exclaimed Ram Singh, removing his turban. "I was really worried. That commander kept staring at you and the children. My word! That was close!"

"Fate has been kind" smiled Kanwar. "It was really nerve-wracking to remain composed under such questioning."

Sakta Singh left two days after the departure of the queen with Ram Singh.

He too ran into a Mughal patrol as he was heading on foot towards Chavand hardly an hour into his journey.

"Hey mystic!" ordered Qutub-Udin-Khan from his horse, as his unit stood under a lofty canopy of spreading banyan trees. "Are you some kind of rajput royal on the run?" demanded the commander much to the laughter of his cavalrymen.

"Royal? Who? Me? Men like me can only dream of royalty" replied Sakta Singh rubbing his beard with his left hand, his long, dense, dreadlocks hanging wildly, reaching almost to his waist, his face smeared with ash, a heavy, black chain of beads hanging about his neck and his right hand carrying a metal jug of water. He however cleverly concealed his lethal dagger on his left thigh that was now draped neat with his clean-washed fiery-orange dhoti.

Two Mughals came trotting to Sakta Singh, dismounted and demanded his rolled-up cloth bag under his right arm. They found betel leaves and areca nuts in plenty. They alighted their horses and left him in peace deciding for some reason not to frisk him for concealed weapons.

"What's the destination in mind?" questioned the commander in a very overbearing manner from the shade.

"Are we under a curfew?" questioned the annoyed 'sadhu'.

"No, I mean where are you off to?" charged the Mughal kingpin.

"I am off to my annual penance in the mountains, My Lord" said Sakta Singh as he squinted his eyes to have a better look at the warlord about twenty yards away.

Qutub-Udin-Khan brusquely waved at him to keep going, deciding he was wasting his time talking to religious men too obsessed with their regime.

Sakta Singh continued his walk, not turning to have a second look, lest the Mughals change their mind for some reason.

"This is weird" opined Qutub-Udin-Khan. "Not a single man or woman we encounter here is linked to this Prathap Singh. Where does he vanish after his attacks?"

"It's the Afghans, Commander. Where else? The Afghans are giving him refuge" said a captain emphatically. "Where else do you think he can flee to? The Sher Shah Suri kindred is still mourning the loss of their principality."

Meanwhile about 50 kilometres away at Zawar, Ram Singh slowly descended down one of the shafts' entrances that barely resembled a rough, lengthy pathway to the mines below that early morning. He led Kanwar and the children tenderly down the broad, dark tunnel that kept stretching for a long distance in the musty darkness.

There were broken rocks, jagged walls and a hard pathway on which they kept treading for a long while. A few rats scurried at the approach of humans in that subterranean darkness.

"What kind of fate is this for a queen?" anguished Kanwar.

"The fate of the kings, queens, princes and princesses of the Hind under Mughal subjugation" opined Ram Singh walking ahead and showing the way to Kanwar and the children with his blazing wooden torch. "Would there not be shouts of ecstasy from the rooftops of the Hind when these Mughals fall once and for all, never to rise again? Invaders! Marauders!"

"Oh, that is not going to happen anytime soon" said an exasperated Kanwar walking gingerly on the hard mine-floor. "It would take an earth-shattering event to bring these giants down... but, fall they will to someone stronger who shall put these aliens in their place."

After tramping on the long, broad, meandering main tunnel for about twenty minutes, the two souls came to a rocky space that resembled a semi-circular stage about four feet high with steps at the extreme ends. There were tunnels leading right and left just before they reached the rocky stage.

"This is where the inmates have to put up" observed Ram Singh fixing his wooden torch onto a niche in the wall.

"My Queen, would you be able to lead a normal life here? The king too?" he queried, feeling very concerned.

"If this will save our lives, yes. We shall exist until we decide otherwise" replied a defiant Kanwar. She made both her children sit on the stage.

"Your highness, I shall stay here until the arrival of the king. I am going to urge him to shift elsewhere. This could be a short-term hideout but not something viable for permanent lodging" he said very candidly. "The royals of Mewar cannot hide here in the long run."

Ten days later, a horse-carriage driven by a young brahmin left a sleepy hamlet on the plains of Mewar in the morning and headed towards the mines of Zawar on the road to Dungarpur. The twin-horse carriage was laden heavily with carrots, cabbages and potatoes. An old woman, with a wrinkled face, clad in a black saree that was half shrouding her head and with her legs stretched sat in the wagon.

The vehicle travelled very slowly given the amount of produce it was bearing. The approaching horses was spotted by the same huge Mughal patrol under the

Banyan shade this time too. However, this time around, the top brass of the Mughal force in Kumbalgarh was present under the canopy that day.

"Father, we are running into trouble" said Amar Singh, the driver turning aside, "watch out."

"Just play it safe, son. Remain calm, I shall handle this" replied the 'old lady'.

Shabaz Khan, Bakshi and Qutub-Udin-Khan came on a short gallop accompanied by ten cavalrymen to intercept the vehicle.

Shabaz Khan came around eying the carriage with suspicion, "So, who are you, old lady?"

"Janvi Singh, My Lord. I am a vegetable farmer" said the woman in quite a feminine voice, bowing her almost fully covered head with her legs still stretched.

"Where are you headed?" demanded the commander again.

"My son, I am proceeding to a village down south" said the lady piously.

"And, who is the man in front?" continued the crafty Shabaz Khan.

"He is my sweet grandson" smiled the lady in a quivering voice.

"What's beneath this produce? You aren't hiding something, are you?" commanded the Mughal heavyweight.

"Commander, let us off-load the whole cart to figure it out" proposed Bakshi.

"Dear me! Would an old woman take on the mighty Mughals by hiding fugitives in a cart?" she posed "At my age?"

"We are wasting time, chasing ghosts, pursuing vegetable-sellers and interrogating die-hard mystics!" vented out Qutub-Udin-Khan.

The trio came around to stare at Amar Singh. Shabaz Khan lifted Amar Singh's chin with the shinning spearhead of his elongated weapon and began staring at him. The clean-shaven head, the black tuft of hair, and a face devoid of expression didn't suggest anything particularly royal.

Out of the blue, Amar Singh began chanting a string of mantras to prove his proficiency in primeval Sanskrit as he took turns to rattle them from one commander to another.

"Enough!" ordered Shabaz Khan as he lowered his spear. "Move!"

The vehicle began its journey again, slowly wobbling left and right as it rumbled forward.

"Had they crossed the line, I would have swung around with my sword" warned the old woman Prathap Singh in his manly voice again. "Hey children!" he said, raising his voice as he permeated his voice into the massive heap of agricultural produce, "Hang on for some time, till we are well out of sight of these patrols."

There was a burst of mocking laughter from Amar Singh, "What did that officer claim? 'We are chasing ghosts, vegetable sellers and religious mystics!' Wow! The royal family has had great success in running into these patrols in perfect disguise!"

"What is destined to be, will be" philosophized the lion of Mewar.

After about a week, Prathap Singh found himself staring into the oblivion as he entered the mines himself. After a short while, he was reunited with an ecstatic Kanwar and the young children.

As he sat on the rocky stage, surveying his new home, he was dumbstruck, "I don't believe this! The Mughals must pay for their wantonness and arrogance. How my hands are tied! This monster is succeeding in its ventures! They swallowed the entire length of the Indus, they grabbed Indraprastha, they swept through the plain of the Ganges, they are in Gujarat, they are invading Malwa and the central heartland and they have subjugated all of the rajput realms! Has not the Hind fallen before their might? What are we to do?"

"Like the old saying goes, My King, 'Always balance courage with common sense'. You will do well to adhere to it. We have suffered enough in the name of confronting these foreigners" counselled his wife.

"As of now, My Liege, you need to lie low. You shall deal with the Mughals in your own way when the opportunity strikes and I am sure you will" encouraged Ram Singh.

"Somewhere, someone has to stop this avalanche! Who will?" mused the king.

There was silence in the mines for a moment that was punctuated by the hissing noise made by the scurrying rats.

"There is enough food supply in here to last for a month, My Lord. We shall need to replenish before we run out. I shall take care of that" assured Ram Singh.

"Be careful" cautioned the king. "Do not put your life in gross danger for the sake of a meal or two. I have lost enough men to Mughal swords."

CHAPTER 29

DESPERATE TIMES, DESPERATE MEASURES

$\mathcal{F}$or about five months, there was neither an attack on the Mughals by Prathap Singh nor did Akbar's servants succeed in locating him. The lull seemed to be getting longer and longer by the day.

"I believe another attack is very much in the offing" remarked Mughal Mir Bakshi as he relaxed in the tent off the Kumbalgarh Fort. "It is always a long, quiet hiatus before an incredible attack."

"All possible loopholes are covered. This fort is secure and so is Gogunda. There is also no way he can access the artillery on this fort and our main forces are way too large for him to take them head on," countered an optimistic Shabaz Khan. "This time around Prathap Singh would be committing plain suicide!"

"Or we shall succeed in the physical capture of his person" chipped in Qutub-Udin-Khan.

"They are too proud to be captured, both men and women. They would prefer taking their lives" replied the senior commander authoritatively. "It's rajput culture. No surrender."

"How come the other rajput domains surrendered to the Mughals?" questioned Qutub-Udin-Khan.

"You are wrong" insisted Shabaz Khan. "They did not 'surrender' to the Mughals. They made an honourable deal with the empire that left both the Mughals and the rajput dominions in a win-win situation. A 'no-war-but-dignified-servitude' agreement that helps them enjoy all their rights while serving as Mughal vassal states is what they signed up for. Mewar is the only exception. The Rana Sanga lineage has been such an exception since the days we Mughals invaded this vast expanse of Hindustan. I think they are born rebels. They consider us aliens and foreigners. We find no acceptance in their hearts and minds. It is this kind of attitude that produces defiance in the face of death. Prathap Singh is a fine example. So were his father Udai Singh and his forebears."

There was silence in the tent as Shabaz Khan got up from his armchair to strap his scabbard onto himself, "Where the head goes, the tail follows, right?" he continued, "Rana Sanga had the nerve to take on Babur… and he was a fine warrior too. He almost whacked the Mughals at Khanwa if not for the treachery of his own kin. No wonder his posterity Prathap Singh follows in his footsteps. The rajputs of Mewar are one of a kind. They are bold lions. They bring about insane fortitude in the face of peril."

Mughal Mir Bakshi was palpably uncomfortable by this time as his commander sang the praises of the rajputs and Mewar, "So commander, are you off on patrol this morning?" he enquired. "You seem dressed for battle."

Shabaz Khan heaved a quick sigh, "I am leaving for Fatehpur Sikri to brief the world ruler" he said. "You two are in command until I return. I hope there is no bungling on your part. Just make sure the orders are followed to the last letter. Prathap Singh is playing it safe. The numbers are not in his favour."

The senior commander hopped on his shiny warhorse and with a kick of his boots, turned around and left for the capital escorted by a 1000 troops on horses many of whom were bearing the Mughal battle standards.

On a cool autumn morning, the Mughal czar began waving to the crowds gathered below the balcony of the royal palace to have a glimpse of the incredible icon ruling most of Hindustan and almost all of Afghanistan. He was briefed tersely about an urgent errand from the mountains of the north-western quarters.

Akbar hurried down adjusting his turban and having a quick glance at his shining white outfit that had the ceremonial belt securing his heavy, two-pronged dagger in place.

The herald announced the arrival of the emperor. The grandees stood in awe. The icon ascended the steps of the throne and was enshrined on the royal seat of power.

"We have an emergency" Akbar said softly trying to control his emotions after a moment's silence. "My half-brother…that over-ambitious warlord Mirza Muhammed Hakim is approaching the Indus from the Khyber with his cavalry!"

"What?" reacted a shocked Mulla Do-Piyazo, "With his cavalry?"

"A 15,000 strong cavalry by intelligence estimates" went on the emperor. "I believe the man wants to barge into Lahore with a show of force."

The court was instantly filled with the loud buzzing of whispers among the most self-controlled courtiers who exchanged glances in disbelief.

"Silence!" ordered the head-courtier as Akbar gestured at him to bring the muttering to an end.

"With all due respect, My Liege, this man should be exterminated at once" recoiled Birbal, wide-eyed with shock moving to the edge of his arm chair. "This is war! This is treachery!"

"Dearie Birbal" continued Akbar, leaning forward. "What is the need for respect here? This scum Mirza Hakim is a traitor! He is a betrayer! A backstabber!"

"We act at once, My Lord!" shot Abdul Karim Kahn bulldozing in with his rude suggestion.

"Abdul Karim, you are to leave immediately for Lahore with a 20,000 strong cavalry" said the monarch raising his voice at the man overseeing the defence of the empire. "You shall be accompanied by Todar Mal and Raja Birbal. Team up with Raja Man Singh and Raja Bagwan Das' forces in Lahore to annihilate Mirza Hakim's fancy army. Rabble-rouser Hakim is to be either killed or captured alive! The artillery, the elephants and the musketeers you need are to be dispatched on intelligence inputs."

As Abdul Karim Kahn, Todar Mal and Birbal began to make their hasty exit, Akbar raised his voice, "Raja Birbal!"

"My Liege..." replied his grandee as he swung around.

"You shall return to Fatehpur Sikri once the army starts advancing to meet Hakim's hussars. Do not stay put" cautioned Akbar.

"As you wish, My King" smiled Birbal with his hand on his sword-hilt.

There was silence for about a minute or two as the top commanders in the court were seen hastening behind the trio.

Abul Fazl said with hesitation, "This advance by Mirza Hakim is going to poison the empire. No doubt about it."

"In one way or the other you are right, my vizier. Poison? Yes, that's exactly what it has come to" observed Akbar.

"The throne is such a temptation for would-be monarchs" mused Faizi the vizier's brother. "How contentment eludes the most blessed among men!"

"Mirza Hakim will pay with his own life for this attempt! He is a maniac!" raged Akbar, his visage visibly upset.

"He was discontent with your secular outlook, My Lord" posed Tansen.

"I lord over this empire. It will be run with my views. My half-brother has no locus-standi regarding any issue in my sovereign state. He is an outcast! Fate has seen to that" said Akbar as he calmed down.

The Mughal plans worked perfectly as its army under Raja Man Singh, Raja Bagwan Das and Abdul Karim Kahn and the rest of Akbar's aristocrats deftly crossed the Indus from the east bank plains to the Khyber well in advance. Hakim's army was intercepted before it could cross the river and was crushed with an awesome assault from the Mughal cavalry. The kingpin was duly captured, chained like a common offender, taken to Kabul and placed under house arrest. His surviving army was scattered to the four winds on the mountains in and around the Khyber.

Birbal returned after an absence of seven days much to the emperor's relief. The dust over the Mirza Hakim's advance took about two months to settle down as the ruling icon wished to have no more loose ends from the mountains of Afghanistan running into the broad plains of Hindustan.

After the deal had been closed on the Mirza Hakim showdown, Shabaz Khan made his appearance bowing gently to his emperor a good two and a half months after leaving Kumbalgarh.

"Commander, is everything under control? What of Prathap Singh?" asked Akbar cautiously.

"Your Grace, there has been no attacks in the last five months" began the very respectful mastermind. "However, we did suffer significant casualties on three different occasions on account of pre-emptive strikes by this fugitive."

"Thrice?" asked an alarmed Akbar.

"Since then, there has been no sign of this man, My Lord. All of Mewar is under Mughal sovereignty" added Shabaz Khan. "We are continuously on the watch to locate him and have him captured dead or alive."

"It could all have been different if only Prathap Singh had made the right choices, couldn't it not have been?" mused the king. "I have a Raja Birbal, a Raja Man Singh and a Raja Bhagwan Das…" The emperor lowered his head in regret, "How lovely to have had a Raja Prathap Singh in this august hall as one of my own! Certain things were not meant to be…"

A Raja Prathap Singh alongside all the grandees at the court? thought Birbal. His sharp, judicious eyes began looking at the emperor in a quizzing manner. He could see the instant discomfort in the expressions of Abul Fazl, Abdul Karim Khan and Mulla Do-Piyazo from the corners of his eye. Todar Mal, however sat as usual with no manifest feelings on his face.

"How immense is the influence of fate! Who could possibly overrule it?" questioned Akbar turning at Abul Fazl.

The vizier hesitated to answer such a philosophical question.

"Fate indeed is potent, My Lord. The choice between fate and destiny however, is something one makes in one's own volition" counselled Todar Mal sensing how no one wanted to answer the question posed by the emperor.

"Raja Birbal" rose Akbar's voice in a figurative manner. "I have pricked my fingers in trying to pluck this one particular rose."

"Your Grace, have you pricked your fingers on the thorns? The fragrance would still linger on your digits. Does not the rosebush grant her perfume even to her needles?" countered Birbal. "The effort should be counted worthwhile nevertheless."

"Should your fingers bleed for the fragrance, My Liege?" posed Faizi. "Destroy the blossom and its quills. Why would you put yourself under the curse of the rose?"

"The rose's odour is utterly intoxicating, My Lord," began Tansen. "You are powerless under its sway ..its incense consumes your heart, your passions, your imagination! Beware of the rose! Its thorns taste your blood, the flaming bush shall steal your soul!"

The potent was moved by Tansen's verse, "Wow! Tansen! Indeed, I have come under the power of one particular rose! I shall certainly extract my fingers? Why should I bleed? Why choose to lose my soul to its sway?"

Akbar turned his attention back to the sturdy Shabaz Khan in the all-black outfit.

"My Liege, we would like to have a garrison built somewhere in the proximity of Kumbalgarh to have a close watch on the proceedings" proposed the stalwart. "We are forced to move troops, animals and weapons every time there is a rebellion in Mewar."

Akbar thought for a moment. He then commanded Abdul Rahim Khan, "Sort this out with him. Think it over and let me know" he said as he turned his head arching his eyebrows at Shabaz Khan.

In the late afternoon that day, Akbar walked in the gardens around Fatehpur Sikri with his magnificos yet again, with Raja Birbal tailing behind very close.

"Birbal, is not the allure of the rose too tempting?" enquired Akbar, stooping to smell the fragrance of a blooming red bud

"Aye, My Lord, it is" came the smiling but serious reply. "Don't allow the crimson to make you captive to 'her' charms. Your soul will know no peace, My Liege."

"So, should I walk away from the blooming flower?" questioned the emperor with interest.

"Yes, for your own good" said Birbal with a cunning grin, "Or else you will be drawn into its mystique spell."

The other members were trailing behind but they were distracted now by the myriad of geraniums, marigold, hibiscus, dahlias, jasmines, poppies, water-lilies, chrysanthemums, frangipanis, mandrakes and a multitude of innumerable roses.

Akbar turned suddenly, "Abdul Karim Khan!" he called.

The man bearing the name came hurrying, "We meet before dinner at Birbal's mansion tonight to sort out the garrison issue. Of course, Raja Birbal will entertain us with his words of wisdom, won't he?" smiled the potentate.

"I shall, My Liege, as long as there remains breath in these nostrils" bowed Raja Birbal.

Later that evening, in the light of glowing glass lights, the aristocrats met in the upper floor of two storeyed complex named after Akbar's pet cabinet member.

Shabaz Khan stood in military stance before the top brass ruling the subcontinent. There were a number of military officials standing in the background of that hall.

"I have gone through this proposal with my officials, My Liege" said Abdul Karim Khan confidently, "We shall establish a garrison at Dewair about 40 kilometres north of Kumbalgarh. It is north-east more to be more precise. We are looking at 30,000 troops at optimal capacity."

"What? 30,000 troops? That is quite a large number inclusive of the logistics involved" voiced a concerned Akbar. "With the commitments in the Afghan mountains, especially the Kandahar region prone to the target of the Persian Safavids, the Hindu Kush disquiet, the trouble in Bengal and the demands in Gujarat… We may not afford that number. Prathap Singh seems missing in action. Anything could have happened to him. Mewar well and truly is under our sway as the commander here vouches. We shall start with 10,000 men. If for some reason the 'lion' resurfaces, we shall bolster that number."

"My Lord, given his audacious track record would you risk another attack by this rajput prince?" cautioned Abul Fazl.

"Nothing has happened in the past five months. Probably he is not keeping well. He could be badly injured or is emotionally distraught. Why keep 30,000 troops doing nothing?" reasoned Akbar, confident of Prathap Singh's disappearance.

"Who knows, My Lord, he is by now terrified of us Mughals?" beamed Faizi the Yemenite, running his left hand hard against his lower lip. "The world is animated with your fabulous victory over your half-brother."

"I'm sure he is terrified by now" seconded Mulla Do-Piyazo sporting his bristling salt and pepper beard.

"A lion that feels threatened could be more aggressive than a normal one" observed Akbar. "It could be more formidable than before. Watch out."

"I intend to pull back the 50,000 men and the commanders stationed around Kumbalgarh. Not all at once, but gradually. We shall dispatch 10,000 to the Dewair garrisons. The barracks are not far from Kumbalgarh should an emergency or need arise" theorized Akbar. "We shall, on the other hand, have regular patrols in Mewar to monitor and act on anything that might be of suspicious nature."

Shabaz Khan glanced at Abdul Karim Kahn. Pull back the whole army from Kumbalgarh?

There was a sense of acceptance from Abdul Karim Khan. He simply did not want to negotiate with his monarch on this decision.

Akbar went on, "If you three commanders are pulled out, we shall have to dispatch another officer to oversee the Dewair operations."

"So, what's to be done regarding the Afghan rebels, My Lord?" demanded Todar Mal wanting to discuss something other than Mewar and Prathap Singh.

"Once Man Singh and Raja Bagwan Das return from the Punjab, I shall have to take a decision just like I did about Prathap Singh" he glanced at Birbal to his left seated on his armchair. "Raja Birbal is unhappy about us not completely accounting for the remnants of Mirza

Hakim's army. His sword is eager for action yet again on the rugged mountains of the north-west, isn't it?"

Many in the cabinet tried to hide their chuckle.

"Those vagabonds would be crushed once and for all. They think they are safe in their mountain sanctuaries. How foolish! Birbal will again see some action" observed the emperor.

Birbal smiled in a reserved manner deciding not to glory at the accolades being sung from the very lips of his potentate.

"Both the blacksmith and the warrior send sparks flying high, Your Grace" observed Tansen.

"We shall surely send the sparks flying in the faces of those rebels in the Afghan heartland. They should bear the full brunt of the Mughal army all the way to the Persian border. It's almost time. Almost, but not yet…" observed Akbar winking at Birbal.

CHAPTER 30

HIDING IN PLAIN SIGHT

August 1582

The army began withdrawing slowly but steadily from Kumbalgarh. What began with a retreat of 5000 troops per weekend very soon rose to 10,000. Within a month and a half Kumbalgarh Fort and its vicinity was devoid of Mughal presence. Nevertheless, on-the-clock patrols by Akbar's lancers in circuits had an eye on the daily proceedings in and around important towns in Mewar.

The patrols were very frequent around Gogunda, since the Mughals came to believe that the King of Mewar was hiding somewhere in the region.

At one particular hamlet not far from the palace, the population was rounded up by the Mughals and an announcement was made, "The emperor would be willing to consider forgiveness for the fugitive Prathap Singh if he decides to surrender."

One among the crowds was Ram Singh listening with apt attention stroking his unkempt beard and sporting a multi-coloured-turban.

"If you happen to come across this wanted man, you may convey the wish of the world ruler" announced the captain seated on his charger.

It had now been about seven months that had passed without a major incident involving Prathap Singh. A week later, Ram Singh in civilian clothes and Sakta Singh in his ascetic outfit bravely reached the Zawar mines carrying food supplies to convey the tidings of the Mughal retreat.

Deep in the heart of the mine, the king was not in good spirits.

"Your Highness, the Mughals have left Kumbalgarh. Cavalry patrols are the only thing that are repeatedly going around" declared Ram Singh.

"Alright, why this change of heart from Akbar?" questioned Prathap Singh relieved to hear some encouraging news.

"All because we have not acted in the past six months or so" replied Sakta Singh trying not to smile in the dull and damp mines.

"Things are not going well here" declared a sombre-looking Prathap Singh. "My young children are not able to have three square meals a day" he paused for a moment. "They are constantly depressed. They don't sleep, the disturbance of the rats is unbearable and the darkness of these tunnels is getting into our bones. There is a deep sense of foreboding here. Kanwar somehow bears this ignominy for my sake" he looked at her with regret. She smiled and turned her head away as she sat with her back to the wall, He rose from the semi-circular rocky stage, "I think it is better to live in plainclothes around Chavand. The town is a safe bet. It is located neither too south nor too close to Gogunda and quite far from Kumbalgarh. It is in the middle of nowhere."

"Brother, the Mughal patrols have announced amnesty for you if you were to surrender to the empire! This is their latest announcement in all the towns and villages" said Sakta Singh sarcastically.

"Amnesty? Are they in their right senses? They pillage my land, they destroy my life, they slaughter my soldiers, they turn my kingdom upside down and they announce amnesty! Is this not sadism?" pursued an aggrieved Prathap Singh, "The sun would rise in the west if Prathap Singh of Mewar surrenders to the Mughals! That is simply unthinkable! Throw their offer to the winds! Is Amar Singh fine?"

"Oh, he is fine and raring to have another go at the Mughals" answered Ram Singh.

"That is how a rajput must live" conceded Prathap Singh. "You two shall identify a spacious house, preferably a farm house where I and my family can carry on living in plainclothes with immunity against these mounted troop patrols. I shall not in any way give reason for the Mughals to suspect my presence. The masquerades I shall employ will be just out of the ordinary. I want you both to return in a week's time for the departure. As we came, so shall we leave, raising no suspicion whatsoever with the vegetable cart and all."

After a gruelling wait of seven days, the family began leaving in the same modus operandi they followed for reaching Zawar. Ram Singh and his 'wife' Kanwar left with their same two young children. Sakta Singh left the mines alone as a wandering mystic. The vegetable cart bearing the remaining two children buried under a huge load of field produce, with Amar Singh as driver and his grandmother Prathap Singh left after a gap of a day. They destroyed all evidence of their presence in the heart of the mines.

This time around there was simply no interception of any of them on their way back. A distant patrol had a passing interest in the husband-wife duo accompanying the two children. That curiosity quickly evaporated in no time considering the abject outfits sported by the four on foot. Neither the meandering mystic Sakta Singh with his flowing braids nor the horse carriage bearing Amar Singh, Prathap Singh and the children encountered Mughal cavalrymen for good.

This particular house among a string of houses by a mountainside offered ample opportunity for the royal family to pose as farmers and land tillers. Their impersonations blended perfectly with the loyal civilians in the settlement sworn to defend them with their own lives. The house also had the advantage of a secret basement where the family chose to stay night and day with ease and comfort. All their needs were well taken care of. The king's life became well oiled, smooth and running except for his longing for the possession of Kumbalgarh and Gogunda.

His mind began working again, steadily, strategically to carry out a plan. Was it time for him to strike again? Everything seemed peaceful, right? Should he bring back the Mughal armies with a yet another well-orchestrated strike against the hordes of Akbar? Where would he strike? The patrols were unimportant considering the barracks at Dewair. So, were the new garrisons at Dewair his target? His mind began considering the pros and cons of his actions. Would Akbar be tempted to invade Mewar in a grandiose manner again if he were to assault Dewair? Would he be putting this quiet community and his life in danger by his actions? The Mughals must have no rest in Mewar! No rest, yes, that was of paramount importance. Dewair had to be sized up. Prathap Singh dispatched the summons to his aides. The die was cast.

On a cool afternoon, Prathap Singh sat under the low hanging, broad, heavy, grey boughs of a massive banyan tree quite circumjacent to his new hideout. Its mammoth trunk, entwined by the ground-reaching bulky roots that made it look disproportionately colossal, offered enough space to shroud the clandestine meet that was convened by the king. Prathap Singh and his aides were very much in the garb of commonfolk and were absolutely indistinguishable from them in all respects.

"What is the situation in Dewair?" demanded Prathap Singh.

"They are done with putting up more than 30 smaller garrisons to accommodate their troops" informed Ram Singh.

"Are you sure it is 30?" doubted the king.

"Correction, My Lord, it's 32, to be precise" came the reply.

"About three or four of these fortifications form a cluster at a distance of about a 100 metres from each other. They are cramped quite tight" added the ever-smiling Sakta

Singh. "These are the sort of wooden confines about twelve foot high made of slender cylindrical tree trunks."

"These huddles are set in three rows. There are eight of these in a long row roughly at a distance of roughly about a 100 to 200 metres from each other" said a clean-shaven Amar Singh, his head still remaining fully bald. "They are pretty adjacent to each other. I would say these swarms of garrisons are spread over an area roughly about 2000 metres."

"What is the estimate about the troop numbers?" pressed the king.

"It could be between 8000 to 10000, My Lord" said Bama Shah. "Given the size of these structures, 10000 should be a fair estimate."

"We believe the Mughal cavalry units are residing in these command posts" Amar Singh noted. "We saw a plethora of horses harnessed in the close vicinity."

"I counted about 50 elephants tethered to massive stables scattered all around these barracks. I could see them clearly through my spyglass" cautioned Sakta Singh. "They have considerable firepower. The only exception seems to be the artillery guns. We did not see any."

"Are these wooden trunks encompassing these fortifications shaped like sharp-pointed objects at their ends?" elicited the king.

"Very much, My Liege. They have spike-like ends and they are joined one to another in a long, compact rows to make up the enclosures" confirmed Ram Singh. "Let me show you, sire."

He got up and gathered a number of twigs from here and there and snapped them in twos and threes and used a pointed gravel stone lying around to sharpen one of their ends in the form of spikes and planted them in the fashion of a rectangular garrison model. He also placed sticks on the ground by these miniature garrison models to indicate the position of the stables housing the horses and the elephants.

He continued his elaboration, "Every one of these strongholds has a broad door about eight-feet high in the same spiking fashion and they are manned by three soldiers perched on top on a scaffold from the inside. The third garrison on the front row has a major watchtower."

After a silence of about thirty seconds, the lodestar spoke, "I have decided to storm these barracks. The Mughals in Dewair must be put to the sword. Does anyone have a different opinion?"

There was silence among the cool of the drooping branches. The sun was beginning his descent in the west. An aura of orange glow began flooding the horizon.

"I understand we have lived without any major disturbance in the last seven months" went on the king. "However, hatred for the Mughals runs in my blood. It is stirring up my soul. My affections are in deep turmoil" said Prathap Singh as he shared his feelings, "I must act!"

"My Lord, the Mughals must be evicted not just from Mewar but from every inch of the Hind. Never mind what the other rajput clans have done with their honour. I shall be by your side, come what may!" burst out Ram Singh.

"So do I, brother" smiled Sakta Singh, "Death, after all comes in one fashion or the other, doesn't it?"

"My allegiance is something you can take for granted" said Amar Singh cheerfully.

Bama Shah sat observing the proceedings knowing that he was not the kind of person to go into the battlefield though he would be willing.

The sky was turning grey and the waning moon's silvery gaze silently became distinct in the far distance.

"We need our cavalry again" proposed the king to Ram Singh. "But not in a hurry. I would like you to have them ready in a month's time. Make sure we don't raise suspicions. Horses would always raise eyebrows. We are talking about many teams of studs. So, we need to be extra careful. I need all the 1000 steeds and their invincible

Mewari warriors. Exercise extreme caution in this matter. These men and the animals need to be housed carefully in different locations until the day we leave for the attack. The broncos especially must not blow our cover!"

"I understand the gravity, My Lord" replied a serious-looking Ram Singh. "These horses shall be arriving in fewer numbers from Sind through Gujarat or the other corridors and I shall ensure suspicions are not raised. We shall try to hoodwink the patrols."

"Sakta, see to the weapons" rumbled Prathap Singh.

"I shall" replied his brother-in-arms euphoniously and then added his latent smile.

"The Mughals seem to be at disadvantage here" noted Prathap Singh. "Their men in the barracks could be trapped in cramped conditions. Do these enclosures have emergency exits? I doubt it. Yet, there could be. Who is to know?"

"They have a new commander at Dewair, brother" reminded Sakta Singh. "A man called Sultan Khan. Quite a serious hand, I hear. Akbar has recalled Shabaz Khan, Mughal Mir Bakshi and the annoying Qutub-Udin-Khan."

"Really?" smiled Prathap Singh. "The talwars of Mewar shall test the combat fibre of this Sultan Kahn."

Everyone grinned. The king rose, as did the others and walked straight to the safety of the house. Darkness by now was beginning to set in the light of the horned moon.

"We shall finalise the details in the days to come. There would be a briefing. You shall be informed" said the king as he dismissed them.

CHAPTER 31

A DAYLIGHT DISHONOUR!

October 1582

It took about forty-five days for the safe conveyance of the 1000 horses and their cavalrymen from the Sind, traversing numerous routes in Gujarat, Punjab and the plain of the Indus to play the fool on the Mughal patrols and reach their safe havens in Mewar trickle by trickle. It was really tough given the increasing frequency of Akbar's sentinels coming in regular circuit.

The king convened yet another meeting for the final briefing for the Dewair strike by the massive trunk of the banyan tree one late afternoon. He was very relaxed, easy-going but focused.

"We are not going to look for new moons and darkness for this operation. We strike in broad daylight!" essayed the king.

"Would you elaborate, my brother?" asked Sakta Singh.

"The Mughals have left a skeletal strength of their forces in and around Kumbalgarh, Gogunda and other towns to maintain their grip. I believe those forces that were withdrawn were required elsewhere" he said as he intensely stared at his brother "There is nothing to be concerned about our attack even if the Mughals come to know about it at the eleventh hour. Their patrols are scattered all over Mewar."

"You mean they won't have the time to put together an army to resist us?" questioned Ram Singh.

"Precisely!" conceded Prathap Singh, "We are safe launching a brazen attack on these constricted Dewair garrisons in daytime. Since these barracks are set in the open plain, we don't have much advantage striking in the night. The advancing horse hooves would give us away anyway, be it day or night. Mughal patrols that challenge us enroute to Dewair must be neutralised."

"Would not the garrison troops be all the more ready to take on us if we choose to engage them in the day?" cautioned Bama Shah.

"Yes, they would scramble and be out of their confines to mount their horses. Such a scenario would be in our favour as we don't have to catapult ourselves into these enclosures to battle them in cramped spaces" suggested Prathap Singh "Once in the open, they would be jostling for positions and become nervous targets for our assault!"

"They do have an able commander!" countered Amar Singh.

"The horses could be reined in but the bulky elephants need ample time to get into battle stations. Would they get into formations to challenge the charging rajputs on horseback in a hurry?" said the hero from Mewar. "Once disoriented, it would be very difficult to get them into proper array. We must watch-out, however. There could be infantry present as well within the walls of these garrisons. We must be prepared to take on all three – the cavalry, the elephant-borne and the infantry."

"You have the very best of the veteran warriors who survived the battle at Haldigatti, My Liege" said Ram Singh with great pride.

"That's fine" smiled Prathap Singh in a reserved way. "I shall entrust you all to protect the horses with enough battle-gear. We could face a shower of arrows from these forts. All our men are to be shrouded with chainmail suits for extra guard. The sword, the spear, the bow and quiver are to be borne by all our warriors. The shield is to be slung on the back."

Four days after the second meeting, on a full moon night around twelve, 300 Mewar rajputs led by Ram Singh armed to the teeth and clad in impenetrable armour pulled up 20 kilometres from the house of Prathap Singh. They had killed 30 Mughal troops on horseback who were on patrol as usual, expecting it to be another dreary night. They were caught unprepared and had to pay with their own lives. Prathap Singh and Amar Singh joined the 300 shortly and the posse breezed through the moonlit night at a steady pace. About an hour later, at Udaipur they were joined by a contingent of 400 similar cavalry led by Sakta Singh. Finally, at about five in the morning this combined mass of cruising cavalry reached Eklingi where they were joined by the remaining 300 men on horseback led by an able captain. This unit too had to slaughter about 20 Mughals on patrol on their way to join the rest of their compatriots.

On reaching the banks of the Banas at Haldigatti, Prathap Singh came to a halt. Memories of the colossal battle with Akbar's military came flooding into his soul. He loitered off on his black steed for some time in the stone cluttered valley in the shadow of the Aravalli mountains leaving the rest to stare after him. The pain, the anguish, the slaughter, the loss and the trauma overwhelmed him for a moment. Did he not suffer the death of so many thousands of his men at the hands of Man Singh and his Mughals? Did not these banks turn into rivers of blood? Was not death stalking this valley that fateful day? Not to mention the thousands that died on the Mughal side too. The memories were overpowering his emotions. He returned to the contingent.

"We shall rest for a while" he said, dismounting. "You may all get off. The horses need a respite before we can proceed with the journey."

Ram Singh in full battle gear ambled towards his king, "You were right, My Lord" he said softly. "Why should you allow the Mughals free rein in Mewar considering the brutality that was unleashed against the rajputs here at Haldigatti?"

Prathap Singh shook his head, "They must feel my vengeance! They must pay the price for invading the realm of my ancestors. The Mughals have no place in Mewar. I would even boldly premise that they have no stake in the wide realm of the Hind!"

Amar Singh and Sakta Singh too joined the king in walking around the valley for some time in the cool of the approaching dawn.

"My land is courteous. My land is peaceable. My people are gentle, they are kind" mused Prathap Singh addressing Sakta Singh and then he exploded like a cannon-shell.

"The rajputs shall be ruled by a rajput! Not a foreigner! Not by a Mughal! No, never! On my dead body, no!"

The sudden outburst from the king startled many a horse. They began to prance, neigh and run wildly. This could have had a domino effect but the troops managed to pacify the animals with a lot of effort.

It was dawn and Prathap Singh hopped on his black stallion ever so lightly after almost an hour's break "Let's move" he commanded and the whole contingent started trotting for some time before settling down into a steady gallop.

They passed over mountains, valleys, hills, rocks, gullies, through thick woods, clearings and open plains. Three hapless Mughal patrols enroute of this thundering cavalry fell in no time to the spears of Pratap Singh's men.

It was around nine in the morning when the garrisons of Dewair slowly inched into the horizon in the distance.

"We shall break into the formations now" ordered the king and immediately the contingent broke up into three units. Amar Singh broke away from his father to head the last contingent made up of 300 cavalrymen.

Prathap Singh led the first 300 and Ram Singh and Sakta Singh led the largest with 400 men.

The body of three cavalry units heading straight for the garrisons immobilized the guards manning the doors for a moment. They realized the disaster that was heading straight for them out of nowhere! They found the use of their hands and sounded the alarm to indicate the imminent attack. Repeated alarms from the bugles had the resident troops, who just had their breakfast, rushing out in concern from their dorms in all garrisons. Arming themselves instantly, they rushed out of their miniature fortresses in total haste to witness the approaching mass of speeding horses. By this time, the three units of Prathap Singh's men were just about 300 metres away from the three rows of these bastions. In sheer panic, sporadic firing of arrows from the Mughals ensued. Mewar's rajputs restrained themselves from firing their arrows into the direction of the garrisons on the wing from their horses until the targets were within arrow range. Most of the incessant Mughal arrows missed while a few landed harmlessly on the well-protected armour of the advancing Mewar cavalrymen by now. The rajput arrows fired from dashing horses too missed their marks except for a few which accounted accidently for a small number of Mughals who fell.

Sultan Khan, the commander had by now rushed out and boarded the howdah of his war-elephant, with his mahout on his seat. He charged straight at Prathap Singh's cavalry with a dash of bravado. The three divisions of the rajput cavalry by now had reached the encampments.

Amar Singh's unit reached the last row of these fortresses only to find hundreds of panic-stricken Mughals rushing towards the stables, ascend their steeds and flee for dear life! However, many other hundreds who chose to challenge Mewar's cavalry led by the crown prince were killed after a very brief clash.

There was a tremendous trumpeting by the 50-odd Mughal war-elephants which were stupefied by the incredible charge unleashed by Prathap Singh. Many, unable to bear the hysteria, broke free from the stables and were running amuck with their chains yet fastened on their feet. Scores of horses too were overexcited by the noise of the charging steeds and began neighing and skipping madly in the stables. Ram Singh's contingent, which charged through the second row of the garrisons, was successful in cutting down scores of very disoriented Mughals, both cavalry and infantry, who were left to their own devices under such a circumstance.

Amid this noisy chaos, a battle broke out between the combined forces of a few thousand Mughals who succeeded in getting onto their stallions and Prathap Singh's unit. The spears of Mewar pierced through many a Mughal ribcage, many a Mughal heart, lung, liver, intestine and many went straight through their sturdy necks and some others managed to impale horses. Akbar's military was found wanting in all aspects to counter the spearheads of Prathap Singh's audacious rajputs. The Mughals found no time for strategy, tactics and simple common sense in the storm of the attack. Hundreds of others lost their lives and limbs in this sweeping assault. Unnumbered scores sustained grievous injuries. Mughal blood flowed freely and lavishly around these garrisons which were a silent witness to this calculated ruthless onslaught.

Prathap Singh came around the elephant of Sultan Khan. Amar Singh appeared with his troops from the oncoming direction.

"Amar!" yelled Pratap Singh, pointing to the elephant howdah "Kill this Mughal!"

The king and his troops proceeded to deal with the rest of the disoriented Mughals who were fighting to stay alive. Not more than 2000 of Akbar's men were left to fight the 1000 cavalry led by Prathap Singh. The remaining had fled for good!

The passion-possessed crown prince aimed a sharp spear right on the blank forehead of his enemy's war-elephant. He flung it with immense force. The spear rammed straight into the centre of the animal's brow and got lodged there. The shell-shocked pachyderm shook its mangled head violently, throwing the mahout on the ground and trampling him to death. It staggered like a ship out of control, trumpeting wildly and ran towards the safety of the mammoth-stables. Sultan Khan hung on for his life.

"A horse! A horse! Get me a horse!" he shrieked from the unsteady elephant that by now had a steady, voluminous stream of blood coming down the sides of its temples, the spear still embedded deeply in its strong, broad head. It suddenly tumbled gently down on its left side to die by the stables.

Sultan Khan alighted safely and jumped onto a horse that was kept ready by his cavalry which kept fending off Prathap Singh's attacks. The angry Mughal commander raised his shining talwar, "Come rajput! Where are you?" he screamed in madness and charged into battle at Prathap Singh's men.

Two Mewari cavalrymen who rushed to finish the Mughal found they had met their match in combat skills. He quickly put an end to their lives with the swashbuckling strokes of his sword.

Amar Singh charged forward and engaged the enraged Mughal singlehandedly. The sparring was intense and engrossing. Amar Singh's blood burned with the fervour of his father Prathap Singh that day. His moves became legendary, tiger-like, swift, deadly and agile. Sultan Khan was aghast at the proficiency of such a young rajput.

A slight hesitation on the Mughal's part saw Amar Singh's sword come down in lethal force on his foe's helmet, shattering it and sending the commander crashing to the ground along with his steed, his sword flying off to a short distance. Amar Singh dismounted and slammed his talwar with crushing force on the breastplate of his enemy. Sultan Khan, who was bleeding copiously from his head by now, collapsed on the beige soil. Amar Singh's talwar then proceeded to amputate the commander's head in one single, heavy blow.

A glimpse of the dead headless commander sent thousands of shell-shocked Mughals flying out of the battle zone in great haste towards Ajmer their major bastion. Their stallions galloped at great speed, sending clouds of dust billowing up in their wake as they fled for their lives.

Akbar's men lost the battle well and truly with their backs turned to the rajputs of Mewar despite their superior numbers!

A long bout of silence followed. It was broken by the approach of the king and his cavalry "Bravo, my son!" exclaimed the king of Mewar. "You have proved that the blood of lions flows in your veins! I am proud of you!"

Amar Singh threw the Mughal commander's head down in disgust.

Prathap Singh looked at Ram Singh, "How many did we lose?"

"We lost 20 brave souls" said his aide with a heavy heart.

"Remove their remains. Perform the last rites without any undue delay, right away! Let us make haste to return. Ajmer is not too far. Akbar's henchmen have fled on horseback. They could return with vengeance" ordered the king.

The cavalry proceeded to fetch long, wooden trunks from the garrison hedges for the cremation.

"Set fire to each of these complexes" commanded Prathap Singh, "I want these structures to be burnt down! Nothing should remain."

Oil found within the fortresses was doused on anything standing and set ablaze. Within thirty minutes, thirty-two garrisons went up in a blaze of netherworld-fire. The spectacle of the blazing firestorms was absolutely astonishing!

Prathap Singh was defying the mighty Mughals and getting away with it. The sight of the 20 dead rajputs on the burning pyres hardened his heart into never reaching a compromise with Akbar. The Mughals remained a foreign race in his eyes.

The whole wide area was littered with the remains of dead Mughals and scores of swords, spears, shields and arrows. The weapons outnumbered the lifeless bodies.

Having completed the formalities, the king addressed his troops, "We shall remain on guard against these aliens. They will try to wreck revenge for this attack. They won't take this lying down. You cavalrymen shall return to the safety of your hideouts in the Sind until you are called for. You shall deliver death to any Mughal patrol infantry or cavalrymen that challenge you enroute. Make sure you are not being followed or being observed. That is very important. Keep shifting your hideouts if you feel unsafe. If for any reason you are taken captive by these foreigners, stay faithful. For a rajput, death is more honourable than disloyalty. Never betray your king, his family, nor his commanders. Farewell."

Shouts of "Long live Maharana Prathap Singh!" filled the air.

The Mewari forces left the battle zone at Dewair that morning with the garrisons still on conflagration and their dead reduced to ashes on the pyres.

CHAPTER 32

TOO MANY RODS IN THE FIRE

October 1582

The Mughal czar sat high on his regal throne encompassed by his colourful courtiers that fine morning. The court was bustling as usual with delightful ambience. Most of the men present in the royal hall had their eyes fixed on the monarch. Standing before him in silence were Shabaz Khan, Mughal Mir Bakshi and Qutub-Udin-Khan donning black military fatigues and holding long, upright lethal spears.

The undulating air from the waving of the fans to his left cooled the emperor's face as he took one long look at the frustration on the faces of his commanders.

"Your Grace, Prathap Singh has destroyed the garrisons at Dewair. We have lost more than a 1000 soldiers.

Commander Sultan Khan is martyred. Seven horseback patrol units in Mewar have also been eliminated," began Shabaz Khan's in a terse manner.

The emperor rubbed his right eyebrow for a moment. He turned towards the rajputs and the Mughals in royal attire on his right. He kept staring at them for some time. They returned his stare in solemn silence.

He then faced his stalwart, "Commander Shabaz Khan, the three of you shall leave for Dewair right away with a force of 5000 cavalry. Accord a proper burial for the bodies of Sultan Khan and the others, if you can locate their remains. You are to return once the protocols are completed. Proceed."

As they were leaving through the main entrance into the throne room, Abul-Fazl the vizier began, "Must we not—"

Akbar cut him short rudely. "This is not the day to discuss Prathap Singh, vizier. We shall have such a deliberation another day." He then smiled at him in a respectful manner.

The rest of his courtiers held their peace. Man Singh Amber having returned from the campaign in Punjab did not bat an eyelid. Birbal, for once, chose silence. Todar Mal, the astute, was ever watchful and Mulla Do-Piyazo and Faizi kept exchanging glances. Tansen looked at his emperor with concern at his strange loss of temper. Abdul Karim Khan thought this carnage could have been avoided had the Mughal mainstay forces not been pulled back.

Birbal felt the urge to counsel the scion given his clout with the emperor. He, however, decided on holding his peace again. The bustling sound of the court returned as the emperor regained his composure.

The three commanders and the 5000 cavalrymen left for Dewair that fair morning with broad, blazing battle standards of the Mughal empire displaying the ascending tawny male lion with its long, swaggering tail, the rising Sun behind it and the vertical white strip with three red and green triangles.

Shabaz Khan was mad with fury as he rode his chestnut brown horse swiftly. Neither Mughal Mir Bakshi nor Qutub-Udin-Khan dared to pose any questions given their superior's short temper.

The contingent reached the battle-site at two O'clock in the afternoon the next day. They could see slender plumes of dark smoke rising into the sky a day after the attack from about a kilometre away! They could also see vultures hovering high in the sky over the burnt garrisons. Many corpses were being plundered by these arial scavengers on the ground already. Quite a few jackals and wolves were also found chewing at the dead bodies strewn all over the two-kilometre wide site. The scene was one of utter devastation. It was total carnage! All the garrisons were destroyed beyond salvation. The smoke kept ascending very slowly producing a surreal feeling. The only living souls found in that eerie location were the bewildered war elephants that survived the onslaught and were left as they were by the forces of Prathap Singh.

As the cavalry came trotting around the three rows of the destroyed garrisons, they had no difficulty locating the remains of Sultan Khan in the foremost row.

"Commander!" called out Mughal Mir Bakshi.

Shabaz Khan came around on his steed to the entrance of the third garrison in the front row.

Sultan Khan's head was nailed to the lintel of the door with a long iron peg straight through the centre of his forehead. His headless body was left hanging from the watchtower by a heavy rope. Large crowds of cavalrymen gathered to have a look at the macabre spectacle.

"May I do the same thing to you, rajput!" growled Shabaz Khan in deep anger. "We will get you! You just wait! Would I not hang you in the same manner? It won't be long! It won't be long!"

At this horrific sight, the Mughal cavalry began yelling, "Death to Prathap Singh! Death to Mewar!"

The entire company went about digging mass graves for their dead and conducting the burials. Sultan Khan's body was buried in an isolated grave far from those of others.

Having completed the rituals in about two hours, Shabaz Khan and his cavalrymen loitered around for some time, gazing at the distant terrain for human activity with their spyglasses. With one final look at the graves, Shabaz Khan led the cavalry brigade that late afternoon on a gentle trot towards the stronghold of Fatehpur Sikri. The surviving jumbos were led away by some of the Mughal cavalrymen doubling as mahouts.

Meanwhile, on a star-filled night in Chavand, Kanwar, sat on an armchair close to the bed gazing at her lord sleeping blissfully on a cotton mattress in the basement of their hideout. The room was filled with the miniscule lights of multiple circular oil-filled earthen lamps. Her anklets kept chiming due to the repeated movement of her left heel being lifted by the ankle of her right heel.

Prathap Singh awoke, turned over on his back and pulled her closer by seizing both of her bracelet-decked arms.

"So, is everything fine, my love?" he wondered.

"Shouldn't I be the one asking you that, My Lord?" she countered. She then pushed his hair covering his forehead back into its place after releasing her right hand forcibly. "How did things go at Dewair?" she enquired.

"Kanwar sweetie, everything went fine. Sometimes plans work to perfection. Such flawlessness shocks you. The strike was a great success. We lost very few men. We destroyed their garrisons and put them to flight."

He rose, washed his face and sat on his bed.

"So, would there be another strike, My King?" she insisted still seated on her chair.

Prathap Singh drew a big heaving sigh, "I hope not. I don't wish to strike, My Queen. I have incensed them enough. They are bubbling with wrath. I must lie low for some time. Quite a long time. We will not be staying here for long. We have to move. Kumbalgarh, Gogunda and Chittor are calling my soul! Would I ever set foot there again?"

He rose again pulling her left hand. She rose. He stopped, pulled her face close and spoke looking straight in her eyes, "I have no idea when we would return to the throne of my ancestors. It may not happen in my lifetime, my love. I cannot fight fate."

She encircled his neck with her silver-bangled hands, "I never, ever asked you to fight fate. I always urged you to go with its flow."

"I will, my dear" he answered, "with you by my side" he placed her glowing-red henna painted left hand on his right cheek firmly. "Your love is my fire."

He kissed her stunning nose, bearing a dazzling, diamond pin many times. "I believe we shall soon be leaving for a place far away from here. Maybe the banks of the Indus. I am not sure where. I am working out the details. We are leaving. We have to. It is dangerous to be put up in one place for far too long." He then left for the terrace to get a breath of fresh air.

It was a bright day in March 1583 when the Mughal court gathered in session. The ostentatious display of power, might, authority and glory were there for all to see.

Akbar, the monarch felt he had waited long enough. He contemplated action against Mewar again. Something was holding him back "Prathap Singh is repeatedly going too far. However, there is troubling news from the Hindu Kush and beyond. The Afghan rebellion is simmering again. Those tribes in the heights are up in arms at the moment. Mirza Mohammed Hakim tasted military defeat at the hands of my Mughal army a year ago. He was humbled by Man Singh Amber, Raja Birbal and Raja Bagwan Das. He is currently under house arrest. His very existence is quietly instigating these Yousufzai ruffians. Desires don't die that easily, do they? Maybe, I should have him executed" surmised the Mughal chief on a scathing tone.

"I believe every time the empire takes action, these rebels make a beeline for the mountaintops in the central highlands. They still have sympathizers among the tribesmen of the Tajiks, the Uzbeks and the Kyrgyz. It may not be necessarily your defeated half-brother" observed Abdul Rahim Khan. "Once they reach these realms, it is difficult to hunt them down. They return to the Afghan mountains after we wind up our campaign. It is an endless cycle, My Lord."

Birbal rose from his seat, something he normally did not do "We need a string of garrisons all along the mountain range on the other side of the Hindu Kush from the north to the south-west all the way to the Arabian Sea blocking the exit of these rebels through the narrow passes, My Lord."

Akbar smiled "If we chop the head of this nefarious snake, the body will lose its venom. We shall deal with the head first. Prathap Singh on the other hand, has mastered the art of surprising us time and again. We should not walk into his trap repeatedly like fools. Should we not prefer a long break in our pursuit of this rajput?"

"Would that not embolden him, My Liege?" asked Faizi with his narrow cherry-red beard that flowed down his chin to his chest.

"It will and it shall. Nevertheless, overconfidence could ultimately be his undoing. Let's bank on that" proposed Akbar. "Mewar has no political or military alliances with the other rajput clans. The fiefdom stands totally cut-off in its rebellion against Fatehpur Sikri. My flag flies over Mewar's terrain. On the other hand, there are thousands of Afghan renegades and they seem to be organized and inspired. The latter seems to be the danger right, front and centre."

Todar Mal and Birbal instantly exchanged glances in full view of Akbar.

Mal, the buxom administrator-general cut in. "My Lord, if you do not deal with Prathap Singh's brazen behaviour it would be construed as blatant defiance."

Birbal seconded. "You cannot allow that. This rajput is shaking his fist at your face. His attacks are an open insubordination to your sovereignty. You have to go after him."

"I believe we have already failed in this venture to finish him, haven't we?" remarked an embittered Faizi throwing a quick sarcastic glance at Abdul Karim Khan who was annoyed by this move. "With all due respect, My Liege, we have been trying to annihilate Prathap Singh for about six years now and there is no end in sight. He has struck five times killing scores of Mughals. Hundreds of our troops in fact have lost their lives against him in combat. If our attempts to destroy him cannot be deemed a failure, what word do you use? Did not the emperor Humayun, your father, accept defeat when he was dethroned by the Pathan, Sher Shah Suri? We too have been dealt decisive blows by this 'Sher' Prathap Singh. What stops us from accepting our debacles? Pride, perhaps?"

He again looked at Abdul Karim Khan, the defence in-charge, who was exasperated by now. "Should there not be some accountability for the lives lost on our side? Did our men die in vain?"

A conglomerate of voices advising, "Calm down, Faizi," led by Abul Fazl, rose that morning in the palatial hall. The astute monarch understood the fraying tempers of his intellectuals and the impulsive reactions of seasoned top cats of the likes of the Yemenite Faizi.

"The empire is growing" observed the czar in a calm and composed manner. "More and more kingdoms of Hindustan are prostrating themselves before our military might. This burgeoning phenomenon is keeping me up night and day. I am unable to leave Fatehpur Sikri for practical reasons. Yet, the Afghans sympathizing with the Mirza Hakim narrative must be dealt a death blow. I hope they are not colluding with the Safavids of Persia. I shall see to that. Prathap Singh is observing all our moves in Mewar. He takes calculated risks. When he strikes, he strikes hard. He has certainly defied us in our repeated efforts to capture him. We are distracted in other locations, otherwise the empire's might would have dealt with him long ago."

There was a protracted silence among the cabinet members as the bustle of the throne room filled everybody's ears.

At length, Birbal spoke. "What are we going to do about this fluid menace in Mewar that is costing us hundreds of lives every time he pounces, My King?"

Akbar nodded. "The fruit shall fall when it is ripe. The north-western border is of vital significance than one man who seems to be on the run."

Tansen was inspired that very moment. "An unripe fruit can be felled by a swift flying arrow. Is not this fruit moving in the wind?"

"Very much, my muse!" remarked the exhilarated ruler. "Very much! But this is an instance of an archer galloping on horseback targeting a fruit moving in the wind. Not an easy task. The fruit is swaying back and forth in the strong breeze and we have not been able to bring it down with our arrows. It is a kind of a high-hanging fruit. No wonder!"

Faizi persisted. "So, My Lord, have we failed vis-à-vis Prathap Singh?"

Mulla-Do Piyazo, palpably incensed by the foolhardiness of his colleague, moved in. "Brother Faizi, do not presume failure where there seems to be a deadlock. The stalemate will not endure forever. Why do you make a hero of this rajput? Must you annoy His Highness?"

Akbar looked with concern at Faizi, the royal mentor of the Mughal princes for a moment. Before the monarch could make an answer, Todar Mal decided to air his view. "Victory always seems to be waiting at the turn of the corner" he said in a religious tone. "Perseverance holds the key."

Not one to bolt from an argument, Faizi shot back, "Just how long do you persevere? Will we keep paying Mughal blood time and again in the name of perseverance?" His long, sleek, ruddy beard quivering to-and-fro repeatedly as he spoke, "Your commander was beheaded and his crown nailed to the doorpost of the garrison. Should you still persevere?"

Raja Birbal sensed his opportunity, but hesitated to add fuel to the fire. Nevertheless, he spoke diplomatically. "My Liege, we must keep up the pressure. Prathap Singh's actions could inflame the Afghan anarchists."

Todar Mal kept staring at his lord for a long time. Akbar returned the stare momentarily. There was silence in the courtroom except for the gentle hustle of the courtiers moving ever so softly.

"We shall act." opined a serious-looking Akbar. "I wish to remind you all that Mewar has been fully integrated as a province of the empire. We have a problem with this heroic rajput. His luck will not be permanent. Since we have been used to succeeding militarily over and over again, there is a sense of despondency. I wish to put you all in remembrance — my army eliminated Hemu, my army slaughtered Sikander Shah Suri, my army defeated Daud Khan, my army crushed the Queen of Gondwana, my army also defeated Mirza Mohammed Hakim. Did not the Mughal armies deal with the Lodis? Countless others are lining up to make up this illustrious list of losing to the Mughals! Should I be impressed by a fleeting rajput? In warfare, things always don't go your way. Yes, we have suffered real setbacks against Prathap Singh. He has truly proved himself to be a 'Rana' of the rajputs. Maybe even a 'Maharana'. He loves to be branded 'The rajput lion Maharana Prathap Singh'. I concede that he has outwitted me. The story is not over yet. My Mughal sword was reluctant to decapitate Hemu. It shall not vacillate to behead Prathap Singh should I cross his path in person."

Raja Birbal fully aroused by Akbar's resolve rose and began pulling his flashing sword from his sheath.

"No, not you, Birbal" smiled the czar. "Those vagabonds on the Afghan mountains await your sword yet again, not Prathap Singh. I shall dispatch you to the northern mountains in a short time."

CHAPTER 33

INTO THE WILD AND BACK

January 1584

The efficacy of the Mughal administration was something which made the empire proud. It was well-oiled and produced desired outcomes. Except in cases that got the imperium all tangled up, it lived up to its expectations. Nevertheless, there were times when apex sub-rosa decisions became unofficial rumours in the palace much to the chagrin of Akbar. One such matter was the dispatch of a force 30,000 strong heading to Mewar for hunting down Prathap Singh yet again.

Ironically, this vital information decided upon at a closed-door meet at Fatehpur Sikri by Akbar and his aides reached Mewar well in advance. The prince of Mewar had his rajput sympathisers by now at Fatehpur Sikri who were in the know of the grapevine on confidential matters and who having realized the exemplary courage of a prince of their own race, had this crucial information relayed on to Prathap Singh's inner circle via their interlocutors.

The Mewar overlord wasted no time. He decided to shelve his move to the banks of the Indus. He rather chose to venture into the forests of Mewar.

Early morning, the day after receiving this intelligence, Prathap Singh, Kanwar and the children left together quite boldly as one unit on horseback heading straight for the dense foliage of Mewar's forest fortress.

They were not intercepted either by Fatehpur Sikri's cavalry or infantry patrols. The king was quite sure this was not going to happen.

Ram Singh in a farmer's guise and Sakta Singh in the masquerade of a sadhu accompanied them. They walked across lush green stretches of fertile land enclosed by high rising mountain plateaus. They crisscrossed the low-lying valleys between the hills and the heights. They kept travelling until they reached the outlying areas of the dense jungles of Mewar after two days. The adolescent children were thoroughly exhausted by the journey. The team ventured into the thicket for about an hour's distance till they reached what looked like a safe place to spend the night - a broad, lengthy cave on an elevated rocky outcrop right in the middle of nowhere. Though the entrance was overgrown with the undergrowth, it had a high arching ceiling. It was also spacious and dry but bore the lingering smell of a large animals, probably bears, leopards or tigers. It was large enough to house about eight people. An immensely big Indian almond tree sprouting strong, lengthy boughs and green and red clusters of fruit stood right by the cave offering the much-desired shade. The immediate area surrounding the cave was littered with fully ripe, leaf-shaped pinkish-red almond fruit.

Prathap Singh began clearing the area around the cave. The creeping plants with their lengthy tendrils and vines and the bushes with their bright flowers and the thorny shrubs were hewn down and disposed of. The king, his wife and the four children bid adieu to Ram Singh and Sakta Singh shortly. The family began to settle down in the den in the falling darkness amidst the noise of the creatures that inhabited the dense jungle.

The heavy buzzing sound of the cicadas was resonating through the wide, thick woodland. Other unidentified sounds and noises soon began to emanate from everywhere in that forestland in quite a sporadic manner. In the far distance the family heard what sounded like the heavy, distinct, metallic roar of a tiger.

"Are those a tiger's bellows?" questioned Kanwar in the yellow crackling fire around which the family had gathered.

"They could be" replied her husband with a sense of anticipation knowing fully well that they were indeed the growls of the big cat.

A fire was prepared at the wide entrance of the cave that gave enough light all the way to the end of the facility. Prathap Singh laid his weapons down and sat with his back to the wall near the inlet of the cave. Thousands of fireflies soon commenced flashing their tiny lights in a weird, repeated manner to add a sense of mystery to the darkness that was settling down on the wood. The royals consumed a humble meal in almost near silence in the light of the wooden torches. They later went to bed on the rocky floor which was made with whatever bedding material they had bought with them. The buzzing insects attracted by the light of the burning fire provided immense discomfort for the family trying to sleep that night.

As they were about to ease into sleep in that unfamiliar woodland realm, they were all shaken by the continuous, loud grunting of a leopard in the short distance. Prathap Singh, still resting with his back to the wall, pulled his spear and kept it at the ready on his lap. He could clearly see the clear pair of brilliant yellow eyes of the big cat staring at him from about fifty feet away and then disappearing into the darkness.

How incredibly their lives had been transformed, thought Kanwar. From being luminaries in Mewar they had been reduced to nomads on the run, seeking shelter in the heart of the unknown, surrounded by annoying insects and formidable predators. Would it get worse than this? Who is to know? Being alive seemed to be of paramount importance at that moment. No one wished to think of the future. It was scary.

The queen then began whispering the choicest of curses on the Mughals. She cursed their progeny, their culture and their values. She cursed their roots "Akbar! You villain, may your Mughals become dust on the ground to be trampled by the sons of Hind!" exploded Kanwar with a sudden outburst. Her four children, already in discomfort in the cave, awoke startled from their disturbed sleep.

"Kanwar, dear!" said Prathap Singh as he walked to the spot where she lay. A pair of aesthetic but agitated eyes stared at him in deep anger. He placed his right hand on her saree-covered forehead. "Calm down, my love. Your grief is not going to change anything. Our lives are fulfilling the fate they were born to accomplish. Your anguish is not going to influence its outcome. Go to sleep. We can only wish things change for the better."

She gripped his arm with both her chiming bangle-decked hands, closed her eyes and drew a long, deep breath.

Dawn brought little comfort except for a myriad of chirping birds filling the forest with mellifluous sounds. The king got on his horse and went about exploring the proximity of the cave armed with his spear and sword.

He would have trotted on for about ten minutes when the wood began to encompass him with different sights, sounds and signs. There were scores of black buck, chital and nilgai deer. They were browsing in the near distance. He could also see a few elephants in the far expanse of the forest. He did hear the yapping of what sounded like a bear in the near distance but could not actually see the animal in the thick greenery. Langur monkeys perched atop different trees in the dense forest were seen jumping from tree to tree in wanton freedom. The king could also see quite a lot of peahens and a few magnificent, blue-necked peacocks with their long trail of green and dull-yellow feathers feeding in a clearing not too far away. There were mongoose scampering around, green parrots creating tremendous chatter in the high branches, hawks flying overhead and he could again hear the snarling of a leopard though he was unable to pinpoint it in the branches of the trees or on the forest floor. Flirting butterflies, buzzing bees and sleek-waisted wasps were racing about with their business of gulping nectar from the unnumbered flowers that grew in every nook and corner. Leaf-cutter ants made a beeline on the forest-floor to carry away chopped pieces of vegetation.

He also thought he heard the unmistakable cute purring of bear cubs somewhere among the distant thick clusters of eucalyptus trees. Did he see black blobs whizzing down the trunks in a hurry? He was not sure. He could however see what resembled sleek, brown-yellow, near crescent-shaped beehives projecting downwards sporadically from the spreading branches of those trees.

The whole sylvan region was abuzz with frantic activity that morning. In the midst of that frenzy there was peace. He felt serene, calm and in unison with nature. He began to take in that peace into his emotions, but he knew too well that he was not destined to spend his life experiencing such a state of peace.

He quickly turned around, returned to his family and found his wife and four children walking about in the vicinity of the cave to sample berries on the bushes.

"So, what is to be done, My Lord?" posed Kanwar.

"We stay here for a while to sense if we can hang on. If…" replied the king.

"And what if we don't?" asked Kanwar raising her thick striking bow-like right eyebrow.

"Then, we will have to look elsewhere to stay put. That may probably be the banks of the Indus" said the king in an unconvincing tone as he dismounted.

"Why do you feel so reluctant about the Indus?" assayed Kanwar.

"The Mughals cannot be under-estimated. Their spies could be anywhere, especially in highly populated regions like the Sind" explained the King. "We would be running a big risk."

She kept keeping her husband in an eye-lock for a tense moment as they sat on the floor of their forest dwelling.

"So, could we carry on our business of living in this wood, My Lord? For how long?" she queried.

"We are here for the short term, dear. We live from day to day. Who knows if we could be leaving for a better place all of a sudden?" he replied with a hint of expectation. "Who knows?"

Meanwhile, the special force to hunt down Prathap Singh had well and truly arrived in Mewar with the usual gusto – cavalry, infantry, artillery, war-elephants and a new man in charge, another rajput prince from the Amber region. A trusted aide of the emperor.

The force settled down in the vicinity of the Kumbalgarh Fort. For tactical reasons, the fort itself was secured with enough manpower and proofed against any form of invasion. After a week or so began the usual spreading of the dragnet to capture Prathap Singh with day and night patrols, combing of the towns and villages and the cavalry investigating the numerous hills and mountains for possible hideouts. Nothing seemed to work in favour for the Mughals and their servants. It was quite frustrating for the newly appointed commander and his troops to be put into this task of looking for a man whom the Mughals had failed to neutralise for this long. The force was very demoralized and out of focus.

No one in the Mughal camp ever thought of venturing into the dense woodland in search of the elusive Prathap Singh. It just didn't cross their minds. The apathetic search for the prince of Mewar dragged on for about two months. One final act of rummaging through the villages and towns of Mewar for possible hideouts of the king and his family yielded no results. Eventually Fatehpur Sikri called off the mission after more than three months, much to the relief of the armed men. The Mughals made a complete retreat.

Prathap Singh's family by now had gotten used to the life in the forest. They had become so one with the elements that made up their new environs. Provisions were brought in every fortnight by either Sakta Singh or Ram Singh. The peace and quiet offered by the forests of Mewar coupled with the blissful ignorance of the Mughals of his presence there made it an oblivion from which he was unwilling to relocate.

Three days after the Mughal exit, Sakta Singh with his flowing locks in the company of Ram Singh turned up on horseback in the intense heat of the day at the camp site in the forest.

"The latest force has left for good, My Lord" said a smiling Ram Singh. "Failure was staring them in the eyes."

"They must be feeling the futility of trying to hunt you down by now, mustn't they?" questioned Sakta Singh.

"So, just how many forays would the Mughals keep making before backing off every instance? Every time they come here, it's a spectacle" said Prathap Singh.

"So what of this forest, my brother? Is the day-to-day life getting on reasonably well?" asked Sakta Singh with concern.

"We are blessed to remain alive here" answered the king. "There is great disturbance in the nights from buzzing insects. Two days back a leopard came calling. It was a close encounter. It had to be shouted away."

Loud barks from a group of chital deer nearby and the immediate fleeing of the gentle ruminants again alerted Prathap Singh to the presence of the big, four-legged predator close by. "It's a large male and is getting bolder by the day" observed the king.

"Maybe the next time you have an encounter with the beast you should treat it like your foe the Mughals and send the spear through its heart" suggested Ram Singh. "Leopards are capable of taking on humans, you know. Their necks are super strong."

"The beast lives in its natural state. We are the ones intruding into its domain. So, I shall not harm it in anyway" advised the king. "It is probably missing its usual perch on the branches of this tree" he pointed to the astronomic Indian almond tree with its immense foliage and lovely green and dark red fruit, almost completely blocking the sun's rays from reaching the ground. The chirrups and the alarm calls of the squirrels chasing each other on the tree echoed through the forest.

"We are not going to retrieve Kumbalgarh and Gogunda" said Prathap Singh on a sad note. "That is going to take an immense undertaking. We shall have to be content if the Mughals leave us in peace in this part of Mewar. As for Chittor, I can only dream of the city. Amar Singh will have to attempt retaking it. It shall not happen in my lifetime."

Then the king remembered something which he had forgotten by oversight "There are wild boars in this forest, do you know? Huge ones, quite huge. One particular animal had lower canines half the size of my hand. I slowly crept upon them the other day. Am I excited to see them!"

"Wild boar! Wow!" exclaimed Sakta Singh. "Hunting boars are a sign of martial skills and a test of a man's bravery!"

"It was something I was obsessed with during my youth" joined in Ram Singh.

"I had to slay a boar before my coronation" observed the king. "It's part of our tradition here in Mewar."

"It would be exciting, brother, to hunt down at least one, a big one to pass your time" remarked Sakta Singh.

Kanwar smiled from inside the cave. So, from hunting the Mughals in battle, it's now time to hunt boars? Why not, is it not good if the king has something interesting to do like a boar-hunt? How else does he spend his time?

The two trusted aides got on their horses as the king went about on his own to show them around the surrounding thicket and the distant mountains. They kept talking on horseback for a few minutes before the two confidantes left the king to the care of the forest.

Prathap Singh hardly slept every night. He always kept a watchful eye through the gloom, particularly suspecting an imminent attack from the male leopard or expecting a bear to show up. A healthy fire was kept ablaze throughout the night to scare any advancing predator that was curious enough to investigate the smell of homo sapiens. The worst-case scenario was to have a tiger encounter or a herd of monstrous elephants which would absolutely leave the family horrified beyond words. Except for the male leopard encounters, there had been no run-ins with other creatures of the wood.

Two weeks later, Ram Singh and Sakta Singh showed up early in the morning soon after dawn. Prathap Singh got them seated on the rocky floor of the spacious den.

"I have made a decision to return to Chavand" said the king.

This took everyone by surprise, including his consort. She kept staring at him for a time.

"Back to Chavand, My Lord?" inquired Ram Singh.

"Yes, back to the same secure hideaway" came the answer.

"So, what—" began Sakta Singh.

"I feel it is safe to gamble that the Mughal army would not be returning to Mewar" postulated Prathap Singh interrupting his brother "My haunch is that their tactics have backfired. They are angry at themselves."

"When do you plan to leave, brother?" asked Sakta Singh with a fleeting smile.

"Why not now?" offered Prathap Singh.

"Now? Right away?" quizzed his brother.

After a moment's silence that was shattered by the chatter of the squirrels up in the almond tree, Ram Singh said, "My Liege, we leave now as you say. Let's go."

A mildly bewildered Kanwar and the kids packed whatever little belongings they had with them and mounted the horses. So, off they went leaving the beauty of the forest to itself and the almond tree to the male leopard who had felt its absence ever since the family moved into the cave.

Three hours later, the family was housed safe and sound in the sprawling basement of the Chavand safe haven. As they settled down to its comforts Kanwar and the children felt relieved by the very thought of being free from the annoying bugs.

Life began limping back to normalcy for the royal family after their return from the woods of Mewar. In fact, it became very typical sans the fortresses of Kumbalgarh and Gogunda.

Two months down the line, there was no sign of any Mughal military activity in Mewar - no patrols, no largescale invasion, no commanders entering towns and villages in pomp and splendour to throw their weight around. The king began venturing openly in broad daylight. He was beginning to lose a sense of caution about Akbar's war machine. The only thing that was possibly a source of concern was betrayal by traitors in Mewar who could exchange information about his location for a monetary benefit. Even that concern wore away with the reassurance given by the painful scars Mewar had borne, especially in Chittor. No rajput worth his salt in Mewar would dare to engineer such a treachery. The king, the queen, Amar Singh, Sakta Singh and the rest of the cabinet including Ram Singh and Bama Shah began openly meeting under the outstretched arms of the monumental banyan tree. The tree's shade became the fixed location for frequent briefings, meetings and intense discussions. The public in the proximity became aware of the royals' presence. Many started filing in to greet the king, the queen and the other royals. This had to be regulated with the deployment of guards. Word started spreading thick and fast about the royals being safe and sound and the king in absolute gung-ho. All of Mewar was now aware of Prathap Singh's presence at Chavand.

Six months into the arrival at their cellar hideout, life seemed to have taken a completely new turn with no sign of the Mughals in the horizon.

"The other rajput fiefdoms must have now been briefed about my presence in Mewar" noted the king as the truncated cabinet met one evening on the terrace of the safe-haven in the cool breeze "Surely Akbar must have taken cognizance too. I am sure he would have."

"He would very well have, brother" replied an ever-smiling Sakta Singh. "He doesn't have the appetite to come after you, does he?"

"Who knows?" replied Prathap Singh "We should always be ready to take evasive action. Nothing is certain. The Mughal emblem is the lion. What if the lion lies crouching, hidden from our sight? We could be making a big mistake. Let us be wary every day."

Another two months passed without any major untoward incident involving the Mughals and Prathap Singh. The king wished to spend the rest of his days in relative peace and quiet, having made his military gallantry very clear to his foes and taking the moral high ground. His fame had spread far and wide even into the realms of Persia.

"It's almost a year since the Mughals quit from here" noted Prathap Singh. "I have no idea what is going through Akbar's mind. I need to govern these areas of Mewar that are free of Mughal interference. I need a decent-looking palace. If it can be called that way."

"You mean another fortress like Kumbalgarh?" demanded Amar Singh.

"Are we not going a bit too far in putting up a palace here at Chavand?" questioned Sakta Singh. "It might trigger a large-scale action by Fatehpur Sikri."

"My people are without a king, without direction, without leadership. They need to know that I am still defying the Mughals. They need to know that rajput honour, values and culture are still being upheld. Imagery carries immense power. We have a moral obligation to project such boldness" countered the king.

"My Liege" began Ram Singh "Your expectation is just. You should have a royal residence here. My suggestion is that you wait for another month and should the Mughals refuse to show any indication of action, you proceed with the construction."

"That sounds good, brother" said Sakta Singh. "Just another month."

"So be it" agreed the king.

With no action happening yet after another month, Prathap Singh proceeded with the construction of a solid residence just on the outskirts of Chavand that could function as his palace and provide some privacy for the queen and the children. A place to receive people, have meetings and plan future action.

The king moved in once the palace stood on its legs. Finally, Kanwar and her adolescent children had the princely comforts to which they were used to.

The king openly began reinforcing his residence with the remnants of his army that had survived Haldigatti and his repeated assaults on Mughal targets. They approximately numbered 2000 troops. There was no way in which he could take on the Mughals with such a miniscule force. The Mewari cavalry in Sind stayed put in the vicinity of the region to avoid running into the regular Mughal army.

Days turned into weeks. The sun rose and set day in and day out. The steady drone of the passing days became a typical event at Chavand. Things began to be taken for granted. There was laughter, sweetness, joy and happiness in the royals' household once again. The weeks gradually turned into months. This cycle almost repeated itself for about two years. There was peace, quiet, tranquillity and serenity in that part of Mewar. There was simply no sign of the Mughals. Were they gone for good? Any glimpse of an approaching fearsome Mughal army would have to be spotted far well in advance for an evacuation of Prathap Singh, Kanwar and his children. Still, the very premise of going after the king of Mewar to crush any sense of insurgency being given up by Akbar made no sense. But why? Neither Prathap Singh nor his aides had any clue.

The massive Mughal army that Prathap Singh had been expecting for quite a few months was now heading from Fatehpur Sikri armed to the teeth for the mountains of the Hindu Kush and not into Mewar. The emperor was pleased to dispatch his favourite bureaucrat Raja Birbal to deal with the Afghan firebrands who were repeatedly launching guerrilla attacks on Mughal targets in the north-western regions of the empire for quite some time. The army was 20,000 strong and was composed of infantry, the cavalry, the archers and a healthy number of war-elephants. The battle-hardened commander seated atop his impressive, armoured tusker felt his blood rushing to slay the Yusufzai tribe that openly claimed that Mirza Mohammed Hakim, the deceased half-brother of the emperor's lineage ought to rule them and not Akbar and his dynasty.

"They should be finished once and for all by my army led by Birbal" observed the czar. "Hakim's henchmen shall fly like dry leaves in a storm."

"They sure will, My Lord" joined in Todar Mal.

"These Yusufzai hoodlums are as good as dead!" stated the vizier, Abul Fazl.

"You spoke about the head of the snake, didn't you, My King?" spurred on Mulla Do-Piyazo, his face enclosed in his thick, luscious beard.

"If those Afghan vandals believe that their insurgent theatrics is going to make me buckle under their demands, they got it all wrong" Akbar's eyes enlarged in irritation. "My brother is dead. I have sent him to his grave! Maggots must be feeding on his defunct body!"

There was silence in the royal hall for a moment. The hustle of the courtiers tangled in the official deliberations became the only voice to be audible in the courtroom.

"Your Majesty should have considered incarcerating Mirza Hakim for life. Was he not your brother? You could have avoided this eruption" reasoned Faizi, his sleek red beard gushing with logic.

"Mirza Hakim was also the blood of Humayun and the blood of Babur" reasoned Tansen "Would not the tree crash to the ground once it dies by its roots?"

"The blood of Babur and the blood of Humayun?" demanded Akbar in a fractious manner as he felt the cool breeze of his courtier's fans. "My sibling Hakim dared to rise his heel against me, advancing towards Punjab with his huge cavalry. He was a grave threat to the real Babur dynasty. His life was duly snuffed out!"

Many hundreds of kilometres away, the battle against the Yusufzai did not go well for the Mughals in and around the mountains of the Hindu Kush. In fact, it was a complete disaster! The rebels already infuriated by the death of their champion the previous year, laid in wait for the Mughals expecting a full forward rush into the narrow passes of the rugged mountains. They had also occupied strategic positions on the mountain range to target the elephants.

Birbal, after declaring an amnesty if the rebels surrendered, went after the lean force of the Afghans that was about 8,000 strong, mostly infantry with some 500-odd cavalry troops. The rebels deftly retreated drawing the main body of the Mughals into the narrow passes where Akbar's army was brutally ambushed. Most of the Mughal elephants were annihilated. Birbal's pachyderm was speared and brought down. The famed administrator was surrounded and neutralized before he could unleash his death blows on the Afghans. His body was dragged into the mountains and eventually quartered into pieces. The Mughals subsequently lost about 8,000 men in battle. The surviving troops fled for their lives on horseback or took to their heels to the Mughal garrisons on the western banks of the Indus. It was a definitive military defeat for the Mughals. The Afghan renegades clearly humiliated the army led by Akbar's famed commander.

Two days later, the emperor was in horrific shock when the news of Birbal's demise and the defeat of his army was conveyed.

There was silence in the court for a long time. Akbar rose, trying to digest the tragic news. He dismissed the court and left for the Diwan-E-Khas with the rest of his cabinet.

His tears were uncontrollable. "I feel I have lost my son" he said amidst the discharge from his eyes. "What about the body?" he demanded of the messenger.

"The remains were not found, Your Grace. The Yusufzai dragged away the body. We could not trace it" came the blunt reply.

"Would not his soul be at ease had we managed to secure the mortal remains for a cremation?" mourned Akbar. "How I wish I had kept him back from this assault. He was so eager to go."

Faizi, increasingly impatient with the blows the Mughal army had been taking was not too pleased "This is a big failure by our intelligence, My Lord" he observed much to the angst of Abdul Karim Khan. "We have lost a very important member of the council, haven't we?"

"They had been waiting to repay us for the death of Mirza Hakim, what else?" noted the king. "These vagabonds will be crushed under my wheel!"

Todar Mal jumped in "We dealt a decisive blow to Mirza Hakim's army four years ago, My Liege. Were they not defeated by the Mughals? The problem again is the sanctuaries the Yusufzai enjoy among the tribes of the Kyrgiz, the Uzbek, the Kazhak and the Tajik. Persia too remains a safe haven. You should confront the Persian Safavids!"

"I will go after these savages nevertheless. Birbal did not shed his blood in vain. I will wipe out every Afghan thug who hides in the mountains! Every last one of them!" warned Akbar.

"You have cut-off the head of the snake a year ago" said Mulla Do-Piyazo. "This is just the tail wagging before it stops moving forever."

CHAPTER 34

PEACE, TOTAL PEACE?

The news of one of Akbar's greats' demise on the mountains of the Hindu Kush reached all the realms of the rajputs. There was intense speculation in Mewar's new capital about the clash in which the top dignitary lost his life. Details began emerging in Mewar over a period of months bit by bit about the botched Mughal offensive in the north-west that led to the military fiasco.

"So, the Mughals lost in the Afghan mountains, didn't they, brother?" demanded Sakta Singh at a cabinet meeting in the spacious hall of the Chavand residence.

"I think Akbar foresees a strategic threat from the Tajik, the Uzbek and the Kyrgiz tribes infested with his half-brother's ideology. He has a haunch that they are backing the Afghan rebels. So, Mewar and its king have been shelved for the time being. How long this intermission would last is something we cannot guess" responded

Prathap Singh. "We have enjoyed quiet for a long duration. We don't want it to end."

"But battling these lanky tribes in the Hindu Kush and beyond is no easy task" observed Ram Singh.

"Who cares if Akbar is kept occupied in those rugged mountains as long as he leaves us in peace. Would it ever matter?" shot Amar Singh.

"Why are you so cynical, Amar?" enquired the king. "Learn to scrutinize everything in your proximity. One thing or the other is bound to affect you, especially in the event of you becoming king."

Proximity? Thought Amar Singh. Mewar was neither too far from Fatehpur Sikri nor from the Hindu Kush. May be a bit far from the Hindu Kush, right?

"We need to be alert for a week or two to see if the Mughals would try to bolster the morale of their troops with an invasion into Mewar" cautioned Prathap Singh. "One thing can easily lead to another."

There was an air of expectation for a big Mughal push into Mewar yet again. Mewar's sleuths were kept on their toes for a possible sweep by Akbar's military into their territory. Prathap Singh, Amar Singh, Sakta Singh and Ram Singh went about in different routes in the middle of the night quite close to the Mughal-held territory to feel if they could sense an oncoming attack. Nothing materialised. There was no sign or indication of such a move. The anticipation began to dissipate slowly and eventually die down.

"We shall continue to be on guard" Prathap Singh warned his military. "Letting our concentration down now is tantamount to preparing our own funeral pyres."

A week later at Fatehpur Sikri, the emperor summoned his cabinet for a briefing in the Diwan-E-Khas. His top grandees were present for the closed-door meeting.

"There has risen a threat from the north-west by some vested interests to challenge the Mughal throne" began the emperor on a serious note. "I shall be leaving shortly for Lahore and then on to the Hindu Kush mountains to take stock of the matter first hand."

There was a pause for a moment from the ruler and then he continued "What Birbal predicted is true. We need a string of bastions all along the mountain range from the Hindu Kush to Kabul to Kandahar and all the way to the Persian border. These passes on the porous Afghan mountains are aiding the conspirators to move back and forth freely and rush reinforcements."

Mulla Do-Piyazo wondered how long the emperor would be gone.

"Crown Prince Salim has bloomed thick and fast into a young man. Should I not say, in fact, a man? Raja Bagwan

Das has pruned his skills in the art of warfare. He is well-trained in the arts and culture and has become fluent in Hindustani" beamed the czar. "The council shall run the empire in tandem with the heir-apparent. There are other things that have engrossed us. Kashmir under the Shah Mirs is ripe for a Mughal deathblow. The Safavids must be driven out of Kandahar once and for all into Persia to secure the gateway into Hindustan. Kabul must be secured well enough to tighten our grip over the Afghan highlands. Then there is this problem of the Hindu Kush rebels. These issues demand that I be present in the north-west for a longer duration. Prathap Singh and his set up can be ignored for quite a while. He is now quite adept at giving us the slip. We cannot afford to run in vain circles."

Vizier Abul Fazl's eyes lit up at the mention of the Safavids "The Safavids are heretics. You should not spare any effort to eject them out of Kandahar and from all the hilltops of the Afghan homeland!" He secured his slipping black shawl back into its place across his chest on his right shoulder.

"So, we shall focus our undivided attention on Kashmir, Kandahar and Kabul, not to forget the outer fringes of the Hindu Kush!" surmised Akbar. "I shall leave with Abdul Karim Kahn, Man Singh and Raja Bagwan Das."

Faizi, moved with inspiration uttered, "It's high time that we Mughals put our foot down in a decisive manner to crush our foes, My King!" His widened eyes shone with eagerness, "Might is always right! That is the only way the world runs."

Abul Fazl echoed his compatriot's sentiments "We need to overwhelm our foes with supreme military force to give them a sense of reality, Your Grace. We need to score definitive victories where we suffered setbacks."

"Yes, Your Grace. Kandahar, Kabul, Kashmir and if fate agrees even Prathap Singh of Mewar" cut in Man Singh with his usual ominous voice. "Would His Majesty be pleased to dispatch the Crown Prince to hunt down Prathap Singh after settling these urgent issues if and when that would suit him?"

"We can have a discussion about that once this order of business concerning the north-west is over," replied Akbar. "Salim shall lead the army on his own into battle one day, but not this early. Let's see how things work out."

CHAPTER 35

DAWN IN THE DISTANCE

A string of events began to manifest in the Mughal empire two months after the unfortunate death of Birbal. The emperor's brother-in-law Raja Bagwan Das led the heavily-armed Mughals into the Kashmir region in April 1586 to a decisive victory against the Shah Mir dynasty that ruled the pristine mountainous valley. The people of Kashmir had to accede to the Mughal demands to be made a province of the empire. The other option of annihilation was simply not that appealing to the Kashmiris. Mughal bureaucracy wasted no time in stamping out every trace of pre-Mughal influence on the province to emboss their dominance. With the annexation being a done thing, the Mughals began to orient the populace into forcing the new reality on the ground into their hearts and minds.

Akbar relocated to Lahore. He began to personally have a close-eye on the situation in the north-west border, straddling Afghanistan. He summoned his warrior aristocrats for military briefings and laid bare his goals. He breathed fire into the souls of his commanders.

The Mughals under Raja Man Singh and Raja Bagwan Das thrust into the region encompassing the Khyber and the Bolan passes, Peshawar, Kabul and the adjoining regions. Their military completely crushed any opposing militia that came up to challenge them. The armed forces under Raja Man Singh went about probing every valley, pass and mountain cave to hunt down the proponents of Mirza Hakim dynasty mercilessly. The Yusufzai were simply overwhelmed this time around. The setting up of the Mughal administration in these realms went about in earnest. Like the Kashmir region, Akbar's administration immediately began implementing measures to bring the conquered territory under firm Mughal subjugation.

Meanwhile in Mewar, things had conveniently settled down to a routine. Prathap Singh ruled in what was left of Mewar free of the Mughal presence. His drastically reduced military played the role of patrolling the much-reduced borders of Mewar to have eyes and ears on the ground to act as an early warning system to protect the king. He too regularly went on night patrols to scour the land for signs of approaching Mughal armies. Nothing ever materialised. Not even a small-scale attack seemed to be in the offing. Prathap Singh went on with his life, as did his queen, Amar Singh and the other sons and daughters. The years rolled on.

The year 1589 was a tragic one for the empire with three Mughal greats – Todar Mal, Tansen and Raja Bagwan Das passing away leaving voids that were very difficult to fill.

It was early 1590. Akbar mused over the loss of his greats one late afternoon in the rose gardens of Agra "Man buds, man blooms, man blows and man bows... Is everything so ephemeral? Who would have thought Raja Birbal would go? Not to forget Fakir Azio-Din who went way ahead of his time."

"Man can act only for a short time, Your Grace" counselled Mulla Do-Piyazo, as he walked alongside Akbar. "Let go of those who are destined to go."

"I was hoping they would stay around to uphold the dynasty" said the sovereign in a low voice as he glanced behind him to direct Do-Piyazo's attention at the sleek-looking Salim ambling alongside the cabinet members.

"Oh! There would always be others who would fill the gap" replied the advisor in an equally loud whisper. "Fate will always see to that. He is coming up fine, Your Grace. You need not worry. He will have his circle of men. He is almost ready to mount the horse. I feel he has a clear head on strong shoulders."

Faizi, following close behind bearing the dark ostentatious baton of the supreme tutor, joined in "There are no accidents, My Liege. Life always sends you the right person at the right time. Prince Salim will have his right people to guide him. Never burden yourself with that."

A short time later, as evening approached, the monarch and his men sat on armchairs on the widespread palatial grounds sipping tea and one or two indulging in the hookah.

"Only memories remain, don't they?" quizzed the monarch as he brought up the deceased grandees again.

"And memories can haunt you enduringly night and day on end, My Liege" felt Faizi, seated right, pulling the hose off his middle-aged lips and sending dense smoke to hang about his mouth, his red beard dangling below his chin complementing his flowing burgundy outfit.

"How is one to keep off haunting memories?" demanded the king.

Abul Fazl, seated left of Akbar leaned close to the czar and looked into his eyes "Your Grace, you need to remind yourself that we would all inevitably become memories. That should suffice you" he paused for a moment and wishing to divert the emperor's mind asked, "When are you going to go after the Persians in Kandahar?"

"Let Kashmir and the Hindu Kush stabilise for good" replied Akbar. "We have more or less brought everything under control in these two regions. Man Singh keeps shuttling between Fatehpur Sikri, Delhi, Lahore and the north-west mountains. I shall act against those Persians for sure."

"Would His Majesty forget his foe, the rajput prince?" probed Faizi, tilting his head, and widening his eyes with a strange grin.

"Prathap Singh?" wondered Akbar.

"Very much, Your Grace" replied Faizi still smiling.

"He is not forgotten. However, I feel he would live out his life in southern Mewar. He is not a threat anymore. He is probably losing his sheen."

"One Mirza Hakim was liquidated, My Liege" poked Faizi with a dry sense of sarcasm as he inhaled a huge dose of the tobacco.

"Aye, he was" concurred Akbar as he gazed at the nearby thicket of mango trees laden with heavy green fruit. "Prathap Singh is not Mirza Hakim. Prathap Singh is not a traitor" Akbar swung his head and smiled at Faizi. "Backstabbers deserve the death they face. The king of Mewar is opposing us because we are his enemies and not his family. There is a big difference."

The monarch kept staring at the crown prince who had taken an ardent liking to the hookah, blowing the smoke as he sat to his extreme right, smiling as he partook in the pleasure.

Akbar began to be filled with an ominous sense about other things.

He summoned Salim to the Diwan- E-Khas one Friday afternoon for a one-on-one briefing.

"Are you getting a grip of the empire's reins?" dug Akbar at the prince.

"I am beginning to have a firm grip" smiled the prince sporting a near-perfect straight nose, thread-like sideburns and slender lips. "I am aware of the intricacies that characterize the various arms of the government. I am well-versed with the military echelons. I know the top brass of the armed forces. I am fully known to your trusted aides and most of all I know the boundaries of the glorious empire."

Akbar nodded ambiguously "Someday the mantle of responsibility to rule this dynasty shall fall on you in all likelihood."

"I would feel humbled with such a responsibility" replied the attractive crown-heir knowing fully well there was no one else to challenge him for that role.

"I am, in fact, living out my life in securing the integrity of the empire's confines" said the emperor very solemnly. "Almost all of our foes have been vanquished or neutralized, except one."

"Prathap Singh?" queried Salim.

"Yes. Mewar is, however, now our domain. The Mughals own all rajput realms. The king of Mewar, however, runs his own miniscule administration on a tract of land, free of our intrusions. He wishes to block our access to the western sea from his end" observed the crowned head.

"I am fully aware. So, he is running a state within a state, right?" demanded Salim.

"Not exactly. The south of this vast land is still not conquered by us" smiled Akbar. "Your idea of 'a state within a state' does not really come into question here. Time will take a toll on Prathap Singh" opined Akbar.

"You are not really going after him?" enquired the prince with a sense of curiosity.

"Son, there is no point in looking for a needle in a colossal haystack" said the sovereign with absolute seriousness. "Yet, if fate so wills that Prince Salim or may I say emperor Salim should account for the king of Mewar… then it would be your moral duty to see to that, wouldn't it be?"

"Wouldn't it be?" questioned the prince gaping his mouth with an eccentric smile, his eyebrows arched high "It surely will be. I have personally witnessed the man in action when I accompanied Raja Man Singh for the Haldigatti encounter. No doubt the man is all power, passion and patriotism. He is a true rajput lion. Nevertheless, if you give the go ahead, I shall lead an army to account for his head."

"Salim!" exclaimed the monarch with a rush of inspiration. "Indeed, the blood of lions runs in your vein! Of Genghiz Khan, Timur and Babur! You will make a fine potentate! You shall account for fugitives like Prathap Singh if that is what fate wishes. Things shall come to fruition in their own sweet time. Not as of now. Fate always overrules. Bear that in mind."

"I have always borne your wisdom in mind" replied the Crown Prince with a forced sense of humility.

"I sense in my spirit that I have neglected the north-west for quite a period of time" said the emperor as he leaned towards his son.

"Go on" egged the prince.

"I believe a conspiracy has been hatched somewhere beyond the Afghan mountains to unseat the line of the Babur-Humayun-Akbar bloodline and replace it with a Babur-Humayun-Mirza Hakim dynasty" shared the potentate with an uneasy sense of foreboding.

"Have you confirmed this? I mean is this backed by intelligence, Father?" said Salim suspiciously.

"My hunch is, the Persians are hand in glove with this intrigue" shared a dejected emperor. "A cartel has been gathering against this dynasty from beyond the rugged mountains, Salim."

"What do you think we should do? This could be very serious. The army must be on standby" replied an alarmed prince.

"There will be no knee-jerk reaction from Fatehpur Sikri. I shall spend more time to secure the northern borders out of Lahore" confided the emperor. "The army top brass would also have to move along with me. I need you to have a firm grip on the empire from Fatehpur Sikri. You shall be the de-facto ruler. All matters that pertain to the well-being of the empire shall be under your jurisdiction. Things will boil down to your choice, your judgement and your discretion."

"I shall bolster you, Father. The empire's betterment is of paramount importance. Proceed with your plans" grinned Salim.

"I am sure you would keep the empire in good stead, my son. May fortune be kind to you" said Akbar as he kissed his son on his supple cheeks.

Akbar departed for Lahore on the howdah of his elephant to oversee the smooth functioning of the Mughal administration in the newly conquered regions and to monitor the Persian border areas for any stealthy attempts by some insane Caucasian alliance to unseat him and his dynasty. He loved the weather and the culinary delicacies of Lahore. The change of air made him feel absolutely euphoric. So great was his contentment that his stay almost became a permanent feature in Lahore. He stayed put for quite a long duration, for about five or six years while having an eagle eye for detail regarding the empire's borders in the north and north-west. He returned occasionally to Fatehpur Sikri to check on Salim's running of the empire. Otherwise, it was it was all the heir-apparent Salim's show for all practical reasons.

The army under Abdul Karim Kahn and Man Singh Amber with their deputies in the likes of Shabaz Kahn spread their large patrol units all the way from the coast of Gwadar to the Khyber and Bholan passes and well beyond to crush any incoming intrusion. A quarter of the Mughal army was shifted with the sole purpose of completely blockading the north and north-western border all the way to the coast of Gwadar to bulldoze the purported invasion by the so-called Caucasian confederacy.

The Persian fort that cropped up from nowhere in the Kandahar region aroused Akbar's suspicion deeply. His deference to Persia for the good relations and the cultural and historic connections since the time of his father not being in the way, he finally decided to strike in the autumn of 1595 to overrun the Persians at Kandahar city to double-check their reaction. Man Singh and Abdul Karim Kahn did a perfect job of forcing the few thousands of Persians in the fort to surrender without a fight with a massive show of force from the Mughals. The Persians clearly lost their nerve and buckled. The Safavids ruling Persia did not react to this act of belligerence by the Mughals. The Persian influence over India was done for good.

There were times when one Prathap Singh flashed through the emperor's mind during his Lahore stay. The emperor smiled to himself. How the times had changed! What had become of Mewar's king? Had he vanished into oblivion?

Those six years were years of peace and tranquillity in what was left in the kingdom of Mewar. The unchanging routine that Mewar lapsed into had become an everyday event.

"Amar Singh is well and truly ready to take over the reins of the kingdom" declared Prathap Singh to his men-at-arms in a meeting one bright morning in his mansion as his son sat at his right. "Life has become very predictable. I only wish I had a large, potent military to war against the Mughals. I am greatly impeded."

"You have braved the Mughals, brother. You almost gave your life for Mewar" smiled Sakta Singh. "You are a real hero in words and deeds. We are grateful that we now live free of the Mughal yoke."

"I still feel anguish in my heart for the way in which the princes of Hind have squandered away their honour to the Mughals" mourned the king.

"It is too late, My Liege" said an aging Ram Singh. "It is way too late for that. The Mughals are on the verge of swallowing all of Hindustan."

Later that night, as he stood on the wind-swept terrace of his residence, Kanwar walked up to her king with her chiming anklets and bangles. "You should now focus on living your life out in peace, My Lord. Don't ever bring up the idea of taking on the Mughals again. You don't have the numbers."

"I am fully aware of that, my dove" said her lord softly. "I wish to spend the rest of my life loving you, loving my sons and daughters and ensure that Akbar's men don't set foot on this side of Mewar… How long do I have?

How far would I go? I hope my end is what they call a 'beautiful death'."

"Come now, why do you have to philosophize this early in your life?" questioned his queen. "You have a long way to go. The end is not to be reckoned. You have a long time ahead of you... and not to forget myself."

She turned to go downstairs when her incense-smoked long tresses of her hair conveyed a whiff of their exhilarating perfume into his nose. He gently seized her silver bangle-decked left hand with his right, as she turned to leave, drew her close and gazed into her eyes in the stillness of the starry sky embedded with a waning crescent "I wish I had finished the Mughals at Haldigatti..." remarked the king.

Her enchanting smile held him in a trance "Let bygones be bygones. History shall remember you with kindness."

She turned swiftly and was about to head for the stairs to the house below when Prathap Singh caught hold of her long-flowing strands of her glistening mane as she began walking. He followed her lifting her undulating hair to his nose to inhale the intoxicating odour they were giving away "Had Kanwar, Queen of Mewar, accompanied me to battle at Haldigatti, her very presence would have moved me to kill all my foes" he said with a lovely smile on his face as he walked behind her.

Kanwar reached the top of the stairs on the way down with Prathap Singh in trail, still holding her jet-black locks in his hands. She stopped and turned around "I wish I had accompanied you to that battle, My King" she complained with a tired smile. "It is however, well and truly late for that."

CHAPTER 36

TO EVERY MAN HIS DESTINY

The year 1595 AD witnessed the passing on of Faizi, the tutor of the emperor's many sons, Salim being the prime among them.

The sovereign dearly missed the bright red turban and the slender cherry-red beard flowing down the Yemenite's chin. He thought that just about when the horizon was about to come into view, his greats were leaving him one by one.

"Life is not fair" he said softly to Abul Fazl, as they strolled one bright night, before dinner on the ghostly, outstretched cobbled courtyard of Fatehpur Sikri. A swarm of heavy, liquid-loaded, matt-black clouds began inundating the atmosphere above Fatehpur Sikri and the surrounding regions at an alarming speed. They blocked out the full moon in an instant. "Why would your brother have to go now at such a young age? He would have made the perfect guide to the crown prince" demanded Akbar as a gust of cold air began rushing into the courtyard forcefully.

"If fate has so predestined his death, My Liege… can we contend? Are we that powerful?" mused Faizi's younger brother. "Is not the course of the human life predestined?"

"Man should have the power to rewrite his own fate" replied the emperor. "There are myriad of things a man could change if he were bestowed with such a privilege."

"I know not even one that had such an honour, Your Grace" said his vizier with a grin.

The smell of rain in the air and the distant thunder made them haste their steps towards the royal quarters.

"Would his liege be staying at Fatehpur Sikri for quite some time?" enquired Abul Fazl as the rain began drizzling gently.

"So it seems" replied Akbar surrounded by a host of well-built military personnel as his vizier boarded the horse carriage awaiting him. "Let's hope I am able to govern the empire from Fatehpur Sikri rather than from Lahore or the Khyber and the Bolan."

"That would be perfect, My Liege" said the vizier as the barrage started to come down in a torrent. His four-wheeled wagon with a driver in command drove into the wet night drawn by two huge white stallions.

In the environs of the Aravalli, the endless dawns and the never-ceasing dusks began to take a toll on Prathap Singh, who was beginning to feel that he was missing the vigour of being the king of Mewar.

So, is this how I live out my life, day in and day out? With a very limited military force left to defend myself and keep me out of harm's way? Is this not mere existence? All my raving and ranting at the Mughals won't change anything on the ground, will it? Days, weeks, months and now years are rolling by… So that's it? You get your children married-off. They have their children and the cycle repeats itself. Is this not all chasing the wind?

Heavy monsoon rains began lashing all rajput domains in mid-1596. After a gap of about three months, heavy torrential rains flooded Sind, Gujarat, Rajputana and the Punjab in November and early December.

The king could not follow the very predictable routine anymore by the last week of December, 1596. At a meeting with his men, he brought up the idea of venturing into the forests of Mewar for a hunt as a means of using his time in a better way.

"I wish to return to the very area where I hid. The place is teaming with game. It is a perfect spot for hunting" proposed Prathap Singh. "I wish to do something different. I am tired of this monotonous life."

"I am all too ready" replied Sakta Singh at once with his usual boyish smile, his aging process never took a toll on his perennial smile. "Let's go."

"I shall come too," said Ram Singh. "It would be exciting to visit the cave you abandoned. We could spend the night in the forest if we don't come across good game."

"Overnight?" probed Sakta Singh.

"I mean if we don't find proper game" clarified Ram Singh.

"There is plenty of game in the forests of Mewar" assured the king. "You would be coming across scores of them once you reach the centre of the forest. Amar Singh can handle things here for a day or two in our absence. I am sure the Mughals are not planning any surprises being privy to our hunting plans."

"They are busy hunting down their foes along the Persian frontier, brother" winked Sakta Singh. "Mewar has disappeared from their thoughts."

The king and his two aides were up and ready on the morning of 5th January 1597 for the hunt. So were their warhorses.

"So, nostalgia is calling, My King?" probed Kanwar.

"Not exactly nostalgia, dear Kanwar" answered Prathap Singh as he adjusted his belt. "I need to get away from this mundane routine that is going on for many years. I need a change."

"Beware the male leopard, My Lord" cautioned Kanwar. "He took a special liking for you about ten years ago!" She broke into a ringing laughter.

"That leopard! His offspring are probably roaming the forests, my dove. He is dead and gone in all likelihood" replied Prathap Singh in a light vein.

"Nevertheless, be on your guard. We heard the roars of a tiger the last time we were there" insisted Kanwar with wide eyes.

"I sure will be on guard. Amar shall be in-charge in my absence. I shall return in the night, if not, I will be here tomorrow morning," assured Prathap Singh.

With a quick customary kiss to her regal forehead, he proceeded to hop on his black stallion. He and his aides galloped towards the dense, thick forests of Mewar that he had abandoned more than a decade ago. They reached the rim of the woodlands after a steady journey of three hours. They halted their cruise temporarily to have a break and refresh themselves with water. After half an hour entering the thick undergrowth, the son of Udai Singh II and his men travelled with steadfast minds towards the core of the hinterland. Deer, black buck, huge bustards, monkeys, peacocks and peahen began appearing sporadically from different sections as they kept dashing forward. The king had not made up his mind as to what to target for his hunt. Too many choices had him thinking.

Prathap Singh and his team entered the heart of the forest in pursuit of game. The king reminisced about his hunting skills when he was a youth.

"I could outrun the wind on Chetak" said the king as they climbed a bone-dry hilltop. "The horse was that powerful."

Sakta Singh was not paying attention to the king's commentary. He was lost in looking out for the chital as the trio kept trotting on and on into deep woods.

The sun had risen, its sharp golden rays were penetrating every nook and corner of the woodlot. Dry leaves littered the carpet area of the jungle. There were plenty of wildlife but the crisp, dry leaves were making approaching them difficult.

The woods were dense with entangling vines. Luxuriant close-packed growth of trees made progress very slow.

The king and his aides reached the location of the cave where he had relocated about eleven years ago. It was completely overgrown with weeds with just the top portion of the structure barely visible above the vegetation.

The almond tree still stood there, but there was no sign of the leopard that used to haunt it.

After a while the trio came into a clearing where they spotted wild boar grazing in quite some distance.

"This is your lucky day, My King" Ram Singh Tanwar observed excitedly. "Your favourite game is waiting for your weapons."

"Brother, I see a large boar among them. It is definitely a male" noted Sakta Singh. "How exciting!"

Prathap Singh ambled a few yards on his horse to take a closer look. Just beyond the herd of rooting wild pigs was the big male with huge tusks protruding from its massive jaws. It was immersed knee-deep in slushy mud looking for edible things. It had been a long, long time since Prathap Singh had brought down such a ferocious-looking animal on a hunting trip.

Then there was this rooting call of a langur monkey on a treetop branch all of a sudden that sent all the deer flying out of the open glen. Peacocks began relaying the alarm with their own distinct, piercing calls. The startled swine stopped feeding and looked around.

The king and his confidantes were about two hundred metres away from the miry stretch. At the sound of the langur and peacock alarms, the large swineherd comprising of females, piglets and adolescent males and females took off squealing hysterically to their right heading deep into the cover of the trees.

The big rusty-brown male with his erect mane running down to his swinging tail, however, stood his ground issuing a warning for the approaching party to back off. It kept staring at the approaching jet-black horse and its rider armed with a razor-sharp spear.

"Stay here. I shall send it to its death" cautioned Prathap Singh as he began to approach the alpha male. The animal began to snort and violently thrust its nozzle into the mud to his left and right sending chunks of semi-solid mire flying into the air. It stood firmly on the slimy ground unwilling to budge an inch.

Prathap Singh realising that the swamp was difficult to negotiate began slowing down his approach to get as close as possible to the huge hog.

The intrepid boar began snorting and gaping its mouth displaying its curling knife-like frontal tusks more than four inches long.

The king accelerated within five metres of the boar and stooped to his right in a bid to impale the animal with his spear. His intelligent quarry, however, was agile enough to bolt forward in the blink of an eye, suffering a gash on its right shoulder and inflict a powerful headbutting jab on the king's right shin. Prathap Singh's horse which was by now veering heavily, lost its balance at the boar's assault and came down on the slush along with the king.

Ram Singh Tanwar and Sakta Singh now began to gallop at the sight of the big beast charging at the king and throwing him off his horse.

The bleeding boar now lunged at the king with full fury. Pratap Singh now just about standing held off the mad boar's very sharp tusks with his steely arms. He could feel the boar's weapons cutting his entwining fingers, making him bleed.

The animal wrestled itself free from his grips with a jump. As Prathap Singh moved back to locate his spear, the boar charging madly a second time and punctured his right thigh penetrating deep with its long, broad, jagged left tusk.

"Hey!" yelled Sakta Singh now within fifty metres of the king. The loud vocal disturbance got the animal distracted and it turned and fled across the watery slush into the woods, with drops of its blood dripping on the slushy terrain.

"You are injured, brother!" said Sakta Singh as he knelt down on the muddy marsh to inspect the bleeding fissure, "It's a deep wound. You are bleeding heavily."

Prathap Singh grimaced with pain as he hopped on his horse with his spear. The three decided to call off the hunt and head back.

Spotting a small rocky depression filled with water near the circumference of the bog, Ram Singh made the king alight and washed the deep wound with water hoping to stop the incessant blood flow. He then tore a large piece of his dhoti and wound the cloth around the wound in an effort to stop the haemorrhage. It seemed to work with the blood flow stopping almost immediately.

Back home at Chavand, the physicians were soon summoned and began attending on the wound sustained by the king.

"So, for the first time in his life the king has been outfoxed by a boar?" remarked Kanwar as she ran her fingers through his hair as he lay on the bed.

"Maybe I take too many things for granted" said Prathap Singh as he forced a smile through the pain.

"You will recover in about ten days" said Kanwar with a smile. "I have not known either a man or an animal that can defeat my Lord."

A week later, the wound had not healed and the infection had spread to the inner thigh region making it impossible for Prathap Singh to walk. He was in considerable pain. He felt serious discomfort. The pathogens had succeeded in affecting his healthy tissues. He was close to being branded 'incapacitated'. He was not too keen to take food.

There was hectic activity at Chavand. A very concerned Kanwar, Amar Singh and the rest of the king's offspring were constantly monitoring his wellbeing. Prathap Singh felt that fate had dealt him a decisive blow. A misfortune from which he probably would not recover. That was his gut feeling.

"I must transfer the regency to Amar Singh" he suggested to Kanwar.

She refused to answer at once. She was in deep distress. No medicines could heal the injured hero.

"I fear the end is approaching, Kanwar" said Prathap Singh.

"Who died from a boar injury, My Lord?" she demanded amidst her steady stream of tears.

"Fate comes in many forms, My Queen. The brightest candle goes out first. Doesn't it?" he replied, struggling to speak.

Things began heading for the worst another week later with the king almost losing his nervous functions and was reduced to being bedridden like a chained, captive lion.

"I have lived. I have loved" he whispered with difficulty as he held the fingers of Kanwar. She began to wonder if her king was hallucinating.

"I lived a rajput and I shall die a rajput" he breathed, "I have not bowed before an alien race. I never subjected my neck to the yoke of the foreigner. The records shall say Prathap Singh was born free, lived free and died free! Prathap Singh never, ever bowed before the Mughals! Prathap Singh the brave that fought for the pride of the Hind and suffered for her honour! I die knowing that I have upheld the honour of the rajputs."

He turned his face to his left to look at Amar Singh, gazing at him for a while. There were tears that came down the face of his son.

"My son, this is the fashion of all mankind. I go as my forefathers went. There is a beginning and there is an ending for all things. The end is unavoidable. Don't spend your time mourning for those whose end came upon them. The end falls upon all" he paused to catch his breath.

"I shall go, my son. The honour of dealing with the Mughals falls upon you. What a privilege it is for a rajput to drive the enemies of his race from his ancestral home? Never, ever compromise with the Mughals. They are a cunning lot. Beware of Fatehpur Sikri! You can trust a serpent but not the Mughals. Mewar looks up to you,

Amar. Mewar and its destiny is now in your hands. Rule her. Cherish her. Love her. Esteem her above everything. This is your calling. Restore Kumbalgarh, Gogunda and Chittor."

Prathap Singh paused to look at his wife. "Kanwar, my life, my everything. I wish I had spent more years with you. That is not to be" cried the king fighting his tears,

"No rajput could ask for a better wife! You are my glory! Now I have to leave you. Stay strong. Do not mourn eternally. I shall have you as my wife in a thousand rebirths! Now I should go. Farewell, my love. It is what it is."

Kanwar moved forward to kiss the king one last time on his forehead right at the place where the hairline met the façade like he always used to do, a long passionate kiss. A faint smile flashed across the face of Prathap Singh as he gazed at his queen.

Three days later Prathap Singh died late in the evening of 19th January 1597 aged 59, surrounded by his family and confidants as the new moon rose over Chavand not far from the Aravalli Range. That very day Amar Singh succeeded his illustrious father to the throne of Mewar. Would the young king live up to the expectations of his people? Would he raise his sword high in battle against the Mughals? Would he look them in the eye? Would he have what it takes to defy Akbar and his Mughals as his father did? The stars were silent as they shone on the sinuous mountains of the Aravalli range that bleak night.

BIBLIOGRAPHY & SOCIAL MEDIA

1. Annals and antiquities of Rajasthan by James Tod: Mushiram Manoharlal publishers New Delhi Volume I, 2001
2. Annals and antiquities of Rajasthan by James Tod: Munishram Manoharla
   publishers New Delhi Volume 2, 2001
3. 'Haldigati' The Thermopylae of Rajasthan - II, https://hritambhara.com
4. Unit 94 --UPSC--The Battle of Haldigati, www.educatererindia.com
5. Battle of Haldigati, www.historicalindia.org
6. 18 Amazing facts about Maharana Pratap that will blow your mind away, https://mythgyaan.com
7. On the history trail: Maharana Pratap and the battle of Haldighati, htpps://sahasa.in

8. Maharana Pratap The Invincible Warrior, Rima Hooja, Juggernaut Publishers, 2018
9. Navaratnas, Wikipedia
10. Mirza Muhammed Hakim, Wikipedia
11. Akbar, Britannica Encyclopedia
12. Battle of Haldigati 1576, Mughal - Rajput War Documentary, YouTube, by Kings and Generals, 2017

www.ingramcontent.com/pod-product-compliance
Lightning Source LLC
LaVergne TN
LVHW091619070526
838199LV00044B/864